THE TEXAS TATTLER

All the news that's barely fit to print!

Police Scour Sperm Bank Records For Mother of Mystery Fortune Heir

A Red Rock "scandal ava-lanche" hit Texas last month when the results of a DNA test declared millionaire family man Dr. Matthew Fortune the father of a child abandoned and left in the care of his own famous ranching clan. Insider sources confirm that he and wife Claudia have separated.

Amidst the rubble of his mar-riage, Matthew holds firm to his assertion of marital fidelity and offers only his donation to a California sperm bank while in medical school as possible expla-nation. Records of sperm bank pregnancies have so far failed to provide a possible mother for the child, Taylor Fortune.

Also on the Fortune front... Ryan Fortune's money-hungry, estranged wife, Sophia, was spotted in a heated lovers' quarrel in the very public lobby of the Palace Lights Hotel...but *not* with her hubby. Looks like Ryan just stumbled upon some fuel for that inferno they're calling a divorce.

Speaking of fire...the red-hot combustion between fearless man-in-blue Sheriff Wyatt Grayhawk and new-beauty-in-town Gabrielle Carter is sending smoke signals swirling around Red Rock. Too bad the only thing Gabrielle can remem-ber is her name—but everyone's calling her Grayhawk's Lady!

About the Author

THE
F RTUNES
OF TEXAS

STELLA BAGWELL

sold her first book to Silhouette in November 1985.
More than fifty novels later, she still loves her job and
says she isn't completely content unless she's writing.
Recently, she and her husband of thirty years moved
from the hills of Oklahoma to Seadrift, Texas, a sleepy
little fishing town located on the coastal bend. Stella
says the water, the tropical climate and the seabirds
make it a lovely place to let her imagination soar and
to put the stories in her head down on paper.

She and her husband have one son, Jason, who lives
and teaches high school math in nearby Port Lavaca.

STELLA BAGWELL
The Heiress and the Sheriff

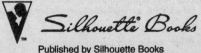
Silhouette Books

Published by Silhouette Books

America's Publisher of Contemporary Romance

Special thanks and acknowledgment are given
to Stella Bagwell for her contribution
to THE FORTUNES OF TEXAS series.

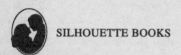 SILHOUETTE BOOKS

ISBN 0-373-38921-3

THE HEIRESS AND THE SHERIFF

Copyright © 1999 by Harlequin Books S.A.

Visit Silhouette Books at www.eHarlequin.com

Printed in U.S.A.

All underlined places are fictitious.

THE FORTUNES OF TEXAS

KINGSTON FORTUNE (d)

- 1st marriage PATIENCE TALBOT (d)
- Teddy §
- 2nd marriage SELENA HOBBS (d)

CAMERON (d)
m MARY ELLEN LOCKHART

HOLDEN ① — LOGAN ⑤ — EDEN ⑦
m Lucinda Brightwater
m Amanda Sue* / Emily Applegate
m Ben Ramir / Sawyer*

LILY REDGROVE
m Chester Cassidy (d)

COLE* ⑪   HANNAH ⑨   MARIA

James a.k.a. Taylor

RYAN

- 1st marriage JANINE LOCKHART (d)
- 2nd marriage SOPHIA BARNES

MATTHEW   ZANE ⑫   DALLAS ④   VANESSA ②***VICTORIA ⑩   CRUZ ③   MAGGIE ④
m Claudia Beaumont
Bryan

ZANE ⑫

DALLAS ④
1st marriage Sara Andersen (d)
2nd marriage Maggie Perez

VANESSA ②
m Devin Kincaid

VICTORIA ⑩

CRUZ ③
Savannah Clark

MAGGIE ④
1st marriage Craig Randall (D)
Travis
2nd marriage Dallas Fortune

† ROSITA and RUBEN PEREZ
Anita   Carmen   Frieda

CLINT LOCKHART
brother of JACE LOCKHART ⑥
Ciara Wilde

MIRANDA
m Lloyd Carter (D)

KANE   GABRIELLE ⑧

---

* Child of affair
d Deceased
D Divorced
m Married
*** Twins
† Affair
‡ Loyal ranch staff
§ Kidnapped by maternal grandfather

TITLES:

1. MILLION DOLLAR MARRIAGE
2. THE BABY PURSUIT
3. EXPECTING...IN TEXAS
4. A WILLING WIFE
5. CORPORATE DADDY
6. SNOWBOUND CINDERELLA
7. THE SHEIKH'S SECRET SON
8. THE HEIRESS AND THE SHERIFF
9. LONE STAR WEDDING
10. IN THE ARMS OF A HERO
11. WEDLOCKED?!
12. HIRED BRIDE

 Meet the Fortunes of Texas

Wyatt Grayhawk: The rugged sheriff didn't trust strangers, especially the young lady who claimed to have no memory and found a haven on the Fortune ranch. But would Wyatt's mission to uncover Gabrielle's past be sidetracked by the allure of the mysterious beauty?

Gabrielle Carter: She didn't know who she was or why she had come to Texas. Although she knew she shouldn't fall for a man who doubted her intentions, she couldn't deny the longings of her heart.

Clint Lockhart: He had a lifelong obsession for revenge on the Fortunes and he'd do whatever it took to get a piece of their family empire.

Hannah Cassidy: When Ryan Fortune proposed to Hannah's mother, Lily, this daughter-of-the-bride decided to plan the perfect Texas wedding. Little did Hannah know that she would soon be meeting the groom of her dreams....

To my family,
and all our unforgettable trips to Texas.
There have been many, and hopefully there
will be many more.

One

Gabrielle Carter gripped the steering wheel, certain the next bend in the road would bring her in view of the Double Crown Ranch. But the curve only opened up to more gentle rolling pastures shaded with huge oaks and dotted with fat, sleek cattle.

She'd never been to Texas. The massive size of the state had surprised her—along with the heat. When she'd stopped earlier in San Antonio for gas, the humidity had been oppressive. Her blouse was still glued to her back, and she didn't have to look in a mirror to know her hair was hanging in limp strands on her shoulders.

She probably should have stayed in San Antonio long enough to rent a room and freshen up before she presented herself at the Fortune family ranch. But she'd already been traveling for nearly four days. Now that her destination was so close she was determined to drive on.

Sweat slicked her palms and her mouth was so dry she could hardly swallow, but Gabrielle knew neither condition was caused by the heat outside the closed windows of her car. She was nervous. Desperately nervous. And as the rental car traveled deeper into the countryside, her mother's words of warning continued to roll through her mind.

I forbid you to go there, Gabrielle! Those people—that family—they're not what you think. They're nothing to you! You're only going to get yourself into a lot of trouble. And when you do, don't expect me to come after you!

Gabrielle's sigh was drowned out by the twangs of country music on the radio. Maybe the Fortunes were nothing to her, she mused. After all, she was a total stranger who lived more than a thousand miles away. Showing up on their doorstep unannounced was probably going to look strange.

Peculiar-looking or not, though, she had to take that chance. Gabrielle tried to swallow the growing lump in her throat.

The road made another slight bend around a group of ancient oaks, and her heart suddenly raced with anticipation. In the far distance she could see a group of buildings. It had to be the Double Crown Ranch. At last! Eagerly she leaned forward and pressed harder on the accelerator. Who was she finally going to meet? What would she say—?

The questions in her head roared to an abrupt halt. A black horse suddenly galloped out of the trees. It wore a saddle, but there was no rider to guide its crazy trek.

Oh, Lord, it was headed straight at her car!

A scream ripped from her throat. She stomped the brake pedal and jerked the steering wheel. Instantly the car spun into a wild skid, and broken images whirled in her vision. The black horse, the green grass and trees, the blue sky all blurred together like an abstract painting.

Frantically she twisted the wheel, any second expecting to hear the sickening *thud* of metal against animal flesh. Miraculously, the car managed to miss the startled horse. But Gabrielle could see the massive tree coming straight at her, and too late she remembered she'd not buckled her seat belt. The impact came before she had time to brace herself. She felt her whole body being pitched forward, and then something hard slammed against her forehead.

Seconds, or minutes, could have passed before Gabrielle returned to consciousness. Hot dusty carpet was pressed against her face. Her legs were twisted awkwardly beneath the steering wheel. Pain hammered behind her eyes and burned like a torch at the back of her skull.

With great effort she pushed herself upright until she was half sitting, half kneeling in the seat. Lifting a hand to her forehead, she tried to focus on her surroundings, but her vision was so blurry she could hardly make out her own fingers.

She'd hit her head. But how? she wondered. Where was she? The pain in her head was so great she could hardly think.

All at once her fuzzy brain managed to register the sickening smell of gasoline. It was all around her, robbing her breath in the tightly closed car.

It took Gabrielle three attempts to get the door open. Once it finally swung wide, she practically fell into the hot, humid air. Outside, she leaned for long moments against the crumpled fender while everything swam around her like an out-of-control carnival ride.

Even outside the vehicle the smell of gasoline was heavy. She had to get away from the foul stench. She had to find someone—anyone—to help her.

Grass, thick and deep, tangled around her ankles as she stumbled away from the car. With each step, her shaky legs threatened to give way, but she forced herself to keep putting one foot in front of the other.

By the time she reached a narrow dirt road, her vision had cleared somewhat, but the pain in her head was still just as fierce. She touched the pads of her fingers against her forehead and felt something wet and gooey. Blood? Had she been in a car wreck? Oh, God, someone help me, she prayed.

"Are you all right?"

The faint sound of a female voice penetrated Gabrielle's

terror, and she turned toward the sound. A petite, dark-haired woman was running toward her. She was panting heavily, and her dark eyes were glazed with fear.

"Who—are you? What happened to me?"

The woman stepped forward and took Gabrielle by the arm. "I'm Maggie Perez Fortune. Here, let me help you get to some shade. My horse bolted away from me and ran right in front of your car. You swerved to miss him and then your car went out of control."

"My car?" she repeated vaguely.

Maggie Fortune motioned behind them. Gabrielle glanced over her shoulder just in time to see a car burst into giant flames.

"Oh, no!" she gasped.

"Oh, God!" Maggie cried. "I've got to call for help!"

The woman helped Gabrielle to the closest tree, where she sank to the ground and leaned weakly against the trunk. She watched the dark-haired woman punch numbers on a cell phone. Where was this place? Gabrielle wondered. She felt so lost, so totally blank.

Though her vision had cleared somewhat, everything was still blurred at the edges. She was obviously out in the countryside somewhere. The grass was green and long—a meadow. And the air was heavy and hot. Very hot.

She glanced back at the burning car. It was totally engulfed in fire now, the flames licking high enough to scorch the overhanging branches of the tree she'd crashed into.

Where had she been going? Where had she come from?

The questions made her head ache even worse, and she dropped her face in her hands and tried to calm the fear that was threatening to consume her.

Her name was Gabrielle Carter. She knew that much. Surely the rest would come to her when the pounding in her head stopped.

She didn't know if she dozed or fainted, but some time later, the sound of Maggie's voice roused her.

"Help should be here very soon." Kneeling down beside her, the woman pulled a white handkerchief from her jeans pocket and dabbed away the blood on Gabrielle's forehead. "Are you hurt anywhere else?"

"I don't think so. My head hurts so badly I can't think. Where am I?"

The woman's lovely features, which looked to be part Mexican, crumpled into a frown. "You mean, you don't know?"

Gabrielle shook her head. "I'm sorry. I—don't. I have no idea where I am or where I've come from."

"You're on the Double Crown Ranch, in Texas. You don't remember driving out here?"

She didn't remember anything! The state of Texas meant nothing to her. Her mind was black, and she was terrified.

"No! Oh, God, what am I going to do?"

The woman gently took her hand and squeezed it. "Please don't worry. It will all come back to you, I'm sure."

She had barely spoken the words when the sound of a siren wailed in the distance. Gabrielle watched with hopeless despair as a fire engine pulled to a stop near the burning car. Two firemen quickly spilled out of the cab, and in a matter of seconds they were dousing the flames with a high-pressure hose hooked up to a water tank.

"Here comes the sheriff," Maggie said, sounding relieved.

Gabrielle looked away from her charred car to see a pickup—sheriff's emblem emblazoned on the side door—roaring up the road. The vehicle pulled to a jarring stop a few yards from where she and Maggie stood in the shade.

A man wearing blue jeans, a white shirt and a black

cowboy hat stepped down from the truck and approached them with long, purposeful strides. He was tall, with long muscular legs that strained against his jeans. His white shirt covered a broad expanse of strong shoulders, and his torso narrowed down to a flat waist and lean hips. Beneath the wide brim of his hat, his features were sharp and angular with high cheekbones and very dark skin. What little Gabrielle could see of his hair was black and cropped close to his head. She thought he looked Native American or Mexican—she wasn't sure which. But she was certain of one thing. She'd never seen a more striking man. No woman could forget a man who looked like this Texas sheriff.

Without smiling, he nodded briefly at Maggie as though he knew her, then turned his attention immediately to Gabrielle. "I'm Sheriff Wyatt Grayhawk," he informed her. "Can you tell me what happened?"

She felt, more than saw, his hazel-green eyes shrewdly sizing her up, and for an instant a flash of resentment joined the throbbing in her head. Couldn't he see she was hurt? Wasn't her physical well-being more important than the details of the accident?

"No. I didn't know what had happened until Ms. Fortune came along and told me."

He looked at the other woman. "You saw the accident?"

"I'm afraid I was the cause of it, Wyatt. I'd been riding down by the creek and had gotten off to rest and water my horse. I didn't see the snake until it struck at him. He jerked away from me and ran off in a mad gallop across the field, and right in front of Gabrielle's car. When she swerved to miss it, the car went into a spin and crashed into a tree. By the time I finally made it up here, she'd gotten out of the car and was wandering down the road."

The sheriff looked back at her, and Gabrielle felt the hair

on the back of her neck rise as though a thunderstorm was mixing in the air.

"Your name is Gabrielle?"

His voice was low, rough and timbered with a Texas drawl. She resisted the urge to shiver. "Gabrielle Carter."

"Where are you from, Gabrielle?"

She swallowed as another wave of helpless fear swamped her. "I don't know."

His eyes, which seemed unusually light for such dark skin, narrowed with suspicion. "What do you mean, you don't know? Surely you know where you live?"

"I don't know," she repeated.

Maggie Fortune said, "Wyatt, I think Gabrielle has hurt her head."

He stepped closer, and Gabrielle had to force herself to stand her ground and endure a closer scrutiny of his unnerving gaze.

"Yes, that's quite a cut you've got there. Let me grab my first aid kit." He sprinted back to his truck and came back with the kit. "I'm no doctor, but I do know a little something about cuts and scrapes. Here's some gauze with some antiseptic. It'll do for now, but I definitely think you'll have to go to the hospital."

Maggie was grateful for his help, more grateful for the distraction from his rapid-fire questions. How come he kept looking at her like he didn't believe she truly couldn't remember anything? Why would she lie?

"So, Gabrielle, do you have any identification on you?"

Identification! She glanced down at her somewhat faded jeans, then quickly jammed her hands in all the pockets, searching for any scrap of paper. There was nothing. No coins or tissues or lipstick. Nothing.

She lifted shocked eyes back to his face. "No. I suppose my purse was in the car. Oh, and now it's burnt!"

The young woman appeared to be genuinely distraught, Wyatt thought. But anyone would be after the jolt she must have taken when her car slammed into the oak. She was not a Texan. At first glance her appearance had told him that much; her voice had proved it. There was no wedding band, no rings of any sort on her fingers. In fact, the only jewelry she was wearing were slender gold hoops in her ears.

"Maggie, were the Fortunes expecting any visitors from out of state?" he asked.

The other woman shook her head at his question. "Not that I'm aware of. But then, people are always dropping in unannounced. You know that, Wyatt."

He looked back at Gabrielle Carter. He'd been friends with the Fortune family for years, and he'd never heard the name Carter mentioned. And if he'd ever seen Gabrielle, he would have remembered. She was not a woman any man would likely forget. He was struck by her beauty, even in this disheveled state.

Her long brown hair was naturally streaked with gold from the sun. The silky strands waved about her shoulders and framed an oval face that was dominated by huge hazel-green eyes fringed with thick dark lashes. Full pink lips quivered as she glanced from him to the smoldering car. Her skin—and he could see plenty of it with the skimpy top she was wearing—was smooth and tanned to a deep golden brown. He tried not to think about the luscious curves beneath the jeans and ribbed knit blouse.

"Well, I think right now, Miss Carter, you'd better let me drive you to the hospital. We'll deal with your identity later."

Gabrielle stared wildly at him, then turned a helpless look on the Fortune woman. "I'm not sure I want to go to

the hospital with him! I don't know where I am! I don't
have any money—''

Wyatt held up a hand to halt her protest, while beside
her the woman said gently, ''Please let him take you. In
my panic, I didn't even think to call an ambulance. And
don't worry about the hospital bill, Gabrielle. The ranch's
insurance will certainly cover it. Especially with me being
the cause of the accident. I really feel just awful.''

''You don't have any choice in the matter, Miss Carter,''
Wyatt Grayhawk informed her none too gently. ''As sheriff, I'm required to see you get medical attention. It's the
law.''

Her heart pounded as she searched his dark, stern face.
Something told her there was very little, if any, compassion
behind his roughly hewn features. This man didn't care if
she was lost or terrified. In fact, the skeptical expression
on his face said he'd doubted her story from the start.

''I guess there's little else I can do then, is there?'' she
said quietly.

''Nothing else,'' he agreed, then reached for her arm.

Gabrielle wanted to jerk away from him. But she didn't
have the strength. And he was the sheriff, she reminded
herself. It wouldn't help her cause to have him riled at her.

''Everything will be all right, Gabrielle,'' the woman assured her as the three of them walked to Wyatt's pickup.
''Wyatt will take good care of you.''

Gabrielle didn't want to think about being under the sheriff's care. He was harder to deal with than the pain in her
head.

''Do you need a lift back to the ranch?'' Wyatt asked
the woman.

''No. I'm going to walk back,'' she told him. ''Maybe
I'll find my horse on the way. You will let us know about
Gabrielle?''

"I'll call the ranch and let you know something as soon as I can. In the meantime, you might let your father-in-law, Ryan, know what's happened."

"I will." The woman waved and headed down the road in the opposite direction from the charred car.

Gabrielle suddenly felt even more lost and alone without her rescuer. At least with the Fortune woman, she'd felt she had someone on her side. With Sheriff Grayhawk she felt anything but safe.

He opened the door of the vehicle and helped Gabrielle up on the bench seat, then skirted around the hood and slid behind the wheel.

"Buckle up," he ordered as he started the engine.

She pulled the straps of the seat belt across her lap, but her fingers were shaking so badly that she couldn't make the two ends catch.

Suddenly two dark-brown hands were pushing her fumbling fingers aside. "Here, let me do it, or we'll never get where we're going," he said gruffly.

She bit down on her lip and turned her face toward the window, but his closeness couldn't be ignored. She could smell the faint scent of his cologne and feel the brush of his warm hands as he latched the seat belt against her.

He was a forceful man in looks and presence. And though her past was a blank, she had a feeling she'd never encountered anyone like him before.

"Thank you," she murmured, once he'd straightened away from her and set the pickup in motion.

He didn't acknowledge her words. Instead, he turned the pickup around and headed back toward what was left of her burned car. The flames and smoke had finally been doused, and the firemen were rolling up their hoses.

Wyatt stopped the pickup. "I'm going to talk to the firemen. I'll be right back," he said without glancing her way.

Through a blur of pain Gabrielle watched the tall, dark sheriff walk over to the two firemen. After a brief moment of conversation he returned to the truck.

"Is there anything left inside the car?" she asked hopefully.

"The metal is still too hot to search through the thing. I'll come back later and see what I can find. Unless you want to tell me what all this is about right now?"

At the question, she snapped her head around, causing even more pain to crush the middle of her forehead. She frowned at him. "What do you mean?"

His brows arched and then he rubbed a hand over his face. "So, you're still determined to play innocent with me. I thought once we got away from Maggie you might decide to come clean."

Gabrielle realized she was in a partial state of shock from the accident, but try as she might she couldn't unravel the strange things this man was saying to her.

"Come clean? I'm sorry, I don't know what you're talking about." She turned slightly toward him, her expression desperate. "Do you know who I am? If you do, why don't you tell me?"

Her voice was rising as though she were very near to hysteria. If she was faking this whole thing she was doing a damn good job, Wyatt thought. But hell, most women were good actresses. Lying to a man came as naturally to them as breathing.

"Calm down, lady. If you've got a concussion, it won't do you any good to get all excited."

Gabrielle's lips parted as she stared at him in stunned fascination. "Excited! How would you feel if your head was cracking and you didn't know who you were or where you were? Oh, I'm sure a big strong man like you would take it all in stride,'' she sneered. ''It would probably be just another day in the life of a Texas sheriff.''

His nostrils flared as his eyes left the highway long enough to glance at her. ''That ache in your head doesn't seem to be affecting your tongue.''

She straightened her shoulders and lifted her chin. ''I don't like being accused. And you were trying to accuse me of something!''

Except for a faint lift of his brows, his features became deceptively passive. ''If you don't know who you are, how can you be certain you aren't guilty?''

She opened her mouth to defend herself, but then a slow, sickening realization struck her. She *might* be a criminal. She might be anything. She just didn't know!

''You're right. I can't be certain of anything,'' she said wretchedly, then dropped her head in her hands.

Behind the wheel, Wyatt tried not to let the despair on her face soften him. She was a hell of a looker, but she could very well be up to no good. In his work he had to be suspicious of everyone. Personally, as a man, there was no woman he trusted. And he was doubly on his guard because of all the trouble the Fortunes had encountered lately.

''You have no idea what you were doing on the road to the Double Crown Ranch?''

Gabrielle strained to remember, but all that came to her mind was waking up with the floorboard of the car pressed against her face and the smell of gasoline choking her.

''No. The name means nothing to me.''

''Does the name Fortune register with you?''

She looked at him hopelessly. ''If I've ever heard of it, I don't know it now. Who are these people? Could I have been going there to do a job?''

His lips thinned to a grim line. "That's what I'm wondering."

The sarcasm in his voice stung her. "What's that supposed to mean?"

"Nothing," he said bluntly. "We'll talk about it later. After you've seen a doctor."

That was fine with her. She was more than a little tired of his innuendos. The pain in her head was making her nauseated, and thinking more than ten minutes into the future was terrifying. She simply wanted to close her eyes and forget the laconic sheriff beside her. She didn't want to be reminded of the fact that she knew nothing about Gabrielle Carter.

A few moments later, his deep voice jerked her out of her jumbled thoughts. "I wouldn't go to sleep if I were you."

She opened her eyes, but didn't bother to lift her head from the back of the seat. "Why?"

"If you've got a concussion you shouldn't sleep."

"I thought you said you were no doctor."

"I'm not. I'm just a lawman."

Her gaze lingered on his rigid profile. "Grayhawk," she repeated. "Is that a Native American name?"

He didn't answer immediately. Finally he said, "My father was Cherokee."

"And your mother?"

"White. Like you."

Even through the haze of her pain, Gabrielle picked up a sharp bitterness in his words. She wondered why, then just as quickly told herself it didn't matter to her if he hated white people, or women, or even her. He was just one man in a big world. Once her memory returned, Sheriff Wyatt Grayhawk would be well and truly out of her life.

Two

The remainder of the trip passed in silence. At the hospital Wyatt escorted Gabrielle into the emergency unit and grabbed the attention of the first nurse he came upon.

"Can he come with me?" Gabrielle asked as the nurse helped her into a wheelchair. She didn't know why she wanted the sheriff to remain at her side. Only minutes ago, she had wished him out of her sight. Yet he was the only familiar face around her, and even if he was unfeeling about her plight, his presence was steadying.

The nurse glanced at Wyatt. "Is he your husband?" she asked Gabrielle.

"No. But—"

"Then it would be better if he didn't. If he's needed, I'll come after him."

He cast Gabrielle a dry glance. "Don't worry. I'm not going anywhere."

Even though the tone of his words was far from gentle, his promise calmed her somewhat. She nodded jerkily at him, and then the nurse wheeled her away.

Wyatt watched her disappear down the hallway, then through a door on the left. For a brief second he almost followed and told the nurse he was going to stay with Gabrielle whether she liked it or not.

Hell, Wyatt, what are you thinking? he asked himself. The woman doesn't need you. Yet, just for a moment, when she'd looked at him with those big pleading eyes, she'd reminded him of a little lost lamb about to go to slaughter.

With another silent curse, he turned and headed to a busy nurses' station across the room. He showed them his badge and asked one of the nurses to page Dr. Matthew Fortune.

She quickly complied and he thanked her, then headed to the waiting area. Even though he didn't want to go there. The frightened look on Gabrielle's face when the nurse had taken her away was lingering in his mind, and oddly enough he was still fighting the urge to go back to the examining room and make sure she was all right.

Forget it, Grayhawk, he muttered to himself. She wasn't a child. Although she was young, he figured she was at least twenty-one or two. And for all he knew that frightened look could have been an act. Just like the loss of memory.

With a tired sigh, he went over to the coffee machine and filled a cup. The strong burnt smell assured him it had been made hours ago, but he took a sip of it anyway. He'd been going since three o'clock this morning—he needed something to fortify him.

Ignoring the vinyl chairs and couch where several people sat flipping through worn magazines, he walked over to a plate-glass window and stared out at the parking area stretching away to the city street. It wasn't often Wyatt personally hauled someone to the hospital. In fact, if it hadn't been for the accident happening on Fortune land, he would have sent a deputy out to handle the investigation.

But the Fortune boys had been his closest friends since childhood. They had stood behind him when others had shunned him for being a half-breed. Without their solid support, he never would have been elected sheriff. And now that trouble had fallen on the family, he was personally checking out every movement on or near the Double Crown Ranch.

In the background, he could hear the nurse on the intercom paging Matthew to come to Emergency. He was still sipping on the bitter coffee when the doctor's voice sounded behind him.

"Wyatt! What are you doing here? Has something happened to Claudia or Taylor? Have you heard something about Bryan?"

Wyatt turned to see the tall, dark-haired doctor hurrying into the waiting room. Wyatt desperately wished he could tell the oldest of the Fortune brothers that he'd located his missing son. But the sad truth was that he was no closer to finding the baby now than he had been six months ago.

Matthew's baby, Bryan, had been taken from his crib during his christening party at the Double Crown nearly a year ago. A special FBI agent had been sent in to handle the case and he'd recovered a baby and the ransom money. But when he'd gotten the child home, everyone was shocked to discover the baby wasn't Bryan. They'd kept the other baby though, since a blood test showed he had the rare Fortune blood, and had named him Taylor.

Wyatt tossed the cup in a nearby trash bin and crossed the small area of the waiting room to greet the other man. "Don't get upset, Matthew. This isn't about Claudia or Bryan or Taylor. Or at least I don't think it is. Do you have a few moments?"

Matthew gestured toward the double doors leading out to the parking lot. "Of course. Let's go outside."

The two men walked out into the heat and took refuge under the shade of a sycamore.

"The reason I'm here, Matthew, is that I brought a young lady into Emergency a few minutes ago. She's had a wreck on the Double Crown. Her car burned, and she has no idea who she is. Or so she claims."

Matthew's finely chiseled features were suddenly frozen with shock. "Oh, my Lord! Was she hurt badly?"

"I don't think so. There was a small cut on her forehead, and she was complaining of a severe headache."

"Didn't she have any identification?"

Wyatt shook his head. "It must have been in the car. I'm going to search it after it cools down, but I doubt there's a chance in hell I'll find anything. Your sister-in-law, Maggie, saw the accident. She was still with the young woman when I got out there to investigate."

"Maggie didn't know her?"

"No. The woman says her name is Gabrielle Carter. I thought it mighty odd she could remember her name but nothing else."

"Gabrielle Carter," the young doctor repeated. "The name doesn't ring a bell with me. Do you think she might have some connection to my son? Maybe the kidnappers sent her to the ranch for some reason?"

Losing baby Bryan had put a strain on the whole family, but Wyatt could see it was beginning to crush Matthew and Claudia's marriage. Especially now that the DNA testing to determine paternity of Taylor had shown Matthew was the father. Matthew claimed it could only be the result of a sperm bank donation he'd made years ago, but Claudia was distraught and skeptical. Wyatt was checking out the sperm bank lead, though.

"I can't rule that possibility out, Matthew. Or she might even have some connection to Taylor. We really won't know until she comes clean with her memory or I can find out who she really is."

"Then you think she's lying?" Matthew asked.

Wyatt grimaced. "I don't know. I just have a gut feeling something's not quite right. But I could be wrong. You're the doctor—is it possible the accident caused her to lose her memory?''

Matthew thoughtfully rubbed his chin. ''It's possible, though amnesia is certainly not something that happens routinely. You say she has a head injury?''

''Her forehead was cut at the hairline and she was complaining of a headache. Could you examine her, Matthew? I'd like to have your opinion before I do anything. And who knows—you might recognize the woman.''

The young doctor glanced at his watch. ''I'm not due for rounds for another thirty minutes. Let's go in, and we'll see what we can find out.''

The two men left the shade and as they approached the entrance of the building, Wyatt placed his hand on Matthew's shoulder. ''Matthew, when you first see this woman, don't let on that you're a Fortune. I want to see if there's any sign of recognition on her face.''

Matthew frowned. ''You sure are a suspicious cuss.''

''I have to be.'' Wyatt grimaced. ''And you should be, too, after all that's been happening to your family.''

The doctor sighed. ''Yes, I know. I just hate all this mistrust. Every time a stranger comes to the ranch, I look at them and wonder if they know where my son is, or if they know something about baby Taylor. I'm even starting to look for clues with my patients here at the hospital! And Claudia—you know what all these unanswered questions are doing to her.''

Wyatt squeezed the other man's shoulder. ''Believe me, Matthew, I understand how hard all of this has been on you. But you can't give up hope now. This woman might just be the lead we've been looking for.''

Back in Emergency, the two men discovered Gabrielle had been admitted to the hospital and taken up to the fifth floor. They headed up together.

Much to Wyatt's surprise, when they walked through the door of her room, she gave absolutely no outward sign of recognizing Matthew. Rather, she planted an accusing look on Wyatt as though he were the direct cause of her being restricted to a hospital bed.

"I take it you haven't done enough to me?" she asked Wyatt. "You've come up here to take my fingerprints or something?"

Wyatt went to the head of her bed and stared down at her. The cut on her forehead had been covered by a bandage, but he could see the whole spot had begun to swell and redden. Someone had undressed her and put her into a flimsy hospital gown. He tried not to notice the shape of her bare breast beneath the thin cotton. But it was next to impossible to keep his gaze from dipping to the full roundness pushing against the fabric.

"Or something," he said, while fighting the odd urge to reach down and brush the tangled hair away from her cheek. He'd been around a lot of pretty women in his thirty-one years—Texas was full of them. But there was something different about this one. Something that, God help him, made him want to protect her.

"I told you I wouldn't leave. What did the doctor say?" he asked.

Sighing, her gaze dropped to the sheet spread across her legs. "He said I had a concussion and that I'll have to stay in here for observation. At least until tomorrow."

"Have you remembered anything?"

"No. But he thinks everything will start coming back to me soon."

She glanced to the foot of the bed where Matthew was busily scanning her chart. "Who are you?" she asked him.

He glanced at Wyatt, then to Gabrielle. "I'm—one of the staff doctors here at the hospital."

"Are you going to be my doctor?"

He smiled gently at her. "That depends."

She motioned to the chart in his hand. "What does that say?"

"It says you've had a trauma to your head. But you're going to be all right."

She looked up at Wyatt and flashed him a crooked smile. "Sorry to disappoint you, Sheriff, but the doc here says I'm going to live."

She was obviously trying to be flip and indifferent, but Wyatt didn't miss the quiver at the corner of her lips. She was as frightened as hell. But whether it was from her loss of memory or because she was up to something, he had no way of knowing.

He pulled his gaze from hers and glanced at Matthew. "Have you seen enough?"

"Yes. I've got to start my rounds." He came to stand by Wyatt and looked down at Gabrielle. "Has your vision cleared any, Miss Carter?"

Her eyes squinted as she tried to focus on the doctor's face. "At times it's clear, and then it gets fuzzy again. Right now you look a little blurred."

"That's understandable." He slipped a penlight out of his lab coat and shined it in each of her eyes. "I imagine you've got quite a headache."

"They gave me something down in Emergency. It's beginning to ease a little."

"That's good.

She swallowed nervously as her gaze vacillated from one man to the other. "Doctor, what if I don't remember tomorrow? Is there something you can give me or do to me to make me remember?"

Matthew patted her shoulder. "Don't worry about your

memory, Miss Carter. Just rest and let your body try to heal itself. Right now that's the best thing you can do."

She nodded, and Matthew made a motion to Wyatt that they should leave the room.

"I'll be back later, Gabrielle," Wyatt promised. "After I've searched your car."

He saw her study his face, then deliberately turn her head toward a window to her right. The light coming through the slatted blinds spread a soft glow behind her, and the sight of her tender profile hit a spot smack in the middle of Wyatt's chest.

"It's a cinch you'll know where to find *me*," she said quietly.

He cleared his throat while mentally shaking himself. "Just make sure you don't try to sneak off from this place. I'll find you wherever you go."

Outside in the hallway, Wyatt deliberately put several feet between them and Gabrielle's door before he questioned his friend. "Well, what do you think, Matthew?"

"I think you were rather hard on her."

Wyatt's eyes widened with surprise. "Hell! I already know I'm not a pleasant man. What I need to hear from you is whether Gabrielle Carter is faking her memory loss."

"I don't think so."

Wyatt let out a long breath. He'd never wanted to believe anything so much in his life. But several reasons held him back. The biggest one being Gabrielle was a woman. And a white one at that. "You *think*. You can't say for certain?"

"No. Like I said before, amnesia isn't something doctors encounter routinely. And even when it's genuine, it's tricky to deal with."

"Have you ever seen this woman before?"

Matthew shook his head. "Never. I'm sure of it. But

Wyatt, I really think you're barking up a wrong tree here. Miss Carter hardly seems the sinister type. I can't imagine her being connected to Bryan's kidnapping, or even to Taylor's winding up on the ranch.''

''You couldn't imagine your own child being stolen from its crib either!'' Wyatt bluntly reminded him. Then, muttering a curse under his breath, he shook his head. ''I'm sorry, Matthew. I know I'm scratching at a wound that hasn't healed, and I don't want to hurt you any more than you already have been. But we can't afford to trust this woman. At least, not until I find out more about her. It might turn out she's the mystery mother of baby Taylor.''

Matthew quickly shook his head. ''Her chart reads she's a virgin. Apparently she told the admitting doctor she had some abdominal pain. Since she couldn't remember her medical history, she agreed to a full physical—including a gyn—just to make sure there were no internal problems. So it's clear the woman hasn't even had sex with a man, Wyatt. Much less given birth to a child.''

For some reason Matthew's words spread a dull flush over Wyatt's dark face. The idea of Gabrielle Carter being pristine and untouched had never occurred to him.

''That doesn't make her innocent in other ways.''

The young doctor sighed as he pinned Wyatt with a regretful look. ''You'll never trust women, will you?''

''Not in this lifetime.''

Matthew threw up his hands in a gesture of surrender. ''All right, Wyatt, so what if you find out Miss Carter was up to no good when she headed out to the ranch? What are you going to do—arrest her on suspicion?''

Gabrielle's pale, haunted face crept into Wyatt's mind, but he pushed it out. If he wasn't careful, that lost, vulnerable look in her pretty eyes would lead him right down a path to ruination.

"I don't know," Wyatt answered. "I'll have to see what tomorrow brings."

Gabrielle could leave the hospital. The doctor had given her the release a few minutes ago. But what was she supposed to do? The only things she possessed were her jeans, top and a pair of clunky sandals. She had no money or car. No home to call for help. At least, if she did, she couldn't remember who her family was, or where they were.

At the moment Gabrielle could only think of two options. Walk until she found a shelter. Or throw herself on the mercy of the Department of Human Services. Neither choice held any appeal. But she had to have some sort of shelter until her memory returned, or until she could find a job and care for herself.

There was a telephone beside the head of the bed. She supposed she could use it for local calls. But there was no directory that she could find. And besides, she had no one to call.

You could call Sheriff Wyatt Grayhawk.

She cringed at the sound of the little voice inside her head. The man had promised he'd be back, but it was nearly noon and she hadn't seen him yet. It was pretty obvious he'd decided she wasn't worth bothering about. Besides, she'd rather ask a stranger on the street for help than ask that man.

"Gabrielle! Great—you're up and all ready to go!"

At the young woman's voice, Gabrielle swung around from her spot at the window. Maggie Fortune stepped into the room.

Relief flooded through Gabrielle. "I'm so glad you came! The doctor has released me and I need a ride to some sort of shelter. Would you mind dropping me off?"

The dark-haired young woman walked over to Gabrielle.

"I would mind very much. I wouldn't think of allowing you to go to a shelter."

Gabrielle's brow puckered with confusion as she looked at the other woman. Maggie Fortune was casually dressed in white slacks and a red blouse, but Gabrielle could see her clothes were expensive, as was her wedding ring and the rest of her jewelry. She was obviously well-to-do. Surely she wasn't going to suggest that Gabrielle go with her!

"I have to do something, Ms. Fortune, until I get my memory back. And so far it's no better than it was yesterday."

"Call me Maggie. Does your head feel any better?"

Gabrielle nodded. "It still aches, but the throbbing isn't fierce like it was yesterday. The doctor read my brain scan this morning, and he says there is no serious injury."

"But what about your memory? Can't he do something about that?"

Gabrielle grimaced. "He believes it will gradually come back to me on its own after my brain gets over the shock of the accident. That's why, for now, I've got to find a place to stay."

"Of course you do. That's why you're coming out to the Double Crown Ranch with me." Gabrielle opened her mouth to protest but Maggie was waving her hand before she could utter one .word. "Don't argue, Gabrielle. I've already talked it over with my husband and father-in-law. They and the rest of the family want you to come. We all feel guilty about putting you in this awful situation."

Feeling suddenly weak, Gabrielle walked over to the bed and sank down on its edge. "I—don't know what to say. From what you said, the whole thing was an accident. I certainly don't hold you or your family accountable."

Maggie smiled gently at her. "I told them all that you

would feel this way. And I also assured them I wouldn't come home without you.''

"But…I'm sure I'll be able to stay a few days at a shelter. And by then I'll probably remember everything and be able to go home. If not, I can surely find a job somewhere.''

Maggie shook her head. "You can't work in your condition. You need time to recuperate.'' She walked over to Gabrielle and gently squeezed her shoulder. "I promise— my family is nice. And the ranch house is so big you won't possibly be in the way. Now get your things and let's go.''

Gabrielle suddenly chuckled and held up her empty palms. "I don't have any things. Whatever I had with me must have burned in the car.''

"Oh, my goodness! I wasn't thinking. You poor thing, you don't even have a toothbrush. Well, never mind, we'll go shopping for whatever you need.''

"Oh no! I—'' Gabrielle's words halted as a knock sounded on the door.

Both women turned to see Sheriff Grayhawk entering the hospital room. Today he was dressed more like a lawman. A revolver in a hand-tooled, leather holster was strapped low on his waist. His shirt was khaki with a sheriff's department emblem on the sleeve. On the pocket over his heart was a shiny round badge with a star in the center.

Gabrielle had thought he looked tough yesterday. Today, he was formidable.

"Hello, Wyatt,'' Maggie greeted him.

Not bothering to remove his black Stetson, he nodded at the woman, then planted a direct stare on Gabrielle. "I see you're dressed. Are you leaving the hospital?''

Her heart pounding madly, she nodded at him.

Maggie spoke up, "Gabrielle has been released by the doctor, so I'm taking her out to the ranch.''

"Is that what you want to do?'' he asked Gabrielle.

She opened her mouth to speak, but once again Maggie beat her to it. "She wanted me to take her to a shelter. But I wouldn't hear of it."

The sheriff's eyes narrowed on Gabrielle's newfound friend. "Does the rest of your family know of your intentions to take Gabrielle out to the Double Crown?"

He made it sound as though she were a leper who should be banished to a dark cave somewhere, Gabrielle thought.

Maggie frowned at him. "We discussed it last night. Ryan and Dallas insist on it. They think it's the least we can do to help Gabrielle. And so do I."

"I see," he said.

Did he? Gabrielle wondered, then choked back a sigh as he glanced at her, then back to Maggie.

"I want to talk with you alone for minute," he told Maggie.

She excused herself, and Wyatt ushered her out of the room.

Gabrielle remained on the bed, staring at the door he'd carefully closed behind him. She had no idea what, if anything, he'd discovered in her car. But two things were becoming very clear to her: he still mistrusted her, and he did not want her going to the Double Crown Ranch.

But why? she asked herself. What was going on out there that could possibly involve her?

Neither Wyatt nor Maggie appeared too happy when they returned to the room, and Gabrielle felt even worse than she had before the Fortune woman had shown up to help her.

"Look, Maggie, I don't want to cause any problems for you. I'm sure Sheriff Grayhawk agrees that I should stay at a shelter and—"

"Don't worry about Wyatt," she said to Gabrielle. "He understands the situation. In fact, he's going to drive you out to the ranch himself while I go do some shopping. So I'll see you in a little while.''

Maggie quickly left the room, and Gabrielle's eyes flew to the sheriff's face. His dark, chiseled features were stoic, giving her no clue as to what was going on behind his intense eyes.

''Are you ready?'' he asked.

She slipped from the bed, but was instantly swamped with dizziness. Her hand instinctively shot out for something to steady her and landed smack in the middle of Wyatt's chest. She jerked back as if she'd touched fire.

Wyatt instantly grabbed her by the shoulder. ''What's wrong? Are you going to faint?'' he asked roughly.

She squeezed her eyes shut and prayed for the spinning in her head to stop. It would be bad enough to faint. But to helplessly wilt in front of this man would be totally humiliating. ''No. I'm a little dizzy. Just give me a moment.''

''This is a hell of a way to be leaving the hospital,'' he muttered. ''You can't even walk down the hallway. Who is the idiot doctor that signed your release papers? I'm going to go find him—''

''I'm all right!'' Her eyes flew open and she straightened away from him with a weak jerk. ''There's no need for you to get so angry.''

Her words brought him up short. He wasn't angry, but he supposed he probably appeared that way to her. Well, that was okay with him. It wouldn't do to let her think he was actually concerned about her. She needed to know he was a hard man, who wouldn't blink an eye about cuffing her hands behind her back—if she turned out to be a criminal.

Three

"Stay here. I'll get a wheelchair," he ordered.

Moments later Wyatt was back, and Gabrielle had no choice but to allow him to push her to the elevator, then out to the sidewalk to his waiting truck.

As they traveled away from the hospital, Gabrielle focused her attention on the passing buildings and streets, hoping something might spark her memory. But after several blocks whizzed by, her spirits sank to her feet. Nothing about the city looked familiar.

As though he were reading her thoughts, he asked, "Recognize anything?"

"No. But I have a feeling I don't recognize this place because I'm not from around here."

His expression remained unmoved as he negotiated the pickup truck through heavy traffic. "I could have told you that yesterday."

She thrust a heavy wave of hair back from her face before fixing him with a stare. "How?"

"You hardly sound Texan. Californian, I'd wager. You have that West Coast look about you, too. Tanned skin, sun-streaked hair."

"I'm sure there are tanned women with streaked hair around here," she pointed out.

"Yeah. But you're different. And I think you know it."

She was different because she had amnesia! she wanted

to yell at him. Instead, she asked, "What did you find in my car?"

The pickup was a four-wheel-drive vehicle with a shift stick in the floor. She watched the corded muscle in his arm work as he shoved the stick into a lower gear. She instinctively knew he was a strong man. She could still feel the grip of his fingers on her shoulder when he'd steadied her in the hospital room.

"It's in that sack beside you. That was all I could find. I'd say the only reason it didn't burn was because it was sheltered by the metal glove compartment. Also I managed to find the VIN number on your car," he said. "It's being run through a computer."

"What will that tell you?"

"Where the vehicle came from. Who owned it."

A pent-up breath whooshed out of her. "Then you might find out who I am."

His lips twisted as he glanced at her. "You said you're Gabrielle Carter. Is that not true?"

He saw her fingers grip the paper, saw her gaze at the clump on her lap as though it was the only thing she possessed in her life. And maybe it was, he thought. The notion bothered Wyatt. Way too much.

"I *am* Gabrielle Carter," she said resolutely. "But who is she?"

He motioned toward the sack. "Maybe that will give you your answer."

Slowly, she unrolled the top of the brown paper bag and peeked inside. "A book?"

"More than just a book."

Gabrielle carefully lifted the article out of the sack. The leather cover was charred around the edges and streaked with smoke, but the words on the front were still visible: Holy Bible. What had she been doing traveling with a Bible? she wondered. Was she a religious zealot? She didn't feel like one. Then again, she was obviously spiritual. Several times in the past two days she had found herself silently praying. Perhaps the book was a family heirloom that she hadn't wanted to part with.

Trying to ignore Wyatt's watchful eye, she quickly opened to the front pages of the book where a family tree would normally be registered. Her heart sank when she saw the entry lines were empty.

She rubbed her fingers back and forth across her forehead. "What do you think I was doing with a Bible?"

"Who knows? Maybe you came here to do missionary work." His gaze cut a skeptical path from her neck all the way down to her feet. "But in that getup, I very much doubt it."

Her face flaming from his blatant inspection, she looked down at herself. Even though her black ribbed top had a scooped neck and no sleeves, there was nothing indecent about it. Nor about her jeans. The sandals were a little funky and the heels a bit high, but from what she'd briefly seen on a few women in the hospital lobby, they were in style.

"You have a certain image of a missionary woman?"

The faint smile on his face was more smirk than anything. Gabrielle wished she had the strength and the nerve to reach across the seat and slap his jaw—lawman or not.

"Yeah. And it sure doesn't fit you."

She breathed deeply and tried to stem her rising temper. "Why don't you want me to go to the Double Crown Ranch?"

"Are my feelings that obvious to you?"

"Very."

They were finally leaving the city behind. Wyatt reached to shove the gearshift into overdrive, and, once again,

Gabrielle watched the rhythmic movements of his body. For the first time she noticed there were no rings on his fingers. A watch with a silver band encrusted with squares of green malachite circled his left wrist, but other than the distinctly Native American piece, he wore no jewelry. She was not surprised at the absence of a wedding band. There was nothing about the man that said he belonged to a woman. Or ever would.

"The Fortunes are my good friends," he told her. "I don't want them to be taken advantage of."

His words stung her hard. Why, she didn't know. What this arrogant sheriff thought of her shouldn't matter one iota. But it did. "Do I look like an ax murderer or something?"

"Or something."

She wanted to scream at his short, noncommittal answers. "What does that mean?"

"The Fortunes have had their share of troubles lately. I don't want your presence adding to them."

Still gripping the Bible, she squared around in the seat to look at him. "What sort of troubles?"

"I'll let them tell you."

She sighed and turned her gaze back to the passing landscape. They were in the countryside now. The land was gentle and rolling with thick green pastures shaded by large hardwood trees. Cattle and horses could be seen on either side of the highway. Cowboy country. Sheriff Wyatt Grayhawk certainly looked like one.

"You're not a man of many words, are you?"

He glanced at her, and Gabrielle was instantly bowled over by the grin on his face. His teeth were a startling white against his dark skin, and the corners of his eyes crinkled with faint amusement. She couldn't imagine how potent he would look if he were to really smile.

"Sometimes it takes more than words to get your point across," he said.

Well, he'd certainly been getting his point across to her loud and clear. In his opinion she belonged in a police lineup rather than as a guest at the Double Crown Ranch.

Sighing, she put the Bible back in the paper sack. "So this is it? This is the sum of what I have in the world."

"It was a miracle the Bible survived the heat. Count yourself lucky you were conscious enough to have gotten out when you did."

She'd been so busy concentrating on her memory that she hadn't thought much about the accident. Wyatt's suggestion reminded her just how blessed she'd been to survive the fiery crash.

"I do. And I will remember…everything. Eventually. The doctor said I would. And when I do I'm going to take great pleasure in telling you so."

His brows lifted skeptically. "Telling me what, Miss Carter?"

She drew in a deep breath, then heaved it out. "That I— I'm not a criminal!"

He shrugged. "I never said you were."

The drawled words had her teeth grinding together. "You didn't have to. I could read it all over your face."

Beneath the brim of his hat, she could see his dark brows arch ever so slightly.

"I'd be careful if I were you, Miss Carter. You might just read me wrong."

Her gaze was drawn downward to the chiseled lines of his lips and she wondered how many women had looked at this man and wanted him. Plenty, no doubt. His long lean body and hard-edged features oozed with sensuality. But Gabrielle knew a sexual romp was all any woman would get from this man.

''What does that mean?''

He flipped on the turn signal, then glanced at her with narrowed eyes. ''It means you'd better not try to second-guess me.''

''You're infuriating!''

His smile was menacing. ''I've been called much worse things. And most of them by women. Your words can't hurt me, Miss Carter.''

She suddenly felt sick and cold inside, and it had nothing to do with the ache in her head or the freezing air blowing from the vents on the dashboard. It wasn't right for any human to be as hard as Wyatt Grayhawk. Surely beneath the badge pinned to his breast was a beating heart. There had to be something or someone in this world he cared about. But so far she could see no sign of compassion in the man.

''No. I'm sure they don't,'' she murmured as she deliberately turned her gaze away from him and fixed it on the narrow country lane they were now traveling. ''A person has to *feel* to be able to hurt. And I can see you're not capable of either.''

She felt, more than saw, him look at her. But he said nothing. After a moment she felt something inside her wilt like a thirsty flower. Whatever happened in the future, she knew she would never forget this man. His dark stern looks, the sound of his voice, the touch of his hand had all burned themselves into her wounded memory.

Less than five minutes later Wyatt parked the truck outside a large house surrounded by a wall built of sandstone. Except for a few shade trees, the structure sat on flat, open land. In the distance, she could see a large barn of weathered wood and another long building that appeared to be horse stables. Nearby were several working pens and numerous outbuildings.

Since she had no memory, she had no way of knowing if she'd ever been on a ranch before. But in any case, she could see this place was a grand-scale operation.

"Is this the Double Crown Ranch?" she asked, as Wyatt helped her down from the cab of the pickup.

A southwest wind was blowing, wet and hot. It tugged at her hair and fluttered the leaves of a nearby cottonwood. She pushed the pestering strands from her face, then glanced at him as she waited for an answer. As usual, she found his hazel eyes watching her, weighing her reactions.

"Yes. This is the Double Crown Ranch. It's the Fortune family homestead."

From what she could see of the house, it was a huge structure with sand-colored adobe walls. Several stone chimneys jutted above the flat tiled roof. In this heat she couldn't imagine needing fireplaces, but maybe Texas didn't always feel like a sauna.

They passed through a wrought-iron gate fastened beneath an arched entryway connecting the sandstone walls. As they walked along a curving stone walkway, she was immediately struck by the lush plants growing all around them. Roses as big as saucers hung from thick green bushes, while clematis and honeysuckle vines draped the heavy beams that thrust from the eaves of the roof.

Gabrielle hadn't thought she was nervous about coming to this ranch, but as she and Wyatt crossed a covered entryway and approached a large, antique wooden door, she realized her mouth was dry and her pulse was racing.

Nothing about this beautiful place seemed familiar, but for some odd reason, she felt a connection to it. As though she were supposed to be here, but didn't know why.

"Maybe someone here will recognize me." She spoke the thought out loud.

Wyatt punched the doorbell. "I wouldn't hold my breath."

"You don't say very much, and when you do it's always pessimistic. Are you always this way? Or am I the only one who sees this side of you?" she asked.

"I'm not pessimistic, Miss Carter. I'm realistic."

Her lips pressed together. "You know, I don't think it would hurt anything if you called me Gabrielle. 'Miss Carter' makes me sound like a dowager."

"I only call my friends by their first name. And I don't know you at all."

Gabrielle felt as if he'd actually struck her across her face. She was alone and lost. Any sort of warmth from him would have been welcome, but it was very obvious he didn't care about her feelings. To him, she was nothing but an unfinished job.

She quickly looked away from him and tried to swallow the hurt. The pain was oddly familiar, as though she were used to rejection. By her family? she wondered. Or a sweetheart? Or maybe, God forbid, she didn't have anybody. No parents or siblings. No boyfriend or lover.

"No. I don't guess you could know me. I don't even know myself," she said quietly.

He was being a bastard. Even he knew it. But something about this young woman was different. She made him itch in all the wrong places, and he couldn't afford to let himself get friendly with her.

Still, the crushed look on her face left him feeling like he'd been kicked in the gut. He didn't want to hurt her. He just didn't want her getting close.

"Look, Miss Carter, I—"

The massive door suddenly swung open and a short middle-aged Mexican woman peered across the threshold at the two of them.

"Good afternoon, Wyatt. I see you've brought our new guest."

"Hello, Rosita. This is Gabrielle Carter. She's just been released from the hospital. Maggie assured me you'd be expecting her."

Except for one white streak at her temple, the plump woman had very dark hair that was pulled to the back of her head in a heavy bun. She had what looked to be a maid's uniform on; so Gabrielle assumed she must be a housekeeper of some kind. She stepped up to Gabrielle and studied her with keen but kind eyes. "Yes. We're expecting Ms. Carter," she said to Wyatt, while continuing to regard her new houseguest. To Gabrielle she said, "I'm Rosita Perez. My daughter Maggie tells me you've lost any possessions you may have had, that everything was burned in the car. I'm very sorry to hear it."

Gabrielle nodded down at the paper sack she was clutching in one hand. "All Sheriff Grayhawk found was my Bible. I think I'm just lucky to be alive."

"I think you are lucky, too," she said, then glanced at Wyatt. "I'll show Gabrielle to her room. Did you want to see Ryan?"

Wyatt shook his head. "No. I won't bother him now. I've got to get back to the office." He glanced at Gabrielle, who looked even more pale and worn since he'd picked her up at the hospital. "I'll be back later. Maybe tonight. Maybe tomorrow."

Gabrielle nodded that she understood, and extended her hand to him. "Thank you, Sheriff Grayhawk, for bringing me out here."

He hesitated only for a second, then reached to clasp her hand in his. Her fingers were small and soft and cool against his warm palm, and for one wild second, he wanted to draw her to him, nestle her cheek against his chest and assure her everything was going to be all right.

But that was the last thing he could allow himself to do. Gabrielle Carter might not be entirely innocent. And even if she was, he couldn't let himself care. He'd been hurt too many times to chance another slap in the face by a woman.

"You're welcome, Miss Carter," he murmured, then glanced at Rosita. "If you need me, call me. Otherwise, I'll let you know what the VIN number turns up."

Wyatt turned and left through the door they had just entered. The housekeeper said to Gabrielle, "Come along and I'll show you where you'll be staying. Then you might want lunch."

"Thank you," Gabrielle told her, then followed her ample figure out of the entryway and into a large great room.

Without a memory, she had no way of knowing what sort of house or apartment she'd been living in before the car accident. But something told her it hadn't been anything like the Double Crown ranch house. One whole wall was dominated by an open rock hearth. The ceiling was high and supported by rough oak beams. The walls were stucco and decorated with numerous paintings and prints, most of which depicted scenes of the Old West. The floor was polished tile, and covered here and there with woven rugs in Mexican and Native American patterns.

Across the room, directly in front of them, a pair of curved, wooden-framed glass doors opened out to a courtyard. Like the front entrance to the house, it was beautifully landscaped with blooming sage, tall clumps of ornamental grass and climbing rosebushes.

"My daughter told us you have amnesia. She feels very guilty about the accident. She wishes she had never gone riding yesterday. I warned her not to go. The night before I had dreamed of a striking serpent." The older woman shrugged and lifted her palms in helpless acquiescence. "I am her mother, but she paid me no more heed than anyone else around here."

Gabrielle wondered if the older woman considered herself some sort of psychic. Frankly, she didn't think she believed in such things. But if the housekeeper had truly dreamed of a striking snake, it would be an awfully eerie coincidence.

Gabrielle followed the woman into a large kitchen. Something spicy and delicious smelling was simmering on a large gas range. Gabrielle's stomach gnawed hungrily—the dry oatmeal and cold toast at the hospital had been too horrible to eat, and last night's fare hadn't been much better.

"Maggie is my youngest. She's married to Dallas Fortune," Rosita said, clearly in an effort to strike up a safe conversation.

"Is this their house?"

The housekeeper chuckled as she motioned for Gabrielle to follow her down a hall off to the left of the kitchen. "No. Dallas and Maggie live in another house on the ranch. It's a whole lot like this one, just not as big. This is Ryan Fortune's home. He's the father of Matthew, Zane, Dallas, Vanessa and Victoria. But I don't expect you know any of them." She made a tsking sound of regret. "*Pobrecita,* you don't even know yourself."

"Maybe if I have a chance to see some of these people, I might remember something," Gabrielle said hopefully. "I had to be headed to this ranch for some reason. Sheriff Grayhawk thinks I was up to no good. But I don't believe that. I don't feel like a bad person inside—and I think I would if I were really bad. Does that make sense, Mrs. Perez?"

The woman opened another heavy wooden door carved deeply with Spanish designs, and gestured for Gabrielle to cross the threshold before her. The room was massive with more stucco walls and heavy beams supporting the ceilings. On one end was a bed, dresser and chest all made of yellow pine. At the opposite end was a sitting area furnished with a large couch and stuffed armchair covered in tan leather. Like the great room and kitchen, the floor was also tiled; the scattered woven rugs filled the room with deep, rich colors.

With a wag of her finger, the housekeeper said, "No. No. I'm not Mrs. Perez. I'm Rosita. And I'll call you Gabrielle, okay?"

At least Rosita wasn't going to be like Sheriff Grayhawk, Gabrielle thought, but then no one could be like that man.

She smiled warmly at the woman. "Yes. I'd like that."

"Good. And I wouldn't worry about Wyatt Grayhawk. He thinks all women are up to no good."

"Why is that?"

Rosita shrugged and tapped her finger against her chin in contemplation. "He's a half-breed. His Indian blood is always at war with the white part of him. He's never happy. But he's a good man."

Deciding she'd talked long enough, Rosita quickly headed out of the room. "Look around and make yourself comfortable," she called over her shoulder. "I'll come after you in a few minutes when lunch is ready."

After the housekeeper had closed the door behind her, Gabrielle wandered over to the king-size bed and trailed her finger over the coarse spread woven in a southwestern-style pattern. The rich turquoise, burgundy and copper colors were just the right contrast to the varnished pine and light-colored walls.

On the long dresser, there was a matching comb, hairbrush, and hand mirror, but nothing else. As Gabrielle glanced around her, she noticed there were no family photos anywhere in the room, so she assumed it was probably used only by guests on the ranch.

The sitting area was equipped with a small television,

stereo and bookcase filled with several hardback and paperback selections. But at the moment she had no need for entertainment. Her thoughts were whirling with all that she'd seen and heard since she'd arrived, and her headache had increased to a steady pounding behind her eyes.

She found the bathroom, which to her surprise was fitted with a huge old claw-foot tub. At the end, a wooden bench was loaded with stoppered bottles filled with oils and salts and bath gels. The idea of filling the tub with warm water and bubbles and soaking for a long while was a tempting one, but Rosita had already warned her that lunch was nearly ready. Gabrielle would have to postpone the bath for now.

Back in the sitting area, she walked to the long windows overlooking the courtyard and discovered one of them was a door. She didn't open it, but stood gazing out at the beauty of the gardens surrounding the massive house.

"Knock, knock! May I come in?"

Gabrielle turned at the familiar sound of Maggie's voice to see the woman's smiling face poking around the edge of the door.

"Of course! I was just waiting for your mother to call me for lunch."

Maggie stepped into the room carrying two giant sacks with twine handles. The logo of a prominent department store was embossed on the glossy paper.

"She said we could take five minutes and then to come. So hurry and look at what you can," Maggie told her.

"Look at what? What is all this?" Gabrielle asked.

Maggie lugged the two sacks over to the bed. When she dumped the contents, wrapped packages spilled over the mattress.

"It's most everything you'll need for a few days. We'll go back and get the rest whenever you're feeling stronger."

Gabrielle's hand lifted to her throat as she stared in stunned fascination at the pile of packages. "This is all for me? An extra pair of jeans and a top would have been plenty!''

Maggie's smile was gentle. ''We don't know how long it will take for your memory to return. You'll need several changes. And a woman has to have makeup and toiletries and lingerie.''

Gabrielle was still too overcome to move, so Maggie took the initiative and opened one of the boxes. ''Look at this! I thought it was darling. See if it will fit, and you can wear it for lunch.'' She thrust a pale blue flowered dress at Gabrielle.

''Oh, do you dress up for meals here?'' she asked, then glanced down at her jeans and top. Wyatt's implication that she more or less looked cheap was still a fresh wound. ''I guess I do look pretty awful.''

''You don't look anything of the sort. I just thought the dress would lift your spirits. Anyway, we hardly ever dress up for meals around here—everything is casual. Everyone is always so busy that no one knows who is going to show up. Unless there's some sort of special occasion going on. But parties have been pretty few and far between here lately. Wyatt doesn't think they're a good idea.''

There was a dressing screen in a corner between a chest of drawers and the bed. Gabrielle went behind it and quickly began to shed her clothes. ''Wyatt? You mean the sheriff?'' she asked Maggie, wondering why he would have any say about this family's social life. It didn't make sense.

''Yes.''

Gabrielle tried to digest the response as she smoothed the long cotton shift down over her thighs. The dress was sleeveless with a scooped neck and slit up one calf. It fit as though it had been made for her.

''I know this will probably sound silly,'' Gabrielle spoke up from behind the dressing screen, ''but I don't understand why the sheriff would care if you had parties.''

Maggie remained silent for a few moments, then she

said, "Well, it just wouldn't be safe. It would be inviting more trouble."

Gabrielle stepped out from behind the screen, and Maggie smiled with approval at the dress.

"You were saying something about more trouble," Gabrielle went on. "Are you talking about my car accident?"

The other woman quickly waved her hand. "Oh, no, Gabrielle. My nephew Bryan was kidnapped from this house nearly a year ago. So far the law officials haven't been able to find him. And Wyatt is afraid the person or persons responsible for the act might try to strike again."

Gabrielle was frozen by the woman's disclosure. Wyatt had told her the Fortune family had been having some trouble, but she hadn't expected it to be this serious or sinister! And he suspected her of being involved in some way! Dear God, the idea of stealing a baby from its own home was repulsive to her. She couldn't have been involved, could she?

"Gabrielle, are you all right? You've gone so white." Maggie rushed across the small space separating the two women and firmly gripped Gabrielle's elbow. "Are you going to faint?"

Gabrielle shook her head and passed a hand over her face. "I—I'm fine. What you just said—it's terrifying. No wonder Wyatt didn't want me coming out here. For all he knows I might have been involved. I don't even know myself," she said desperately.

Maggie patted Gabrielle's arm in an effort to soothe her. "I'm willing to bet you have nothing to do with baby Bryan's disappearance. Or with baby Taylor's arrival."

Gabrielle's face puckered with a bewildered frown. "Baby Taylor? You mean there's something else going on about another baby?"

Maggie nodded. "The kidnappers demanded fifty-million dollars in ransom for the baby's safe return. But my brother-in-law Devin, who's an FBI agent foiled their attempt. The kidnappers escaped, but he did manage to get the money and the baby back. Or so everyone thought, until he got the baby home. We were all shocked when we saw the child wasn't Bryan. None of us had ever seen this baby boy before. But stranger still, he's turned out to be a Fortune.''

Gabrielle's eyes widened. ''But how could that be—if no one knew the child? Did one of the Fortune men have an affair that produced a baby no one was aware of?''

Maggie grimaced. ''That's what Bryan's mother, my sister-in-law Claudia, is starting to think. Even though her husband, Matthew, swears he's never been unfaithful. But the DNA tests prove he's the child's father.''

''So one baby is still missing and the other one is not yet identified? I can see now how my sudden appearance might cause suspicion.'' She groaned with regret. ''I just wish I could remember something—anything that might tell me why I was driving toward this ranch.''

''Don't worry, Gabrielle. Wyatt is a good sheriff. He'll sift through every possible clue to find your background.''

Gabrielle could certainly believe that. She got the impression he'd leave no stone unturned to put her behind bars, or, at the very least, out of the state of Texas.

What had she gotten herself into? Try as she might, she couldn't see how she was going to get herself out of Texas—and away from Sheriff Wyatt Grayhawk.

Four

After being summoned to lunch, Gabrielle and Maggie walked down a hallway and entered a large kitchen. Gabrielle instantly noticed the flavor of the room was distinctly Tex-Mex. Bundles of dried, red chili peppers hung from the ceiling, which was lower in this room. The dishes and containers sitting on the cabinets and work island were made of heavy pottery painted in earth tones of brown, copper, sand, and the pink of rose rock. Along one wall was a row of windows, and beneath them were several large potted plants that appeared to be some sort of desert succulents.

She glanced at Maggie. "Well, I may not have done anything bad, but Wyatt Grayhawk has the impression I have," Gabrielle continued their conversation.

Maggie sighed. "There're a lot of things you don't know about Wyatt Grayhawk."

And I don't want to know, Gabrielle thought, but kept the remark to herself as she and Maggie made their way into a large dining area.

Two men were already seated at a long oak table. Upon seeing the women they both stood, and the younger of the two came around the table to help them into their chairs.

Gabrielle tried to remember where she'd seen him before, then it dawned on her. "Aren't you—"

"Yes. I'm the doctor who was with Wyatt yesterday at

the hospital.'' He extended his hand in greeting. ''I'm Matthew Fortune.''

Gabrielle didn't know what to think. Yesterday he'd never mentioned she'd wrecked her car on his family's property or that he was connected in any way to the Fortunes.

Seeing the bewildered frown on her face, he went on. ''I'm sorry I didn't introduce myself yesterday. But Wyatt had his reasons for wanting me not to.''

Wyatt. Did these people do everything the man told them to do?

''Yes. I'm sure he did have his reasons,'' she murmured. Namely, that he'd been deliberately trying to catch her in the act of lying. Suddenly she couldn't wait to see the man again. She was going to take great pleasure in telling him— sheriff or not—what she thought about his underhanded tactics.

''I'm Ryan Fortune, Miss Carter.''

She glanced up to see the older man had come around the table to greet her. He was about fifty or so, Gabrielle guessed, and was tall and solidly built. He was a handsome man, and though he was obviously rich, there was nothing arrogant about him.

Offering her hand, she said, ''Thank you for having me in your home, sir. It's very beautiful.''

''I'm very sorry about your accident, Gabrielle. My whole family and I are hoping you'll be completely well very soon.'' He smiled at her in a fatherly way, and Gabrielle suddenly didn't feel so bad about being here on the Double Crown.

''I hope so, too, sir. And I promise I won't take advantage of your hospitality. As soon as Sheriff Grayhawk finds my identity, I'll be leaving.''

Ryan Fortune's smile turned to one of compassion, and

Gabrielle got the impression that he was a man who knew what it was like to face overwhelming trouble and endure the pain that went with it.

"Don't be worried about making a hasty stay of it here at the ranch, Miss Carter. As you can see, we have plenty of room. And we want you to be truly well and on your feet before you leave."

"Thank you, sir."

"You're very welcome," he said with another indulgent smile, then returned to his seat at the head of the table.

Next to her Maggie said to Gabrielle, "See, I told you you shouldn't feel bad about staying here. My father-in-law is very kind. And he has a wonderful fiancée, Lily. You'll like her very much."

"Lily isn't officially my fiancée," Ryan said with a proud chuckle. "Not until she puts the engagement ring on her finger. But I'm hoping that's going to be very soon." The older man glanced at his son. "And speaking of lovely brides, where's Claudia? Isn't she going to eat lunch with us?"

The young doctor grimaced. "No. She's eating alone."

Ryan frowned at his son. "It's not often you get to be away from the hospital for lunch. Maybe if I go and talk with her—"

Matthew interrupted with a shake of his head. "No. Don't bother. The sight of me upsets her right now. And I can hardly blame her."

"But, son, you're—"

"I'm sorry, Dad. I don't want to talk about it. Anyway, Rosita's here with the food."

As the housekeeper served them all a tossed salad and burritos smothered with green chili sauce, Gabrielle's thoughts lingered on the two men's exchange. Maggie had hinted all was not well with Matthew's marriage, and she could certainly understand why his wife would be upset. Still, from her first perception of the man, he seemed like the last sort to have an affair. His eyes were too honest and full of hurt.

Not anything like Wyatt Grayhawk, she thought as she stabbed her fork into a spicy burrito. He wouldn't care if he hurt a woman. His eyes were as hard as pieces of steel.

There is a lot about Wyatt Grayhawk you don't know.... Maggie's words had intrigued her, but she wasn't going to stoop to asking questions about him. The less she knew about the taciturn sheriff, the better off she would be.

Later that afternoon, Wyatt glanced up as one of his deputies pushed the paper across his desk. ''Here's the data from the car rental agency, Wyatt. It just came over the fax.''

''Thanks, Gonzolez.''

He waited for the deputy to leave his office before he read the printed information. Once he'd finished, he leaned back in the leather chair and stared thoughtfully at the opposite wall of the small office.

So he'd been right after all. Gabrielle was from California. Without looking at a map, he would guess the address given was somewhere in the Los Angeles area. She'd rented the car six days ago and had informed the rental agency she would return it in two weeks.

That meant she hadn't expected to stay all that long in Texas. But long enough to cause problems, he thought. *If* that had been her intention. And in his job *if* was always a mighty big word.

Sighing, he rose from the chair and walked over to the dusty paned window that overlooked the main street of Red Rock. Late evening traffic was bustling up and down, with folks going home from their jobs and attending to last-minute shopping and errands.

The small town had been uncharitable to him in some ways, but good too, Wyatt supposed. He'd been born and raised nearby on a dusty hundred-acre ranch. His Cherokee father had been a cold-hearted cuss who'd found it easier to show him the back of his hand than to say more than two words at a time to his son. Wyatt had endured his abuse, mostly because he had no one else to turn to, nowhere else to go. And he'd blamed himself for his father's bitter cruelty.

Marilyn, Wyatt's mother, had been a white woman, and from his very early memories he could still recall how soft and beautiful she'd been, with long blond hair and blue eyes. She'd had a gentle voice too, and sometimes she sang funny little songs to Wyatt as she cooked in the small kitchen of their shabby home. She'd always been hugging and kissing him, and often she'd told him she loved him more than anything on earth. And Wyatt had believed her. His mother had always been the one solid thing he could count on.

Many times Wyatt had heard his parents fighting, but as a small child he'd not understood what any of their arguments had been about. Once he'd found her crying and her cheek had been red; she had whispered to Wyatt that soon she was going to take him away to a better place.

But then one morning he'd woken to find his father standing over his bed. His breath had smelled of whiskey and a snarl twisted his bloated face.

That good-for-nothing mama of yours is gone, boy. And she won't be coming back.

But why didn't she take me with her, Daddy?

Because she didn't want a half-breed kid. She didn't want

you! So don't be cryin' and whinin' for her to come get
you. She won't.

For a long time Wyatt had hoped his father was wrong.
Every day he'd prayed and waited for his mother to return.
But she hadn't, and eventually his young mind had been
forced to accept that his father was right. Marilyn Grayhawk hadn't wanted a half-breed son. She'd only married
Leonard because she'd been pregnant, his father had told
him. So Wyatt was the reason his beautiful, gentle mother
had left. Wyatt was the reason his father was bitter and
angry and mean.

With a tired grimace, Wyatt reached up and swiped a
hand through his short black hair. He didn't think of his
parents much anymore. Once he'd reached eighteen he'd
moved out of his father's house. Eventually Leonard Grayhawk had gone back to Oklahoma. And as for Wyatt's
mother, he hadn't seen or heard from her since he was five
years old.

What the hell was he doing? He didn't have time to stand
around recollecting his sorry childhood. Neither one of his
parents had given a damn about him. Neither one of them
was worth a second thought.

Wyatt returned to his desk and picked up the faxed information on Gabrielle Carter. There was a phone number
listed along with her California address. If he was lucky,
someone on the other end would answer.

The telephone rang three times and then he heard Gabrielle's cheerful greeting on an answering machine. There
was a *beep,* then the line went blank. Still Wyatt continued
to hold the receiver next to his ear as though he expected
Gabrielle's voice to come back at him at any moment.

When he finally realized what he was doing, he hung up
the phone with a *bang.* She isn't going to talk to you, Grayhawk, he silently scolded himself. She's out at the Double

Crown Ranch. Planning, well, no telling what. Maybe to take baby Taylor when no one is looking. Even if it was impossible for her to be the child's mother, she might be his aunt. Gabrielle could very well have a crazy sister out there somewhere who'd requested Matthew's sperm and given birth to his son.

The idea was far-fetched, he knew. But so far, he still hadn't traced down all the sperm bank clients who'd received Matthew's sperm. And until he did, he couldn't rule out any possibility.

He rubbed a hand over his face and dialed Gabrielle's number again. This time he listened even more closely to her voice, and as before it made him feel odd in a way he couldn't explain. She sounded so happy and young and carefree. She sounded sweet and gentle. Like a woman who would laugh a lot and smile a lot and care about her fellow human beings.

Slamming the phone down again, he yelled for Gonzolez. The deputy immediately entered the cluttered office and stood beside Wyatt's desk.

"Is something wrong, Wyatt?"

Hell, yes! Everything was wrong, he thought. A woman with big hazel-green eyes and long sun-streaked hair was trying to worm her way under his skin. And he wasn't about to let it happen.

He tapped the paper on his desk with a long, lean finger. "I want you to keep dialing this number. At thirty-minute intervals until you reach someone. If anyone does answer, get their name, address, number, the whole works—and pump them for any info they might have on Gabrielle. Also, I want you to call Bob Adair out at the Los Angeles police department and ask him about the area of the address. Rich, poor, whatever. He'll know."

"I don't ever remember us dealing with an amnesia victim before. Kinda strange that one's come along now. With all that's been happening out there on the Fortune place.''

Wyatt glanced up at the older man. He'd been on the force for many years and had served the sheriff's department well. He hated doing desk work, but Wyatt deliberately kept him busy in the office. It was less than a year until Gonzolez could retire. Wyatt didn't want some idiot out there with a gun or a knife ruining the coming years for him.

"I'm not so sure she has amnesia," Wyatt told him. "But until I can prove otherwise, there's not much I can do about it. Her name didn't turn up any criminal record. But you and I both know that doesn't mean a damn lot. It could mean she's been lucky so far and not gotten caught by the law.''

The older man rubbed his chin thoughtfully. "Maybe. But you know, it would be a helluva thing not to know your family or friends or even yourself. If she does really have amnesia, she's probably pretty scared right about now. I would be.''

Wyatt reached up and pinched the bridge of his nose. As he did, the image of Gabrielle's trembling lips and the lost look in her eyes flashed through his mind. But just as quickly he shoved the mental picture away. He couldn't get soft now. Or ever.

Rising to his feet, he reached for his Stetson resting on one corner of his desk. After tugging it low on his forehead, he said to Gonzolez, "I'm going out to the Double Crown. If you get anything on that number, page me immediately.''

"I'll let you know," the deputy assured him.

Behind the office building, Wyatt walked across a small parking area to his truck. The sun was on the verge of sliding out of sight in the western sky. Still, it was as hot as blue blazes, and without a cloud to be seen there was no chance the drought they'd been enduring for the past weeks would be broken. Much of the pastureland between Red Rock and the Double Crown Ranch would soon burn if rain didn't fall soon, and Wyatt didn't envy the area ranchers.

In the past he'd often thought of purchasing a spread for himself where he could raise a few cattle and horses. Since his father had been a small-time rancher, Wyatt had grown up learning about both. But his hopes of having a family to go with the ranch had died a bitter death, making him shove the whole idea aside.

Leonard Grayhawk had taught Wyatt most everything he needed to know to raise a good herd of cattle, to pick a well-bred horse. But Wyatt didn't know one thing about being a husband or a father. And he'd been a fool to believe he could ever be either.

None of that mattered now. He had a nice, comfortable home in the suburbs. And that was all Wyatt was ever going to need.

He reached the Double Crown just as darkness was falling around the big ranch house. Mary Ellen Fortune, Ryan's widowed sister-in-law, answered the door and ushered him in. For a woman in her fifties, she was still pretty and wholesome with thick red hair that just touched her shoulders. Her blue eyes were bright and her skin was as fine as a porcelain dish.

"It's nice to see you this evening, Wyatt," she said as he followed her into the great room. "Are you here on business or pleasure?"

Mary Ellen was probably close to his mother's age or a little older, and sometimes he wondered if his mother Marilyn would look anything like this woman. Or had Marilyn used herself up? She could even be dead. He didn't know, and he told himself that was the way he wanted to keep it.

"Business," he answered. "I need to see Gabrielle. She is still here, isn't she?"

The older woman smiled. "Yes. I met her earlier this afternoon. She's a lovely young woman. It was such an unfortunate thing for her to have wrecked her car that way. Maggie is still miserable about the whole thing."

"You didn't recognize anything about her?" Wyatt asked her.

"No. I've been racking my brain, trying to think of anyone I knew by the name of Carter, but I can't come up with a one." She motioned for Wyatt to continue following her through the dining area, then down a long hall to their right. "Anyway, I think Gabrielle is in her room. I'll show you where. Would you like something to drink? I'll have Rosita bring coffee in to you."

"If she has some already made. But tell her not to go to any trouble."

Mary Ellen laughed softly. "It's never any trouble for Rosita to serve the sheriff. You're just like one of her five kids."

She knocked on a carved wooden door, and from deep inside the room, Wyatt could hear Gabrielle's voice responding. Then, moments later, the door swung wide.

Her mouth fell open at the sight of Wyatt, then immediately snapped shut to form a grim line. "Oh. It's you," she said none too graciously.

"I think Wyatt has some business he wants to see you about," Mary Ellen told her. She glanced at Wyatt "So I'll leave you two alone. Rosita will be in soon with coffee."

Wyatt thanked Mary Ellen, then stepped past Gabrielle and into the room. He'd been in the other wings of the house before, but never this particular part. The Fortunes had certainly made things more than comfortable for their mysterious houseguest.

"I see you've already settled in. New dress and all."

She turned to see his penetrating gaze scanning her figure, and hated the fact that she felt totally naked beneath his perusal. "Maggie bought me a whole pile of things. And before you start in—I didn't ask for any of it."

His smile was more of a sneer, and Gabrielle's spine stiffened.

"I'll bet you didn't try too hard to make her take them back, now did you?"

"Maybe you haven't noticed, but Maggie is a kind person. I wasn't about to insult her generosity. I'll leave the clothes here whenever I leave, and she can donate them to a church or needy shelter."

He hadn't expected that from her, and for a moment he wondered just how far a woman could take her subterfuge to get what she wanted. A long way, he figured. Especially if it meant getting her hands on some of the Fortune millions.

"Still trying to make me think you're a lost missionary worker?"

She glowered at him while trying not to let his sarcastic question hurt. "I wouldn't dream of trying to make you *think*."

To her surprise a little grin tugged at the corners of his lips. "You know, the longer you stay here, the more I'm going to see you're not the helpless little lamb you want the Fortunes to think you are."

Gabrielle didn't know what sort of temperament she'd had in the past, but right now she wanted to throw herself bodily at this man. She wanted to whack her fist against his broad chest just to see if she could make him feel.

"Yes, I've really been giving them a sob story. By the time I leave here, I'll have a pile of money and Ryan will be writing me into the will. And all because I had the good luck to have a wreck on the Double Crown.'' She laughed then, a mocking sound that made him glower back at her. ''But I'm sure you already know I somehow managed to stage all of that too. I even planted the snake down at the creek so it would strike at Maggie's horse so it would deliberately run wild in front of my car. The whole incident took some doing, but I'll have to admit the timing was perfect. I even managed to get out of the car just before it blew up. I'll bet that makes you good and sick—''

''That's enough!''

She shot him an innocent look. ''Really? I thought you wanted me to…what did you call it yesterday? Fess up?''

He closed the few steps between them and clamped his hand around her upper arm. ''You're treading on thin ice, Miss Carter. Are you deliberately trying to make things worse for yourself?''

Her breasts were heaving up and down like a laboring engine, and she hated him for having such a savage effect on her. ''I may be at a disadvantage right now because I don't know who I am. But that doesn't mean I'm going to stand around and let you harass me. You're nothing but a bully with a badge pinned to your shirt!''

Never in Wyatt's life had a woman twisted and turned his insides like this one, and before he could stop himself he jerked her forward and into his arms. The shocked look in her eyes as her breasts flattened against his hard chest gave him a surge of power and pleasure.

''For two cents I'd shut you up good and proper,'' he muttered harshly as he stared down at her moist lips.

''I wish I had a purse with two cents in it!'' she heaved back at him. ''Then we'd see just what sort of man you really are!''

Wyatt knew he should push her away. But suddenly he was drugged by the warm softness of her body. The sweet scent of her skin and hair drifted to his nostrils and filled his head. Without thinking, his hand spread under her chin. His thumb and fingers clamped into her cheeks, making her lips part temptingly.

From the first moment he'd looked at this woman's face, he'd wondered what it would be like to taste the soft alluring curve of her lips. Now all he had to do was bend his head and bite into their fullness.

"If that's what you want, then you can charge it," he taunted lowly.

Gabrielle's heart pounded as she watched his face dipping closer and closer. She couldn't let him kiss her. She might as well throw herself into a pit of fire!

Just as she started to squirm against him, a knock sounded on the door. Instantly, he dropped his hold on her face and stepped away from her. Her cheeks flaming with anger and embarrassment, Gabrielle hurried to answer it.

While she was at the door, Wyatt walked over to the sitting area and looked out at the courtyard. Darkness had fallen and the walkways between the carefully tended gardens were lit with footlights. But he couldn't see any of it. Gabrielle's face kept swimming temptingly before his eyes.

He didn't know what in hell had come over him. For nearly eight years he'd worked as a lawman, and during that time he'd met all sorts of women. Never had he laid hands on one in such a way. He'd never wanted to. But something about Gabrielle both infuriated and excited him. He wanted to touch her, shake her, rile her. He wanted to know who she was and what she was. Not as a sheriff, but as a man.

"Rosita brought the coffee. She sent cake with it. In case you haven't had supper, she said."

Sarcasm tinged the last of her words, and for once Wyatt didn't blame her. He'd been gouging her since he first walked up on her after the car accident. And that wasn't like him either.

With an inward sigh, he turned away from the window to see Gabrielle placing a tray of food and drinks on the low pine coffee table sitting parallel to the couch.

He said a bit wryly, "It may surprise you to know that Rosita likes me."

Keeping her gaze carefully averted from him, she sat down and began to pour coffee from an insulated pot into two heavy mugs. She was still consumed with the feel of his hard warm body next to hers and the sight of his lips inching closer. It was a blessing that Rosita had knocked. Otherwise, Gabrielle really didn't know how she would have resisted the man.

"Rosita probably likes everyone."

"No. Rosita is cautious and suspicious. And even more superstitious."

She found the courage to glance at him and was surprised that he wasn't looking at her as though he'd like to slap her in irons. "I've already learned that. She predicts I'm going to learn something about myself while I'm here," she told him, then asked, "Sugar or cream?"

"No. Straight."

She handed the mug to him, and their eyes met. Electric excitement raced down Gabrielle's spine. "Rosita also said I would know you before I left here."

One of his brows arched with mocking humor, but inside he felt an odd sort of chill, a sensation closely akin to fear. Which didn't make sense. Wyatt didn't fear anything. He'd endured and survived eighteen years of hell with his father. Nothing could be worse.

"Rosita is always making predictions."

"Do they ever come true?"

He shrugged. "Sometimes she makes a lucky guess."

She carefully studied the closed expression on his face. "Then you don't believe she's psychic?"

"I believe Rosita is a wise old woman who makes her deductions with her eyes and her ears."

Gabrielle was inclined to agree with him. Yet she couldn't dismiss the fact that Rosita had also warned Maggie of a striking serpent.

Turning her attention back to the tray, Gabrielle tilted a pitcher of cream over her mug until the coffee was the color of caramel. "It's odd, isn't it, that I don't know what my house or apartment looks like or who my family is, but I instinctively know I like cream in my coffee."

"Matthew says amnesia is a tricky thing." Dammit, now he was halfway admitting she really might have amnesia. What else was he going to be doing before he left here? he wondered crossly.

She looked up at him. "Then you do believe I have amnesia?"

There was such a hopeful, eager look in her eyes that he felt his resistance close to crumbling. "I'm not believing anything yet. Either one way or the other."

Her shoulders visibly sagged with disappointment. "Why did you come here tonight? Mary Ellen mentioned you had some business to discuss with me."

He leaned toward her and picked up a slice of carrot cake from the wooden tray. "I do."

She waited while he took a bite of the sweet and swallowed it. If he had any news to give her, he was certainly taking his time about telling her. But then, she'd already come to the conclusion that Wyatt Grayhawk did things his own way and at his own speed.

"I've got your home address. Or at least the one you gave the car rental agency."

Her mouth fell open and she quickly plunked her mug

down on the coffee table. "My address! Why are you just now telling me? Where is it? Have you located anyone there?"

Her questions had a frantic edge to them, and Wyatt wondered if it was from fear of exposure or real eagerness to find her past. He wished he knew.

"It's somewhere in the Los Angeles area. The only thing I've managed to get on the telephone is a recording on your answering machine."

"What does it say?"

"The normal thing. That you're away from the phone and to leave a message."

"Oh. Well, that hardly gives you anything to go on."

"On the contrary. It tells me more than you think."

"Like what?"

Hope was back in her voice. Wyatt tried to ignore it. "Namely that you live alone."

"How can you be sure? I might have a roommate. Or a lover."

Wyatt bit into the rich, spicy cake while he pondered Gabrielle's remark. Maybe being a virgin was something a woman couldn't instinctively know about herself. Or maybe Gabrielle was simply testing him, trying to see just how much he actually knew about her.

"You didn't mention a roommate's name on the machine. And as for the lover...I don't think so," he said bluntly.

"Why?" she persisted. "I realize I wasn't wearing a wedding ring. But it's possible I have a live-in lover."

Wyatt's gaze fell to her small hands, now clutching the coffee mug. Her nails were short and neat and painted a pearly color that reminded him of the inside of the mussel shells he used to pick up from the creek bed. The thought of those soft tanned fingers stroking some man as he made love to her was repulsive to Wyatt. Unless he was that man. God help him.

"I said no!"

She reared back at his outburst, her face a picture of bewilderment. "Why is that so hard to imagine? I'm fairly certain I'm of legal age. If there is a man I was involved with, he might be able to—"

"There is no man, Gabrielle. You're a virgin."

Five

Gabrielle appeared so totally stung by his comment, he almost believed she was amnesic. But then, good drama classes could have produced the same expression, he assured himself.

"How could you possibly know such a thing!" she flung at him.

Wyatt couldn't remember the last time he'd felt the heat of a blush steal over his face. But he was sure as hell feeling it now. "I wasn't supposed to know," he muttered. "But it was part of your medical report and—"

"And you just didn't have the decency to quit reading!"

Wyatt could have told her that he hadn't read anything. But he wasn't going to lay any sort of blame on Matthew. She already considered him the equivalent of pond scum. It didn't matter if she believed he'd also invaded her privacy.

"Miss Carter, there are things going on here—"

"I know all about those things! Maggie has filled me in on Bryan's kidnapping and how the recovered baby turned out to be Matthew's son. But a different one. Which he says he didn't know he had. And if you think I had something to do with any of it, you're crazy, you're—"

Her words halted and she frowned. Then, bending her head, she pressed a hand over her eyes.

"What's the matter?"

She didn't answer or look up at him. He moved closer and took her by the shoulder. "Are you ill, Gabrielle?"

"No," she said with moan.

"Then look at me!" he ordered.

"I can't. I can't see you. Everything suddenly started blurring and running together."

The panic in her voice was real, and Wyatt could not stop his hand from reaching up and stroking down the long length of her hair. "Is your head hurting?" he asked more gently.

"Not any more than it's been hurting all day."

He stroked her hair again, loving the way the silky texture slid against the pads of his fingers. "See if your vision is getting any better," he urged.

She lifted her head and turned slightly to look at him. The puckered frown between her brows told him she was still struggling to focus.

"I think you should lie down, Gabrielle. I'll help you."

He took her hand and drew her up from the couch. After two steps she swayed on her feet and clutched desperately at his forearm. "I'm sorry, Wyatt. Everything is spinning. Just give me a moment."

Wyatt didn't bother giving her time. Instead, he bent and picked her up in his arms.

Gabrielle gasped. "What—are you doing?"

"Keeping you from falling on your face."

Gabrielle had no other choice but to wrap her arms around his neck and hold on as he carried her across the long room.

She was not a large woman. She wasn't petite either. Yet Wyatt managed her weight as though he were used to lifting much more. His arms were strong bands around her back and beneath her thighs. The hard muscles of his shoulders flexed beneath her arms.

In spite of his cold words she felt safe and protected by his nearness. Scents of sweet grass and earthy musk emanated from his clothes and rich black hair. The smell filled her like a heady drink of wine. She was gripped with the urge to bury her face against his neck and savor the feel of his smooth brown skin beneath her cheek.

All too soon he was lying her down on the mattress. As he straightened away from her, she instantly missed the warmth of his body and the secure feeling it had lent her.

"What are you doing?" she asked when she realized he was pushing some sort of intercom button.

"I want Matthew to take a look at you."

She started to protest, but before she could open her mouth he was already speaking into the intercom.

He disconnected, then the mattress dipped as he sat down on the side of the bed near her shoulder. "He'll be here shortly," he told her.

"The man has enough troubles without me disturbing him. I didn't come out here to make a pest of myself. Although I'm sure you don't believe that."

Wyatt didn't know what to believe anymore. But he didn't want to take the chance that Gabrielle was simply faking it. If she truly needed medical attention, he would be the first to want her to have it.

"Matthew has been through a hell of a lot these past months. I doubt doctoring you will add to the strain."

She didn't say anything to that, and he told himself he should get up from the bed and put some space between them. Yet he didn't. He liked being near enough to smell her flowery scent, see the fine texture of her skin and the amber-brown flecks in her eyes. Her lashes were too long to be real. Yet he could see they were as natural as the dusky-pink of her lips. Lips he still wanted to taste.

"Wyatt?"

She'd never called him by his given name, and it sounded strangely intimate coming from her.

"Yes."

"I know the Fortunes aren't any of my business. But I frankly don't understand why a man like Matthew donated sperm. He has a wife and a child with her…"

Wyatt considered telling her she was sticking her nose where it didn't belong. But she was already staying here as a guest in the Fortune house. She could easily get the information from one of the family members. And he was beginning to get the feeling it would be better all around if he loosened up with this woman. If she got the idea he was beginning to trust her, she might just let her guard down.

"It happened long before he married Claudia. When he was in his first year of medical school at Stanford," he told her. "I'm not exactly sure what prompted him to donate sperm. I think…well, Matthew is a real family man. He loves children, and I think he liked the idea of being able to help some infertile couple have a child of their own. I'm sure he never believed the donation would lead to anything like this."

"No. I'll bet not," she agreed.

His lips twisted as he looked down at her woebegone expression. "Why the long face? His problem is nothing to you."

She turned her face away from him, but not before he could see her frown was full of hurt. "How can you be so coarse? He's a kind man. I feel sorry for him. I can't imagine having a child and then losing it."

Without warning, thoughts of his mother entered Wyatt's mind for the second time that day. Could Gabrielle ever be the way his mother had been? Could she vow her love, then walk away without a word and never come back? No matter what the answer, he would never risk his heart to find out.

"I can be coarse because I'm a sheriff," he told her. "I'm paid to be that way. If I looked at everything and everyone with a soft heart, things around here would be in a hell of a mess."

"Looks to me like they are anyway," she couldn't help retorting.

If Wyatt had an ego, her words would have sliced it down to nothing. As it was, he didn't care if she thought him inept. She'd probably already been wondering how a sorry half-breed had gotten elected to the office in the first place.

"I'm just a sheriff, Gabrielle. Not a superhero."

Her head turned back to him and she struggled to see his face. "You called me Gabrielle. Does that mean I'm your friend?"

He lifted a lock of her hair that was lying loose on the pillow and studied its rich brown color. "Do you want to be my friend?"

Gabrielle figured being Wyatt's friend was akin to a shot at the doctor's office. It would probably hurt a little, but the end result might be positive.

"It's always better to make friends than enemies. But I don't want to be accused of trying to sweeten you up."

One corner of his mouth curled upward. "I think we both know I'm too smart for that."

A soft knock sounded on the door. Matthew entered the room carrying a black medical bag. As he approached the bed, Wyatt stood and moved out of his way. Matthew examined Gabrielle and asked her several questions about how she was feeling.

After concluding his examination, he asked, "Have you taken any more painkillers?"

"No. I don't much like the idea of putting drugs in my system."

He released the blood-pressure cuff from around her arm. "Well, in this case, I think you should take them. Your blood pressure is a little elevated. That could be from the pain." He glanced at Wyatt. "Have you been harassing her with questions?"

Wyatt's frown was full of resentment. "Matthew, what do you think I am?"

"You're my friend. That's how I know you can be...unrelenting at times."

"He hasn't been harassing me," Gabrielle spoke up, surprising both men. "Wyatt has discovered where I live. So how soon do you think I can go home?"

She didn't know what home was. But whatever it was, she had to go back. She couldn't prey on the Fortunes' hospitality. They already had enough troubles without trying to care for her too.

Matthew lifted her wrist and counted her pulse. "I wouldn't advise you to be traveling for a while, Gabrielle. Remember, you do have a concussion, and sometimes complications from such an injury can linger for several days. Even weeks."

"You mean like this blurry vision?"

"Exactly. And your headaches. As a doctor, I say you need to stay put and let the injury to your brain totally heal. Besides, if you have no recollection of your home, it might be jarring to try to step right back into things." Matthew glanced at Wyatt. "Were you able to contact any family?"

Wyatt grimaced. "No. Nothing but an address. But believe me, I'll keep working on it."

Matthew shook out two capsules from the medicine bottle sitting by the telephone. "Take these—and if your vision doesn't get better before bedtime, let me know. You might have to go back into the hospital for another brain scan.''

Wyatt fetched Gabrielle's coffee mug, and she obediently swallowed the capsules.

''Thank you, Matthew. I'm sorry to have interrupted your evening.''

His smile was rueful. ''It was no interruption, Gabrielle. I was just reading some medical reports.''

''Where's Claudia and the baby?'' Wyatt asked him.

Matthew collected his things and snapped the black bag shut. ''Having supper with a friend. But don't worry, one of the bodyguards has gone with them.''

Wyatt was thinking that it would have been better if Matthew had escorted his wife, but he kept the idea to himself. Matthew and Claudia would have to work out their problems in their own way. Besides, he didn't know anything about marriage—except that most never worked out for the long haul.

Once Matthew said his good-nights and left the room, Gabrielle looked at Wyatt. ''What did he mean, the bodyguard went with her? Do the Fortunes have bodyguards?''

Did she really not know? he wondered. ''After Bryan was kidnapped, Ryan thought it best to post bodyguards on the ranch. Especially since there's no way of knowing if the kidnappers will try to strike again.''

Gabrielle shivered outwardly. ''How absolutely awful to have to live under such a strain. I don't think having money would be worth it. Give me a shack or a tent. I'd rather have peace of mind.''

His gaze lingered on her face as he stood beside the bed. ''Maybe you think that now. But before you lost your memory you might have had different ideas about wealth.'' She was coming here for some reason, he thought, and where the Fortunes were concerned, it probably boiled down to money.

She tried not to let his suggestion rile her. He'd shown her more kindness tonight than she'd ever expected. She was beginning to think he might not be hard through and through, as she'd first believed. Just crusty on the outside.

"I can't say you're wrong, Wyatt. I have no idea what I was before I wrecked my car yesterday. But a person's moral values come from somewhere deep inside. I don't think a crack on the head is going to change them."

Wyatt wanted to believe her. But then, he'd wanted to believe his mother when she'd promised to take him to a better place. "I guess time will tell us about that. Right now, I've got to get back to the Sheriff's Office. If you have to return to the hospital, tell Matthew to call me."

She nodded, and he started toward the door. But just as his hand closed over the knob she called his name, and he glanced over his shoulder at her.

"You need something else?" he asked.

She drew in a deep breath and let it out. "No. I wanted to tell you I thought you played a dirty, underhanded trick yesterday at the hospital."

His brows shot up with interest. "Really? Which trick was that?"

"Telling Matthew to keep his identity from me. That was a bad thing to do. I was already confused enough. And you tried to take advantage of the situation."

He shrugged, and the grin on his face said he didn't feel one ounce of remorse. "So I'm dirty and bad. Maybe if you'll remember that, we'll both be better off."

He opened the door and stepped out, then, on second thought, leaned his head back inside. "By the way, Gabrielle, I forgot to mention there was no criminal record matching your name."

Yet he still trusted her as much as he would a Texas sidewinder, she thought. She shouldn't feel crushed, but the pressure in her chest nearly robbed her of breath. "Obviously that doesn't let me off the hook where you're concerned."

"We both know you were coming here to the Double Crown for something. When you can tell me the real reason, I'll decide whether you're a criminal or not."

Gabrielle didn't bother trying to defend herself with a retort. Instead, she turned her face to the wall and waited to hear the door shut behind him.

Two days later Gabrielle was feeling stronger although her headaches and blurry vision were still striking her without warning. Most of the time she stuck close to her room and tried to occupy herself with a book or a television program. But that was very hard to do when her mind was roiling with questions.

This evening she'd wandered outside into the courtyard. As she strolled through the carefully tended plants and groupings of comfortable lawn furniture, she couldn't help but wonder how much longer her memory was going to remain a blank. She felt as if she'd been dropped out of the sky and left here in this place for some unknown reason. But why?

"Gabrielle, come here, I want to show you something."

Gabrielle turned her head to see that Maggie had entered the courtyard and was taking a seat at a large round glass table shaded with a huge flowered umbrella.

She hurried over to where the other woman sat. "Hi, Maggie! It's nice to see you."

She smiled warmly at Gabrielle. "I was planning to come by yesterday to check on you. But I got busy with my son, Travis. He wanted to go horseback riding, and I decided it would be a good time for me to get back on a horse and put what happened with your accident behind me."

Gabrielle took a seat in the chair directly across from her. "I'm glad you did. I would hate to think it spoiled your pleasure in riding."

"It hasn't," Maggie assured her, then with a sad frown, she added, "but I can see you still haven't remembered. Have any sort of memories flashed through your mind?"

"No. Sometimes it seems like...well, vague impressions come over me. Especially since Wyatt uncovered my address. More and more I'm beginning to think I don't have a family."

Maggie's brows puckered into a frown. "Surely not. You're a young woman. I doubt your parents are deceased. What makes you think such a thing, anyway?"

Gabrielle shrugged. "I can't explain myself. It's just a feeling I get especially when I see you Fortunes together. I don't think I had the connection of a family the way you all do. Maybe I have a family but we're estranged. I just can't remember. And the harder I try, the more my head hurts." She shook her head and sighed. "The Double Crown Ranch is at least fifteen-hundred miles from my address in California. That's a long distance. Especially for a young woman to be traveling alone. What was I doing coming here? And Maggie, Wyatt told me something else that bothers me even more."

Concern in her dark eyes, Maggie leaned forward. "What?"

"What he told me is personal and—well, frankly, it's hard for me to accept."

"What is it?" Maggie prompted.

Gabrielle glanced around to make sure the two of them were alone. "I'm a virgin."

Maggie's mouth fell open. "How does *he* know?"

Seeing where the other woman's thoughts were leading, Gabrielle quickly waved away her assumption. "Not by intimate investigation!"

"Then how—"

"How he found out doesn't matter. What it implies is what bothers me," Gabrielle confessed. "Maybe I actually am a religious zealot. The virginity certainly goes along with the Bible Wyatt found in my car. Or maybe I'm just abnormal."

"Gabrielle," Maggie gently scolded, "you're not abnormal! Why would you think something like that?"

Color flooded Gabrielle's cheeks. "Well, I'm a little old not to…have known a man, don't you think?"

"You don't know how old you are," Maggie argued. "Anyway, being a virgin is something you should be proud of. I know my life would have been a lot less complicated if I had waited to give myself to a man. As it was, I ended up pregnant and married to a man I didn't love."

"I take it you're not talking about your husband now?"

With a dreamy smile, Maggie shook her head. "No. Dallas is wonderful to me and my son. I'm happily in love."

Gabrielle sighed. "Well, it's a cinch there's no man out there for me. If there was, I wasn't *that* close to him."

Maggie reached over and patted the back of Gabrielle's hand. "You're worrying far too much. Things are going to fall in place for you. Just wait and see." She leaned back in the chair and snapped her fingers. "Oh, I almost forgot."

She leaned over for something on the floor by her chair. Gabrielle watched her lift another huge sack filled with packages onto the table. "I went into San Antonio today to run some errands, and while I was there I picked up a few more things I thought you might need."

"Maggie!" Gabrielle gasped. "You've already given me

so much. This really isn't necessary. You're spending far too much—''

"Gabrielle," she interrupted, "my husband isn't lacking for money."

"It doesn't matter if he is rich. I don't want to take advantage." She could already imagine the sardonic look on Wyatt's face when he found out Maggie had spent more money on her.

A lump suddenly filled Gabrielle's throat. She was a stranger to these people, yet they continued to treat her with warmth and caring kindness. Dear God, she couldn't have been coming here to hurt them! The idea was too horrible to contemplate.

"You already gave me everything I needed the day I was released from the hospital. And anyway, I promised Wyatt I'd leave the things here whenever I left to go home."

Maggie stared at her in comical disbelief. "Whatever for? They're yours."

An odd sort of pain crawled its way beneath Gabrielle's chest. Damn the man, even when he wasn't around he had the power to affect her.

"To prove to him that I'm—I'm not a gold digger."

Maggie laughed freely. "Honey, leaving your clothes and things behind isn't going to prove anything to Wyatt, believe me. No woman could prove her worth to that man, so don't bother to try."

Unable to hide her curiosity, Gabrielle asked, "Why do you say that? Is he one of those men who hate women?"

Even as she asked the question, Gabrielle couldn't imagine such a thing. The other night when Wyatt had carried her to bed, she hadn't felt any hatred in him. When he'd stroked her hair, it had been with a gentle hand.

"No. I don't think he actually hates women," Maggie

told her. "In fact, from what I hear he was pretty serious about a girl some years back. But something happened. I don't know what. Anyway, they parted company, and he's been a loner ever since. I guess he lost his trust in women and doesn't think they're worth the effort."

The idea of Wyatt loving and losing a woman was hard for Gabrielle to take in. He seemed too strong and sure of himself to ever be besotted or brokenhearted over a woman.

"One bad romance shouldn't have that much effect on a person," Gabrielle pointed out.

"Well, I don't expect losing his mother the way he did helped matters," Maggie said, her expression thoughtful.

"His mother died?"

Maggie shook her head. "She left when Wyatt was very young. I've heard my parents talk about it. She just up and walked away, and no one ever heard from her again. I suppose it's a possibility she could be dead now."

Gabrielle stared at her in dismay. "Wyatt doesn't know what happened to her?"

"I don't know. You'd have to ask him that. And I wouldn't if I were you. He can get downright mean if you touch his sore spots."

Gabrielle had already learned that to some degree. Still, she wanted to know about him. Why was he so hard and suspicious? Especially of her.

"What about his father? Do you know anything about him?"

"My father, Ruben, says Leonard Grayhawk was a mean man who had drinking bouts. I guess Wyatt was lucky— or determined—to survive his childhood." She gathered up the large department store bag. "Enough about that dismal stuff. Let's take these things to your room. And Gabrielle, no matter what Wyatt says, you're not leaving any of these things behind. You're going to look absolutely too pretty in them.''

Gabrielle followed Maggie into the house. But as she opened the packages of expensive clothing and expressed her pleasure over them, thoughts of Wyatt lingered like a haunting shadow in the back of her mind.

His mother had left, never to contact her son again. And his father had been anything but loving. It was little wonder Wyatt had turned into a hard man. No doubt he'd had to be tough to survive and climb to the life he had now. But surely growing up without love would only make him want to seek it more.

I think he's lost all trust in women.

Wyatt hadn't tried to hide the fact that he doubted Gabrielle. But she'd believed his attitude was because of all the things that had been happening to the Fortunes, not because she was a woman.

So what could she possibly do to gain his trust? Nothing, she told herself grimly. Without her memory, she was helpless. She was at the mercy of Red Rock's sheriff.

And worst of all, he knew it.

Six

Back at the Sheriff's Office, Gonzolez stood in front of his boss's desk and waited until Wyatt finished his telephone conversation before he spoke.

"You wanted to tell me something?" the older man asked as Wyatt hung up and glanced at him.

"Yes. You might as well forget that number out in California for now. I don't think it's going to produce anything."

"The young lady hasn't remembered anything?"

Wyatt leaned back in the leather chair and raked fingers from both hands through his short hair. He was more exhausted than he could ever remember being, but there was so much he needed to do on the Fortune case. And over the past two days there'd been a rash of local brawls that had filled the jail with drunks and assault cases. He still hadn't finished the paperwork on all the arrests.

"If she has, no one has bothered to tell me about it."

"What about those last two women you were trying to locate? The ones who'd requested Matthew's sperm?"

Wyatt heaved out a heavy breath. "Both of them had moved around like gypsies. I had to track them through a long list of old addresses before I had any success locating them. I finally reached one this morning. She told me she was never able to get pregnant and has given up on the idea. The last one I contacted this evening. No luck there either; she had second thoughts and never went through with the artificial insemination.''

"So now what, Wyatt? It's a damn cinch some woman out there gave birth to that child. You think Matthew had a few rolls in the hay and just doesn't want to own up to his wife about it?''

Wyatt shook his head. "No. He's adamant about being faithful to his wife, and I know Matthew. He's not a man who would lie. For any reason. There has to be some other explanation. And it's come down to the woman who registered under the name Brown at the fertility clinic. If we could find her, we might be getting somewhere.''

Gonzolez shook his head. "Well, that whole thing about another baby being delivered for the kidnap ransom is downright weird. If this Brown woman is the mother of Taylor, why would she give her own son away—and keep Bryan?''

"Who the hell knows. There're some crazy people out there,'' he said with a weary sigh, then added thoughtfully, "But oddly enough, having baby Taylor in the house has helped the Fortunes. At least, it did until we learned Matthew was his real father.'' Wyatt reached for his hat, put it on his head, then rose to his feet. "I'll be out at the Double Crown if you need me.''

In the study of the Double Crown ranch house, Ryan Fortune stood quietly with his back facing the cold fireplace. A few steps away from him, a tall young man in his early thirties with short dark hair paced up and down like a caged tiger.

Parker Malone had been a friend of the family for years. He'd played football with Matthew in college, and his father's law firm had handled many legal matters for the Fortunes through the years.

Parker was currently handling Ryan's divorce. With Sophia's greedy claws wrapped around his money and a percentage of his assets, it was going to take a damn good lawyer to break her hold and leave him in the clear to marry Lily. And from all Ryan had heard and seen, Parker possessed one of the best legal minds in this part of Texas.

Unfortunately, during these past few months, he could see the younger man was embittered about marriage. And Ryan could hardly blame him. Parker had watched his parents go through a hellish divorce, and then before he'd reached the age of thirty, he'd suffered through his own divorce. It was no surprise to Ryan that the man was continually advising him to put thoughts of marrying Lily out of his mind. At least until they had Sophia where they wanted her.

"Look, Parker, I know my love for Lily seems foolish to you. And I admit I made a terrible mistake in judgment when I married Sophia. But at the time I was in a black hole. Janine had died and I missed her terribly. I couldn't see what Sophia was really all about. But Lily is different—"

The lawyer interrupted with a shake of his dark head. "Ryan, I'm not putting Lily down. I'm only trying to make you look at things sensibly. You could have waited to buy an engagement ring. We have no concrete promise yet that Sophia will sign the fifty-million dollar settlement we offered her."

"As far as I'm concerned, what Sophia does or doesn't do has nothing to do with buying Lily an engagement ring. I'm going to marry her, one way or the other. And to hell with what it takes to get Sophia off my back."

Parker paused in mid-stride to frown at Ryan Fortune. "That's just the sort of thinking I'm worried about. The woman doesn't deserve a penny, Ryan. It sickens me to think you're going to be giving her fifty million. Nothing is worth giving her more!''

Ryan's faint smile was tinged with sadness as he closed the distance between them and clamped a fatherly hand on Parker's shoulder. "That's where I disagree, Parker. Lily's love is worth everything to me. I lost it once. I won't let that happen again. One of these days you're going to meet someone who will change you. And then you'll know what I'm talking about.''

"I very much doubt—" Parker was interrupted by a knock on the study door.

Ryan moved away from him and called, "Come in."

Rosita stood inside the open doorway. Her gaze encompassed both men, then settled on her boss. "Wyatt would like to see you, Ryan. Are you busy now?"

"No. Send him on in."

The housekeeper left, closing the door behind her. Parker said, "I'd better be going so you two can talk. We'll discuss what's happening with the divorce later."

"No. Stay. Wyatt might have some news we'll all want to hear."

"All right."

A knock sounded on the door, and Wyatt stepped into the study.

"Good evening, Wyatt," Ryan quickly greeted him. "You know my lawyer, Parker Malone."

Wyatt glanced at the young man. "Nice to see you again, Parker."

"Same here." Parker nodded warmly.

"I didn't mean to interrupt," Wyatt said. "But I do have some news on the case. Are Matthew and Claudia home?"

"I think so. I'll buzz his suite and tell him you're here." He started across the room toward an intercom. As he walked, he tossed over his shoulder, "Have you found out something about Bryan or Taylor?"

"In a way. I've discovered something Matthew and Claudia need to know. I'll tell you when they get here."

Ryan nodded grimly.

In less than five minutes Matthew and his wife, Claudia, entered the study. Her shoulder-length blond hair was perfectly groomed, her makeup equally flawless. Yet the desperate look in the woman's blue eyes told Wyatt she wasn't nearly as composed as her appearance would lead one to believe. As for Matthew, his expression was one of a man who seemed resigned for more bad news.

As the whole group turned their attention on Wyatt, he tried to remember the last time he'd been able to report anything positive to these people. He ached for them all. They were his friends, yet even with his sleuthing abilities, he hadn't been able to put things right for them.

"I know you were all hoping I'd be able to uncover Taylor's mother through the list of women I received from the sperm bank. Today, I succeeded in tracing down the last two. There is one name left, but I've discovered the name is phony and so is the address. And from their records she only visited the clinic once and never returned for a follow-up visit."

Grim-faced, Claudia moved away from her husband and came to stand in front of Wyatt. "What did you find out from the two women you did track down? Did one of them give birth to Taylor?"

Wyatt took a deep breath and let the bomb drop. There was no way to avoid it. "No. One of them was never able to conceive and finally abandoned the idea altogether. The other one had second thoughts and decided she didn't want to get pregnant by artificial insemination."

Claudia flinched as if Wyatt had slapped her, then she

whirled on Matthew like a wounded animal. "Bastard!" she said coldly. "You had an affair and all this time you've let me go through this agony—"

Tears choked off the rest of her words, and she ran toward the door. Matthew threw his hands up and hurried after her.

"Claudia, I didn't have an affair! I've told you—"

She jerked open the door, then paused on the threshold, her head held high. "I don't care what you've told me! Wyatt's evidence proves it. I'm not staying in this house with you another minute," she said through gritted teeth.

"But the baby—"

"I'm taking Taylor with me. He might be yours by blood, but you obviously didn't care enough about him to even acknowledge his birth."

Matthew groaned loudly. "Claudia, I didn't know about his birth! There was no woman. Wyatt just said there's one more name—"

"Sure. A phony name," she interrupted as tears began to stream down her face. "Oh, go tell your lies to someone else!"

The door slammed in Matthew's face and he slowly turned to face the three men. "I don't know what to do anymore," he said, his voice defeated, his shoulders sagging.

"I'm sorry, Matthew," Wyatt said. "I was afraid Claudia might react like this. But I had to tell you."

Matthew nodded glumly. "Of course you did. It's not your fault. But dammit, Wyatt, what does it all mean?"

Behind them, Parker spoke up like the true lawyer he was. "Matthew, are you certain you didn't have one fling? Maybe one night you were feeling tired and depressed. You stopped in town for a drink or two, and one thing led to another."

"No! I would never betray Claudia in such a way. I love her! Dad, you believe me, don't you?"

"I've never known you to lie about anything," Ryan told him. "But I can see how it all looks mighty incriminating to Claudia."

He stared in disbelief at his father. "Then you're taking her side in this thing? You think she should move out—away from me?"

Ryan held up his hand. "I'm not saying anything like that. I can see where both of you are being hurt by this whole thing, and my taking sides would only make matters worse."

Wyatt placed his hand on Matthew's shoulder. "I know this probably won't help much right now, but I promise, Matthew, I will find the woman who gave birth to Taylor. If this Brown woman is the mother, I'll find her someway. And then Claudia will have to believe you."

He looked gratefully at Wyatt. "Yeah, I know you will, partner. But by then, will any of it matter? How can I live with a woman who doesn't believe in me?"

"Touché!" Parker bellowed. "If you need a divorce lawyer, Matthew, you know where to find me."

"I just might at that," Matthew muttered, then stalked rigidly out of the study.

Wyatt planted his Stetson back on his head and glanced at the two men left in the room. "Well, I guess I've stirred up enough trouble for one night. I'll say goodbye to you two."

"Thanks for coming, Wyatt," Ryan said to him. "I'm sorry you had to witness that scene between my son and his wife. But you, as much as anybody around here, know what they've been going through."

Wyatt nodded, his lips compressed in a stern, straight line. "Yeah. I'll keep you posted on anything I uncover."

On his way out, Wyatt found himself turning toward the corridor that led to Gabrielle's room.

As he stood outside Gabrielle's door, he asked himself what he was doing. He'd come to the Double Crown only because he had wanted to give Matthew and Claudia the crushing news about the baby in person, rather than over the telephone. There was no reason for him to see Gabrielle tonight. Except that he wanted to.

As he knocked lightly on her door, he cursed himself for his weakness. Young virgins were not his style. And young virgins with no recollections of their past were way off-limits. Yet something about her tugged at him long after he heard her voice and looked upon her face.

"Yes? Come in. The door is unlocked."

For one brief moment he considered turning on his heel and quickly walking away. Then, cursing himself for being a coward, he pushed through the heavy door.

She had been sitting on the leather couch, but the moment she saw it was him, she stood. A silk, peach-colored robe was wrapped around her slender figure and cinched at her waist. Even from this distance he could see the naked outline of her breast beneath the fine material, and his body stirred with unashamed longing.

"I didn't know it was you," she said bluntly.

"Obviously." He walked over to where she stood, his eyes drinking in the tousled hair piled atop her head, the smooth brown column of her throat, the curves of her bare lips.

"Don't you ever rest?"

His lips twisted into something close to a grin. "Only when it's a necessity."

Like the heavy *thud* of a bass fiddle, Gabrielle's heart pounded inside her chest as his gaze continued to sweep over her face and down to the gaping material between her breasts. Not caring how virginal or modest she looked, she reached up with one hand and clasped the robe tightly together.

Her action made the grin on his face deepen, and Gabrielle felt stunned, bowled over by the flash of his white teeth and the dangerous glint in his hazel-green eyes. How many women had seen that same sensual look on his face and been lured into his bed by it?

"Why are you here? Have you found out something else about me?"

The question reminded him who he was and why he'd come to the Double Crown in the first place. It hadn't been to see her. But now that he was seeing her, he didn't regret his decision to walk down here to her room. She looked like a juicy apricot. Sweet and tart and, oh, so ready to bite.

"Scared?"

She lifted her chin a fraction. "Not of you," she lied.

His gaze settled on her lips, and she clutched the robe even more tightly.

"If you're not, you should be," he said slowly, then forced himself to step around her and over to the windows facing out onto the courtyard.

Gabrielle turned and watched the muscles of his shoulders flex as he folded his arms against his chest. He was dressed as she'd seen him last: in jeans and a khaki shirt with short sleeves. The sheriff's badge was hidden beneath his arm, but she instinctively knew it was there. She figured he rarely took it off. Even when he went to bed, he probably pinned it to his shorts. But then maybe he didn't wear shorts—maybe he slept in the raw. The idea of his long bronze body without a thing on it stung every inch of her with heat.

"I had some business to attend to with Matthew and his

family," he said. "I thought I'd check on you while I was here. You weren't feeling well the last time I saw you."

"You surprise me, Wyatt. I thought you believed my blurry vision wasn't real. That I was faking it...along with my memory loss."

"I considered it."

"I'm sure you did."

Irked by his brutal honesty, she walked over to where he stood by the windows. When his eyes slanted down to her upturned face, she felt everything inside her begin to shake. Not with hostility, but from the simple excitement of being near him.

"If you really want to know, I'm feeling stronger," she told him. "But I still lose my vision without any warning."

"So that means Matthew doesn't want you traveling yet."

He said it as a statement, but she answered it as a question. "No. He doesn't. So now I guess you're thinking I'm faking the headaches and blurry vision so I can continue to live here in luxury?"

He turned slightly so that he was facing her head-on. His expression was smooth—neither accusing nor believing. "I think Matthew is a doctor with a kind heart. And right now, well, he's in no condition to make judgments."

Gabrielle frowned at him. "What does that mean?"

"The man has been through hell, and I've just handed him another plate of trouble to digest."

Forgetting to hold the robe, her hand dropped to her side. "What sort of trouble? Have you found his baby son?"

His eyes narrowed as he turned his gaze away from her and out to the darkened courtyard. "No," he said grimly.

"Then—"

"I had to tell him and Claudia that none of the women

who'd requested his sperm at the fertility clinic is the mother of Taylor."

Gabrielle gasped at the realization as to what that meant. Yet she refused to believe Matthew had committed adultery. The sordid behavior didn't fit the man at all.

"Oh, dear. How did they take it?"

He slanted her a sardonic look. "How do you think? Claudia is furious. She's taking Taylor and moving out."

"Oh, no! That isn't going to help matters." Gabrielle spoke her thoughts out loud.

The twist to Wyatt's lips deepened. "No. I don't expect it will. I don't know what the hell Claudia is thinking. If she can't trust her husband more than this, I'm not so sure Matthew needs her."

Gabrielle's mouth fell open as indignation poured through her. "Trust! You of all people are going to condemn Claudia for not having enough faith in her husband? He's fathered a baby somehow, yet you expect her to believe in his innocence? If you can be so open-minded about Matthew, why do you treat me like a felon? I haven't done anything wrong either."

His face hardened, his nostrils flared. He'd seen too much pain tonight. And he'd heard too many lies from too many women in the past to take Gabrielle's accusations lightly.

"Get this straight, Gabrielle. I will never trust any woman. Especially you."

Like a black cloud, rage blinded her to everything but the moment and the provoking expression on his face. Before she could stop herself, her palm cracked solidly against his jaw.

By the time her hand fell back to her side, she realized what she'd done. Her heart was pounding wildly and her breasts were heaving with anger and fear. Yet the conse-

quences of her actions no longer mattered, she told herself.
At least she'd gotten the satisfaction of retaliation.

"You might be the sheriff around here, but that doesn't
give you the right to insult me!"

His eyes glowing oddly, he snagged both her shoulders—and jerked. She stumbled forward. The heels of her
palms landed against his chest, preventing her from falling
completely against him.

Desperately, she tried to lever herself away, but his hands
snatched her waist and yanked her into his arms. Air
whooshed from her lungs as her breasts flattened against
his hard chest.

"Let me go, you bully! You arrogant bast—"

The rest of her words were smothered when, like a hawk
swooping down on a helpless little field mouse, his mouth
covered hers.

For the first few seconds Gabrielle was too stunned to
resist, and then, suddenly, she was consumed with the dark,
forbidden taste of him. If she'd ever sampled anything so
rich or delicious she didn't know it. His hot mouth was
devouring hers as his tongue slid smoothly between her
teeth and against her tongue.

She felt locked in some timeless place where nothing
existed but the feel of his hard body pressing into hers, the
raw hunger of his lips. She wanted to stay forever in the
warm space he was creating. She wanted to cling. Absorb.
Never let go.

His fingers slid inside her robe and clamped around her
naked breast. As the pad of his thumb teased her nipple,
longing coiled in her loins and caused her to whimper in
the back of her throat.

The small, sensual sound penetrated Wyatt's foggy brain.
With a shocked start, he realized his body had already been
set on a forward motion with no intention of stopping until

he'd buried himself inside her. God, what had come over him!

He thrust her aside so forcefully that she nearly stumbled. Stunned by the rapid escalation of her desire, and the abrupt end of their embrace, she sucked in a long breath and tried to calm her racing heart.

Finally she was composed enough to glance around the room. Once again she was shocked to see Wyatt about to walk out the door. Angry, she raced across the room and slammed the door closed before he could step through it. "Where do you think you're going?"

Beneath the brim of his hat, his brows formed a furious black line. "I'm getting the hell out of here!"

"Why? Afraid you might end up wanting a criminal?"

His lips formed a sneer while his eyes bored into her. "Don't try to taunt me into making love to you, Gabrielle. It won't work."

She gasped. "Are you—if you think—" She stopped, swallowed and started again. "That would be impossible. You don't know how to make love, Wyatt Grayhawk. All you know about is sex!"

His harsh laugh stabbed her in the chest. "You seemed to be liking it well enough."

Her already pink face flamed red. "Maybe I did," she dared. "But fires do burn out. What could you offer a woman then?"

"You'll never know," he promised coldly.

Seven

The sun was fierce, but the broad-brimmed straw hat Maggie had thoughtfully purchased for Gabrielle kept the worst of the heat from pounding her head. Yet the sticky heat was the last thing on her mind as she strolled a short distance away from the ranch house.

Getting outdoors was wonderful. Finally, after five days on the ranch, she was beginning to feel physically strong again, and so far this afternoon her head wasn't hurting. If she continued to recuperate at this rate, she might be able to talk Matthew into letting her travel home.

Home. Gabrielle didn't know why, but the word seemed all wrong when she thought of California. She supposed it was because she couldn't remember what her home had been. It might have been a place she loved. But then again, it might have been just a residence—rooms where she slept and ate, but little more. Either way, she wasn't at all sure she wanted to go back there.

Ever since Wyatt had given her the address she'd stared at the small square of paper, wondering, straining to remember. But so far not a glimmer of recollection had flittered through her mind.

With a troubled sigh, she stopped beneath the shade of a cottonwood and leaned against the rough trunk. A good half-mile across the flat pastureland she could make out the images of several barns. Dust mushroomed up from the nearby working pens, and Gabrielle wished she had the strength to walk the distance and watch the cowboys work. She'd never been on a cattle ranch. It would be interesting to learn how the animals were branded and cared for.

Her eyes suddenly widened. How had she known she'd never been on a cattle ranch before? Had she remembered, or did her ignorance about ranch work intuitively tell her? She desperately wanted to believe it was memory. Perhaps this was a tiny start toward her recovery. She had to keep hoping. As much as she loved the Double Crown, she couldn't stay here forever. And now there was Wyatt to contend with.

She had no idea what he was thinking of her now. She hadn't seen or heard from him since he'd stopped by her room three nights ago. After the way she'd slapped him, then kissed him so wantonly, his opinion of her had probably nosedived.

Gabrielle had tried to think just as badly of him. But somehow she couldn't. No matter how hard she tried, it was impossible to forget the way she'd felt crushed in the tight circle of his arms. He'd made her feel so possessed, so wanted. She would have given him anything, right then and there. It was a shocking admission.

And then to accuse Wyatt of not knowing how to make love! Coming from a virgin that must have seemed pretty hilarious to him. He was probably still laughing. But she wasn't. Because she knew she was right. And what could be sadder than a person who didn't know how to love?

Her thoughts coupled with the heat were beginning to sap her strength, so she pushed away from the tree trunk and walked slowly back to the house. Once inside the courtyard, she went directly to her room and stripped off her sweaty jeans and blouse.

She'd just stepped under the spray of the shower when she heard Rosita's muffled voice in the bathroom.

"I can't understand you, Rosita. Just a minute." She opened the shower door and, with a towel carelessly clutched to her front, stepped partially out of the stall.

"Is something wrong?" she asked the housekeeper.

"No. I'm sorry I disturbed you, Gabrielle. I came to your room earlier and you were gone. Then I started to worry that you'd gone outside and fainted."

The older woman's concern for her never failed to touch Gabrielle. In less than a week she'd grown very close to the housekeeper, and she often wondered if she had a grandmother like Rosita somewhere. She would have liked to think so, but something deep inside told her she'd never experienced the motherly concern this woman had shown her.

"I'm sorry I worried you, Rosita. I did go outside for a little walk. But I made it just fine. Next time I'll be sure and tell you."

She waved her hand in a dismissive way. "No worry now. I thought I'd better warn you that you'll be having supper in the big dining room tonight. Lily and her daughter Hannah are coming, and Ryan wants something special cooked. So you might want to put on a dress."

"Oh, is it a special occasion of some sort?"

The old woman rolled her eyes. "I think Ryan wants to give Lily that big sparkly ring he bought for her."

Gabrielle smiled. "Then I'll try to look my best." She started to step back into the shower, then glanced over her shoulder at the woman. "What about Wyatt? Will he be coming?"

A knowing smile spread over Rosita's face. "Not that I know of. But Wyatt has an open invitation to the Double Crown. He's liable to show up any time."

"Oh. Well, I was just wondering."

Rosita's smile deepened. "He is a man to wonder about."

Gabrielle couldn't think of a thing to say to that, and turned once again to step back into the shower. As she did, she noticed Rosita eyeing the birthmark on her hip.

"I know it's rather a strange-looking birthmark. Like a queen's crown," she said to the woman, then laughed. "I'm just thankful it's in a spot that doesn't show."

"A birthmark could never hurt your beauty, Gabrielle. Go finish your shower, and I'll call you when everyone starts to gather."

The old house was gone. The porch had crashed in first, then the remaining roof and walls had followed a few years later. Now there wasn't much more than a heap of decaying lumber and the stones that had once formed the foundation.

Wyatt kicked at a piece of rusty tin with the toe of his boot. Dust flew, and a lizard made a wild scramble for safety.

He didn't know what had brought him out here to this place where he'd grown up. There was nothing here now but memories. And none of them were good. Mostly he could see his father, a big strong Cherokee sitting on the porch, his black hair slicked back from a wide face, a beer in one hand and a favorite hound at his feet.

Leonard had been an intelligent, fairly educated man, but he'd lacked the ambition to use either. Especially after Marilyn had left. Even though Wyatt had been little more than five years old, he could remember his father doing nothing more than sitting beneath a shade tree for days at a time, drinking and talking to his hunting dogs rather than taking care of the cattle or horses.

After Wyatt had grown older, he'd often wondered where Leonard had gotten the money to put groceries on the table or to pay the utilities. In the deepest part of him, he knew his mother had every reason to walk away from this place. Wyatt couldn't blame her for wanting a better life. He just blamed her for not wanting *him*.

A bitter lump filled his throat; he turned away from the pile of broken dreams and headed back to his truck. At the edge of the blacktop road was a faded real estate sign: For Sale. Hundred Acres.

Who the hell would want this place? he asked himself. Not him. He had a nice house in the clean, well-to-do suburbs, a house most anyone would be proud to own. He'd be a damn idiot to want a hundred acres of overgrown land. Property that would take months to clear into pasture and hay meadows. He'd need his head examined for even considering the idea of building a ranch house on this spot. Marilyn had left this sorry place and her son behind. It wasn't a plot of fertile soil. A family hadn't grown from it then, and he'd be a fool for thinking he could build one on it now. Yet for some irrational reason the place called for him to try again.

I don't want a woman. I don't want a family.

Even as he thought the words, the memory of Gabrielle's body crushing against him burned through Wyatt like a red-hot ember. He'd never felt the things that had flooded through him when he'd kissed her. He'd forgotten where they were and why he'd touched her in the first place. He'd forgotten everything except the overwhelming need to make love to her.

You don't know how to make love, Wyatt Grayhawk! All you know about is sex!

Gabrielle's taunt had left him furious. Mostly because she'd been right. Wyatt had never made love to a woman. His connection to women had always been driven by lust. Never by his heart. Even Rita, whom he'd once believed he'd wanted to marry, had given him plenty of romps in bed. But he'd never touched her with love. He wasn't sure he would know how.

Muttering a curse, he twisted the key in the ignition and the engine fired to life. He needed to forget this place. And he sure as hell needed to forget Gabrielle Carter. But when he pulled the truck back onto the road, he turned the nose in the direction of the Double Crown.

Just to check on her, he promised himself. If he was lucky, he would find her with her memory intact and her bags packed to leave. But luck had never ridden on Wyatt's shoulders. And he didn't expect tonight to be any different.

Before supper that evening, Gabrielle met Ryan's fiancée, Lily Redgrove Cassidy, and her daughter, Hannah. She was also introduced to Matthew's younger brothers, Dallas and Zane. Though both were tall and lean and strongly built like their older brother, most of the resemblance stopped there. Dallas seemed every inch the quiet cowboy who never strayed far away from his wife's side, while Zane was the single, outgoing businessman, chatting up everyone in the room.

Gabrielle got the impression that the middle brother, Zane, was very close to Matthew. Several times she noticed him casually tossing his arm around his older brother's shoulder or giving him a fond cuff on the arm. She hoped Zane's appearance would somehow help fill the void created by Claudia's conspicuous absence. But she doubted anything or anyone could make Matthew forget for one minute that his wife had separated from him.

Throughout the evening, Gabrielle tried not to think of the young doctor's troubles and to focus on the happiness she saw on Lily's and Ryan's faces every time they looked at each other.

Gabrielle had never met Ryan's estranged wife, Sophia, but she'd heard enough from the family to give her a clear picture of the woman. And when Gabrielle had learned the woman was considering fifty million for a divorce settlement, it was easy to make her own deductions about Sophia Fortune. The woman was concerned about one thing: money.

However, Lily appeared to be altogether different. There was no doubt she was a beautiful woman. Tall, with a voluptuous figure and beautiful dark hair and eyes, she made a perfect match for Ryan. But it was the love in her eyes when she looked at him, and the gentle way she touched him, that assured Gabrielle she would be right for the older Fortune. Their wedding would be a joy to the whole family. Something all of them needed.

After a delicious lengthy supper, everyone settled down for after-dinner liqueurs and coffee in the great room. When Ryan presented Lily with the engagement ring, the whole group gathered around and exclaimed over the extravagant piece of jewelry.

Awestruck, Lily gasped, "Ryan! Did you insist the jeweler put every stone he had into this ring?"

Laughing joyously, he said, "Nothing is too good for you, Lily. And I told him I wanted everyone to be able to see you were mine." He plucked the ring from its plush velvet nest. "Let me put it on your finger."

Her eyes full of love, Lily extended her slender hand and allowed him to slide the ring onto her fourth finger. The heavy gold band studded with sapphires, rubies, emeralds and diamonds cast sparks of fire as she held up her hand, then twisted it this way and that for everyone to get a view.

"It's…I can't describe how beautiful the ring is. I absolutely adore it." She turned back to Ryan, her expression suddenly full of anguish. "But I'm sorry, darling. I can't wear it now."

Easing the ring from her finger, she handed it back to Ryan. Maggie gasped, while Hannah groaned. Matthew, Dallas and Zane exchanged concerned glances. As for Ryan, he looked as if his fiancée had just slapped him. "But, Lily. Why? You've already agreed that we'll have a December wedding!"

Sadness gripped her lovely features. "Yes. I want nothing more than to become your wife. That's why...I'm afraid to wear the ring. Sophia hasn't signed the divorce papers yet. I don't want to jinx anything by jumping the gun."

"Mother!" Hannah exclaimed, "we've already started planning the wedding. Wearing the engagement ring isn't any different."

Lily turned toward her daughter. "I'm sorry, Hannah. Call me superstitious or silly. I can't help how I feel. I don't want to wear my engagement ring until I know we are well and truly rid of Sophia."

Ryan shook his head. "Lily, it doesn't matter—"

The doorbell rang, and the group looked around at the offending noise. Rosita had already gone home some time ago, so Gabrielle quickly offered to answer it.

Gabrielle was the last person Wyatt had been expecting to answer the door. For long seconds he could do nothing more than stare at the vision she made in a long burgundy dress printed with tiny white flowers. A short crocheted top of the same color was buttoned over the low neckline, giving him discreet little peeks at the plump tops of her breasts. Her hair was coiled into an elaborate twist at the back of her head and rhinestones glittered at her ears.

"Hello, Wyatt," she said huskily.

"What the hell is going on?"

His gruff response didn't surprise her. He was not a man who wasted time with niceties. She closed the door behind her, then stepped out onto the adobe steps. "Some of the family gathered for supper tonight. Ryan has given Lily an engagement ring. Why are you here?"

Why *was* he here? Wyatt asked himself. His body answered for him. He grabbed her hand and jerked her off the steps.

"Wyatt! What—"

Before she could get the rest of the question out, he tugged her behind a clump of pampas grass that towered over their heads and hid them from view. Instantly, his arm hooked around her waist, his fingers clamped under her chin. She caught the glitter of his eyes in the darkness, and then, without warning, his lips were on hers, searching, biting, devouring.

Even if he'd given her time to resist, she wouldn't have. For the past three days she'd hungered for him. For this. It was crazy! Crazy to want him this much.

Her bones turned to mush, forcing her to grab onto his shoulders. His hands cupped her bottom and jerked her hips against the hard bulge in his jeans. She moaned at the intimate contact and dug her fingers tighter into his shoulders. Lifting his head, Wyatt sucked in a harsh breath. "Get in the house and tell them you're leaving with me."

Gabrielle didn't question his hoarsely whispered order. She was in no condition to resist him.

In the entryway she smoothed her hair, pressed her fingers against her puffy lips, then drew in a steadying breath before heading into the great room.

Ryan still had Lily cornered in a big armchair. Thankfully, they were too deep in conversation to notice her return. Matthew, Zane and Dallas were watching some sort of news report on television. She didn't see Hannah anywhere, but Maggie was wandering around the room, collecting empty glasses. Gabrielle hurried to intercept her as she started toward the kitchen.

Bending her head down to Maggie's, she whispered next to her ear. "It was Wyatt at the door. He's taking me somewhere."

Maggie glanced at her sharply. "Where?"

"I don't know."

The other woman released a troubled sigh. "Be careful. That's all I can say. As a sheriff, Wyatt is wonderful. As a man, he's downright dangerous."

No one understood that better than Gabrielle. "I know."

She discreetly made her way out of the great room and back out to the front entrance of the house.

Wyatt stepped out of the shadows and caught her by the elbow. The simple touch of his fingers left her trembling, and she wondered wildly why and how things between them had escalated into this.

Without speaking, he guided her out of the front yard and through the iron gate that separated the sandstone wall surrounding the house. In the dark shadows she could see his truck gleaming in the patches of moonlight filtering through the cottonwoods.

When they reached the vehicle, his body pressed hers back against the door, and once again his lips ground down on her mouth. The sudden, unexplained onslaught of his desire was in itself like a dizzying ride. She clung to him and kissed him hungrily. She could do nothing else.

But a voice in the back of her mind kept droning on and on, asking what it all meant and why it was happening now. Telling her she had to stop it…stop him before it was too late and she had no chance to turn back.

"Wyatt," she whispered as she gasped for breath—and sanity. "What are you doing?"

His fingers touched her cheek, and she felt a part of her heart melt like warm chocolate. "Isn't it obvious?"

"Yes. No." She sighed and the erotic scent of his skin filled her head, fired the longing that was already burning through her body like a bright flame. "You left here furious three days ago."

One corner of his lips twisted upward. "You've been counting?"

"No."

"You can lie better than that."

Her nostrils flared with anger even as her lips trembled to kiss him again. "You would say that," she whispered. "If you think I'm so bad, why do you have me here...like this?"

"Maybe I like bad girls." His head bent closer and his hard lips brushed temptingly against hers. "And you are bad, Gabrielle. You've put some kind of spell on me, and I'm not going to be able to rest until you do something about it."

She swallowed as a shiver of anticipation slid down her spine. "Like what?"

His white teeth gleamed against his dark skin as a goading grin spread across his face. "What do you think?"

Her knees threatened to buckle as his fingers stabbed through the holes in her lace top and stroked the tender flesh of the tops of her breasts.

"I think you're starved for sex."

He was starved for *her*. But he couldn't tell her that. To admit he wanted only her would put a whip in her hand. It would let her own a part of him he wouldn't let any woman see, much less possess.

"Then you don't know anything about me."

No. She didn't. But despite that she had let herself want him. Need him. When it came to desiring a man, how did a woman stop herself? she wondered. Moreover, she wasn't at all sure she wanted to stop.

"I don't believe anyone knows you, Wyatt Grayhawk."

He didn't reply. Instead he tugged her away from the door and opened it.

"Get in," he said. "I'll take you for a drive."

"Where?"

"Does it matter?"

It didn't. And somewhere in her mind a flicker of memory or feeling said that before her amnesia she had never met a man who treated her the way Wyatt was doing. She was sure she'd had pride and independence. Yet she was just as certain that if she'd met him before, she would be reacting the same way she was now. Not because he was a Texas sheriff who could deal her some misery. But because each time he was near, every feminine particle inside her surged and boiled, and—God help her—softened with need.

"No," she whispered.

Something like triumph flickered in his eyes and then quickly faded as he reached to help her into the high cab. Gabrielle didn't have a clue what was going on in his head. But for tonight, she wasn't going to try to figure out the man, she was simply going to enjoy him.

He started the engine and headed the truck away from the ranch. Gabrielle recognized the inside of the cab as being the same vehicle she'd ridden in when he'd carried her to and from the hospital. Tonight he must have had the two-way radio turned off. They rode in silence for a while.

Since he was dressed in a blue chambray shirt with the sleeves rolled back against his forearms and his badge nowhere in sight, she wondered if he was off-duty, and asked him as much.

The question gave a wry twist to his lips. "A sheriff is never off-duty."

"You're not wearing your badge," she pointed out.

"It's on me. You just can't see it."

She turned her head away from him and gazed out at the moonlit landscape slipping past her window. This was a night to make love, she thought, outside in the moist heat, with the stars shining down like diamonds. She breathed deeply and tried to shake away the erotic images dancing behind her eyes.

"Have you ever had to use these rifles?" she asked, glancing at the rack of weapons behind their shoulders.

"On a few occasions. There've been hostage situations. A bank robbery that ended in a high-speed chase. But with the exception of drunks and domestic fights, it's mostly quiet around here."

"Then you've never been wounded?"

His head turned toward her. The lights on the panel illuminated his mocking expression. "Why do you ask? Think I might have some scars you'd like to see?"

Heat burned her cheeks. "Actually, I was wondering if your job was dangerous."

"Any time you pin on a badge, you're putting yourself in danger. But I've never been shot. Just stabbed a couple of times."

She gasped. "Stabbed! With what?"

"A knife. A switchblade."

The mere thought of someone driving a steel blade into Wyatt's flesh tore at her. "How did that happen?"

"I was a deputy then. Trying to break up a fight."

"Where were you stabbed?"

"In the shoulder and thigh."

He said it as though it were an everyday occurrence. But

then, perhaps being stabbed wasn't the worst thing Wyatt had been through in his life.

"What happened to the person who did it?"

"He's in prison now. Serving time for a different crime."

Thank God, she thought with a shiver.

"Are you going to worry about me now?" he asked in a goading tone.

Yet she got the impression that underneath, he really wanted to know how she felt about his job. "I think I will. A little. But," she went on as her eyes roamed his strong profile, "I also think you're a man who can take care of himself."

He liked her answer. Liked it too much. "I always have, Gabrielle."

Eight

Wyatt pulled into a wide circled drive and parked in front of a large, split-level brick house.

"What are we doing here?" she asked.

He killed the engine and looked at her. "This is my house."

Not his home or where he lived. Just his house. "Very impressive," she said as she peered out the windshield.

He opened the door and helped her to the ground. "It's nothing like the Double Crown ranch house."

She held on to his hand as they started up a short sidewalk. "I doubt anything around here is comparable to the Double Crown ranch house," she told him.

At the covered entrance, he unlocked a wide oak door and ushered her inside to a small foyer. While he shut and locked the door behind them, she stood to one side and waited, expecting him to switch on a light. When he reached for her instead, her heart flipped, then raced into a mad gallop.

"You've hexed me," he said as his tongue slid provocatively down her jawline, then up to the corner of her lips. "Right now I'm acting like one hell of a fool."

"For wanting a woman?" she asked, her head tilting back as his lips began to explore the smooth skin at the base of her neck.

He more than wanted Gabrielle. She was like a fever, scalding and tormenting his insides. Ever since he'd kissed her three nights ago, he'd realized he had to have her. Not just once, but over and over.

"For wanting you," he answered her. "You don't know who you are or what you are. You might have been planning to take the Fortunes for millions. You could even have Matthew and Claudia's baby son hidden away somewhere. But I don't give a damn. Maybe I will tomorrow. But not right now."

She'd come with him knowing how he felt about her. She should be ashamed for allowing him to accuse her of such heinous things while touching her as if he owned her. But, God help her, she couldn't resist him. All she had to do was look at him and it was like a potent drug had been injected into her veins.

Yet deep down she kept telling herself he couldn't touch her this way if he truly believed she was a criminal. He just couldn't.

She sighed, and his lips returned to hers. He kissed her fiercely, hungrily until her knees gave way and he lifted her into his arms. He carried her out of the foyer and across a large area into what sort of room, she didn't know. The house was dark and silent except for her own shallow breaths and the roaring thuds of her heartbeat in her ears.

Seconds later he eased her down on a soft leather couch and reached for the twist of hair at the back of her head. One by one, he removed the pins, and her hair tumbled thick and heavy onto her shoulders. He slid his fingers through the silky brown strands, then buried his face in the waves.

"You smell like a flower," he murmured. "Sweet. So sweet."

"Lilac," she whispered.

Slowly, he loosened the buttons on her top and pushed it off her shoulders. Then, bending his head, his tongue lapped the soft skin exposed by the low neckline. She shivered with longing, and he lifted his eyes to her face.

"Are you frightened of me, Gabrielle?"

He was a fierce man, but oddly enough she felt utterly safe and protected in his arms. "No."

"You've never made love with a man before."

"I only know what you've told me," she said. But deep inside she knew she had never been touched the way Wyatt had touched her. She had never felt this way before. Nor would she ever again, unless Wyatt was the man making love to her.

Wyatt hadn't expected her innocence to mean anything to him. Women had come and gone in his life. He hadn't really cared when or how they had entered womanhood. But as he looked into Gabrielle's eyes, he could see she trusted him; she was willing to give herself to him when, more than likely, she had turned many others down. The idea pierced something deep in his chest, a hidden spot he didn't want to acknowledge.

Shoving the unexpected emotion away, he reached for the single button at the back of her neck. When it opened, she lifted her arms, and he tugged the dress over her head, then tossed it onto a nearby coffee table.

When he turned back to her, what he found was enough to make him groan out loud. She was clad in two little wisps of scarlet lace. The lingerie was hardly enough to cover her nipples or the tempting *V* between her thighs.

His eyes lit with sensual pleasure, and he traced his fingertips along the edge of the lace molded to the mounds of her breasts. "If Maggie bought you these things, then I feel sorry for Dallas. The poor man probably never gets any rest."

Gabrielle thought she would be embarrassed to let him see her this way. Yet she felt nothing close to it. Her body was giving him pleasure, and it thrilled her to know how much the sight of her delighted him.

"She wanted me to feel sexy."

"Who the hell did she think was going to be seeing you?"

"Myself," she answered, then the corners of her lips tilted slyly upward. "Or maybe you."

He snorted. "No one thinks I'm this gullible," he said; even as he pushed her back against the leather couch.

Gabrielle trembled as his hand left her breasts and slid across her bare midriff, then down to her belly button and lower still.

"If you think this is a mistake, maybe we'd better stop," she whispered.

He lifted his head and there was a feral gleam in his eyes as they searched her shadowed face. "Stop? How the hell do you think I can stop now? This started the moment I first saw you. It has to end sometime. Somewhere."

End. What a strange word. He believed making love to her would end things between them. Whereas Gabrielle thought of their coupling as a beginning. But then, she had to remind herself Wyatt wouldn't be making love. Sex was all he wanted from her.

"I'm not like the other women you've known," she whispered, biting down on her lip to stop its quivering.

To her surprise his features suddenly softened and his hands lifted to cradle her cheeks. "No. You're not like them," he whispered. "You are far more potent. More dangerous. But I have to have you."

His lips settled over hers, and she sighed inside and slipped her arms around his neck. It didn't matter that he only wanted her body. Where he was concerned she had no shame or pride, just hungry need.

Seconds later, his tongue stabbed between her teeth and

plunged into the warm intimacy of her mouth. She embraced the connection, welcomed the weight of his body as it settled over hers.

Minutes later—Gabrielle was so lost in him that she couldn't be sure how many—he was suddenly easing away from her, then standing beside the couch.

"Damn it all to hell!"

She raised up and pushed her tousled hair off her face. "What is it?"

He jammed his hand down into the front pocket of his jeans and dragged out a small black box—a pager.

"I'm needed." He moved to the end of the couch and switched on a lamp. At the same time he reached for the telephone sitting beside it.

"Where?" she asked, her voice still husky with desire.

"I don't know yet."

He punched in a number, and Gabrielle sat up and reached for her dress. Before she could get it over her head, he said, "Something has happened out at the Double Crown. We've got to go."

Fear shot through her. "What? Is someone hurt?"

"I don't know. Ryan told the dispatcher it was urgent."

She stood and wriggled the dress down over her hips, then looked around for her top. The piece of crocheted lace was buried beneath a throw pillow. She reached for it.

"Put it on in the truck," he told her, then grabbed her by the hand and quickly led her out of the house.

As he gunned the truck out of the drive, Gabrielle fastened the seat belt across her lap and tried to ignore the pangs of regret slashing through her. Making love to Wyatt would have been a mistake, she told herself fiercely. It was probably all for the best that this emergency had intervened. But the practical reasoning didn't ease the empty ache inside her.

Wyatt broke the speed limit on the way to the ranch, but Gabrielle managed to twist her hair back in place and button her top before they entered the house. As for her bare lips, she had no purse or makeup with her to repair the ravages of Wyatt's kisses.

But as the two of them quickly entered the great room, she could see her disheveled appearance would never be noticed. Everyone was trying to talk at once, and Ryan looked grim and pale. Lily clung to his arm as if she were afraid both of them might collapse if she let go.

When the group spotted Wyatt, the room went instantly quiet. They all rushed toward him. Gabrielle stood by Wyatt's side, wondering what more could have happened to send this family into such an uproar.

"What's happened?" Wyatt asked, directing the question at Ryan, flanked on both sides by Matthew, Dallas and Zane.

Matthew handed a plain white envelope to Wyatt. "This was found on the front steps a few minutes ago."

"Who found it?"

"Maggie," Dallas said. "She thought she heard a cat meowing out in the front yard. When she went to investigate, she found the envelope."

Wyatt searched the front and the back before he opened the flap. "Where are those damn bodyguards? Aren't they supposed to be watching the house?"

"There was only one on duty tonight," Ryan told him. "And he was in the courtyard. He didn't see anything. He thought he heard a vehicle, but he figured it was one of the wranglers or the foreman coming to see me. He didn't look."

"Useless," Wyatt muttered. "You'd be better off with a dog."

"I've already fired him," Ryan assured him.

That might prevent the next person down the road from being hurt, Wyatt thought, but it wasn't going to help the Fortunes tonight.

Inside the envelope was a small square of paper with a short message and a Polaroid snapshot taped to the bottom. "Is this Bryan?" Wyatt asked as he read the ransom note.

"It's been a year, but I know that's Bryan. The picture has to be recent," Matthew added hopefully. "That can only mean he's alive!"

At least the child appeared safe and healthy in the photo, Wyatt had to agree, but what had taken place since the picture had been snapped was anyone's guess. "I think we all have to believe Bryan is safe. Has the FBI been notified?"

Dallas spoke up. "Yes. Right after we paged you."

Wyatt read the message once again. The kidnapper was asking for several million dollars to be dropped off at midnight, five days from tonight. The money was to be in a brown paper bag. The location was not far from the ranch, where two county roads intersected. At the crossing there was a row of mailboxes facing east, and the money was to be deposited in the last one, marked Box 51.

"It's been a year, you know," Ryan said weakly. "A year today that my grandson was taken from us. I should have been expecting something bad to happen today."

Matthew turned to his father. "Dad, we can't look on this as bad. If we deliver the ransom, this might finally be our chance to get Bryan back!"

"I agree," Dallas put in. "At least this is some sort of contact from the kidnapper."

Ryan sighed and passed a hand over his forehead. "Yes. Yes, I know you're both right," he told his sons. "It's just that I feel so damn helpless." He looked to Wyatt for guidance. "What do you think, Wyatt? Should I start making arrangements for the cash?"

Wyatt let out a long breath. One minute he'd had Gabrielle in his arms and had been on his way to heaven. Now he was faced with a ransom note and a desperate family.

He glanced at Gabrielle. Her face was pale and pinched, her eyes full of dark shadows. She hadn't spoken one word since they'd returned to the ranch, and he wondered what was going through her mind. Was she thinking of what had almost happened between them? Or did she know something about this ransom note? God, he wished he knew.

Turning his attention back to Ryan, he said, "Let's take one thing at a time, Ryan. First of all, I'll need to see how the FBI wants to handle this. I expect they might advise you not to pay the ransom."

"By God, I don't give a damn about the money!" Ryan exploded. "I want my grandson, my flesh-and-blood, back in this house where he belongs!"

Seeing how distraught Ryan was becoming, Lily patted his arm. "Darling, Wyatt understands that. He's simply saying the FBI will probably be against the idea."

Zane nodded in agreement. "I remember them saying that once a ransom is picked up, there's no insurance the kidnapped victim will be turned over unharmed."

Gabrielle felt chilled at the very idea of anyone hurting a baby. But she also realized anything could happen.

"Wyatt, are there any clues in the picture?" Gabrielle asked.

Wyatt carried the message into the kitchen where a bright light hung over a small breakfast area. Everyone followed and gathered around as he placed the photo in the middle of the table.

"There's a newspaper next to the baby. But I can't read

the date,'' Wyatt said. ''Is there a magnifying glass around here?''

''Mother has one in her mending basket. She keeps it in the kitchen,'' Maggie said quickly. ''I'll get it.''

Wyatt peered closer at the picture. The baby was sitting on a cheap couch that was ragged in places. Wedged under the edge appeared to be part of a woman's high heel shoe. The carpet—what little could be seen of it—was a garish red shag.

''The paneling and the carpet remind me of the sort you see in a trailer house.'' Wyatt spoke his thoughts out loud.

''From the looks of that high heel, do you think the kidnapper is a woman?'' Matthew asked.

''The shoe could have been put there purposely to make it appear that way. Or the kidnapper could be so stupid, he or she didn't even notice the shoe. But the paper was obviously put there to show the date.''

At that moment Maggie returned and presented the small magnifying glass. Wyatt thanked her, then tilted it over the area of the newspaper.

''Why, it's the *San Antonio Star!*'' Lily gasped.

''And the date is today!'' Ryan added excitedly.

Matthew sagged against the table, his relief almost too great to bear. ''Oh, thank God! Bryan is alive and well.''

Wyatt glanced up at the doctor. ''Have you told Claudia about any of this?''

He shook his head. ''No. We only received the note just before you arrived. I wanted to wait and see what you thought about it all before I told her. But now—this is even better news than I expected!''

''It is good news,'' Wyatt agreed. ''The fact that Bryan is alive and seemingly well taken care of after all these months makes me believe the kidnapper has no intention of physically harming him.''

"But we can't take that for granted, can we, Wyatt?" Dallas asked.

Wyatt glanced across the table at Matthew's younger brother. "No. We can't take anything for granted in this case. After all these months had passed without any more demands for ransom, I was beginning to think the kidnapper had decided he wanted a baby more than money. But now it's obvious he or she has an evil, greedy mind. They want a baby, money—or both. They already have the baby. Who knows what they'll do to keep him or get the money."

"Since it is a San Antonio newspaper, do you think my son might be close?" Matthew asked him.

"Probably closer than we think," he answered grimly.

Beside him, Gabrielle shook her head and blinked her eyes. The image of baby Bryan was blurring into streaks of color. Pain was gathering in her forehead and shooting through the top of her skull. Not wanting to interrupt, she quietly slipped away from the group and hurried down the hallway to her room.

Once there she switched on a small lamp at the head of the bed and shook out two of the pain capsules the doctor had prescribed. She swallowed them down with a drink of water from the bathroom, then lay down on the long leather couch.

A few minutes passed before there was a soft knock on the door, then Maggie entered the dimly lit room.

"Gabrielle, are you ill?"

"It's my head again," she told the other woman. "Everything suddenly began to blur and then the pain started pounding."

"I'm so sorry," she said, coming to stand beside the couch. "Is there anything I can get for you?"

"No. I took my pain medicine. Hopefully, I'll feel better in a few minutes."

"Wyatt noticed you were gone and asked me to come look in on you."

Gabrielle sighed. "He's probably thinking I was feeling guilty and couldn't face all of you."

"Guilty? About what?"

"The kidnapping. I'm sure he'll associate the note with me somehow."

Maggie's short laugh was incredulous. "How could he? You were gone with him when it arrived."

Gabrielle pressed her fingertips against her throbbing forehead. If only she could remember! "That will hardly make any difference to Wyatt. He'll have the idea I gave a signal to someone, or something like that."

Maggie shook her head. "If it's any consolation, none of us Fortunes believe you're in cahoots with anybody."

"It does make me feel better to know you all believe in me. But…"

"But Wyatt's opinion is what really matters to you," Maggie finished knowingly.

A lump of tears formed in Gabrielle's throat. She hated herself for becoming so emotional. Now wasn't the time. She needed to be strong for this family and try to help them in any way she could.

"It shouldn't. I know," she mumbled.

Maggie sat down on the end of the long coffee table and studied Gabrielle's troubled face. "I'm not sure what your feelings for Wyatt are, Gabrielle. But I must warn you. He eats young women like you for breakfast. You only have to look at him to know he has no problem finding a willing woman to satisfy his needs."

And she'd almost been one of those "willing" women, Gabrielle thought miserably. Was he capable of simply using her, then tossing her aside?

Yes. For her own sake, she had to believe so.

"Maggie, do you think Wyatt has ever wanted a wife or children?"

Maggie contemplated her question for a moment. "I'm not really the one to ask. My husband knows Wyatt much better. You see Wyatt and the Fortune brothers grew up together. The Fortunes helped Wyatt get elected. They've all been friends for years. But as to what I think…well, if Wyatt ever wanted a wife or family he hasn't shown it. But then, he's not a man who wears his emotions on his sleeve either."

Gabrielle didn't say anything, and Maggie regarded her more closely. "Are you wishing he was interested in you that way?"

Gabrielle swallowed, then glanced at Maggie. She still couldn't see clearly, but enough to tell Maggie was looking at her with concern. "I don't know," she whispered, her voice full of misery. "My home is in California. But I have no recollection of it. I suppose I'll have to go back there…to try to find my family. If I have any. Even if Wyatt did want me that way, I couldn't very well stay here without knowing about my past. It's all so frustrating."

"I can't imagine what you must be going through. Not knowing if you have parents or siblings. And if you do, you wouldn't recognize them."

Gabrielle was certain she wouldn't recognize anyone from her past. Her memory was too dead. "A few minutes ago when we were all looking at the picture of baby Bryan, I kept wondering if I have a mother somewhere, and if she's wondering and worrying about me. Or if…she doesn't give a damn where I am. Since Wyatt told me there's been no missing persons report filed on me, I have to think the latter."

Rising to her feet, Maggie shook her head. "You're trying to think too much, Gabrielle. Your head can't heal with such a jumble of thoughts whirling around inside it. Do you want Matthew to take a look at you?''

Gabrielle sat straight up. "Goodness, no! It's only a headache. He has far more important things to deal with now. Did Wyatt say anything else about the ransom note after I left? What does he think about it all?''

"Right now, I think he's viewing the whole thing cautiously. And he wants to discuss it all with the FBI before the drop-off date for the money. Which will be Saturday night.''

"It sounded like your father-in-law is adamant about paying the ransom.''

She nodded. "Ryan will do anything to get his grandson back.''

Gabrielle could only wonder if she'd ever been loved that much. Some vague feeling inside her said she'd never been a cherished family member. "I guess now there's not much for your family to do, but wait.''

Maggie smiled hopefully. "This time I'm keeping both fingers crossed and praying Bryan will be returned. It's about time something good happens to this family.'' She started toward the door. "I'm going to join the others and let you rest. If you need me, yell.''

"Thank you, Maggie.''

Maggie's hand paused on the doorknob. "You know,'' she said, glancing back at Gabrielle, "something just dawned on me. A few moments ago when you were talking about having a family, you mentioned wondering if you had a mother, but nothing about a father. Maybe subconsciously you know you don't have a father?''

Gabrielle's aching forehead puckered into a deeper frown as she tried to summon the merest flash of memory. "You could be right, Maggie. I might not have a father. For all I know, I might not have anyone.''

* * *

Rosita swatted at her husband Ruben's hand as he lovingly patted her round behind.

"I don't know why you're feeling frisky tonight, old man. You've been breaking yearlings in this heat all day. Maybe I've been feeding you too good."

Ruben laughed and rubbed his midsection. He'd always been built like a bull, the only difference now that he was sixty-three was the slight paunch hanging over his belt. Eating his wife's good cooking all these years had taken its toll. His black hair had turned mostly salt-and-pepper, along with his beard and mustache, but he was still much of a man. And he loved his devoted wife. His desire for her had never waned during their long marriage. Ruben would be the first to admit his greatest pleasure in life was coming home in the evenings to her and their small home.

"Maybe you just look too good for this old man to keep his hands to himself," Ruben told her.

Her face flushed with pleasure. "Ruben, I have to tell you what I saw today. At the ranch house."

Ruben, who was used to his wife's predictions and visions, wasn't surprised by her urgent tone. "Hmm. What was it, *querida?*"

"Gabrielle. You know the young woman who can't remember—"

"*Si,* I know. What about her?"

"I went to her room this afternoon to speak with her. She was in the shower, and when she stepped out, I saw her hip. There was a birthmark on it—a crown-shaped birthmark just like the one that all the Fortunes have."

Ruben looked at his wife. "What did you say to her? Did you question her about it?"

"No. I didn't let on like it was anything. I told her a

birthmark couldn't mar her beauty. What do you think, Ruben? Should I mention it to Ryan or Matthew?''

He frowned. "I don't know, Rosita. What good would it do if the girl can't remember? Do you think she doesn't know anything about the Fortunes having birthmarks like hers?''

Rosita firmly shook her head. ''I'm certain she doesn't know anything. If she did, the amnesia has wiped it from her mind.''

He rubbed his mustache thoughtfully. He had worked for the Fortunes for many years. He owed them much and thought of them as family. He didn't want to cause them any more problems than they already had. ''It could just be a coincidence. If she is some long-lost relation, they'll find out sooner or later anyway.''

Rosita grimaced. ''That's what I was thinking. Besides, they've already got so much trouble to deal with. What with Claudia and the baby moving out, and Ryan trying to get rid of that hell-cat Sophia. No,'' she added more firmly. ''I'm going to keep what I saw to myself. If Gabrielle really is a part of the Fortune family, it'll all come to light. Anyway, they think I'm a crazy old woman.''

Nine

For the next few days Wyatt barely had time to eat, much less sleep. Most of his waking hours had been spent on the phone with the FBI. The special agent assigned to the case had finally agreed to allow the ransom money to be dropped. He and Wyatt were still making preparations as to how to handle the switch. In the meantime, two more federal agents had been posted on the Double Crown for security reasons.

Along with the Fortunes' problem, there had been several local arrests that had required Wyatt's attention, and he'd testified in court at two different trials. There was also the ongoing search for Gabrielle's background, which had so far turned up no further information. He'd questioned her landlord and neighboring tenants, but none of them knew anything about Gabrielle's personal life. Nor had any of them seen or heard anyone at her apartment. Wyatt had decided there wasn't much left to do in her case but hope her memory returned.

If she ever lost it.

He tried to ignore the nasty voice in the back of his mind, but it was difficult to do. Especially when he was this tired and his brain was on the verge of overload. All week he'd been trying to make some sort of sense of everything that had happened on the Double Crown this past month. Gabrielle's wreck and supposed amnesia. The anniversary of baby Bryan's kidnapping and then the ransom note delivered to the ranch on the same night.

Was it all only coincidence? Did Gabrielle just happen to show up at the same time the kidnappers decided to yell for money? After months of silence?

He didn't know what to think anymore. When Gabrielle entered his mind, his desire for her got in the way. He knew that where she was concerned, he was placing his neck on the chopping block.

The ransom note had arrived four days ago. He hadn't seen Gabrielle since she'd left the kitchen that night. Maggie had told him she'd suffered another episode of blurry vision and headache and had gone to her room to lie down. By the time he'd finished discussing the ransom note with the Fortunes, it had been too late to stop by her room.

The next day Wyatt had called the ranch. Without having to ask, Rosita had informed him Gabrielle was still in her room with a headache. After that he'd gotten too busy to call. Yet Gabrielle had not left his thoughts for more than five minutes. And this evening he decided he had to see her for himself. Fool or not, he missed her.

Gabrielle stood outside the huge round pen watching Ruben hold a branding iron over a spray of freezing nitrogen gas, then stick it to a young horse's hip.

"Aren't brands supposed to be hot, Ruben? I thought cowboys built a fire and heated the iron in the coals."

Beside her, the old ranch hand smiled patiently. "That's the only way it could be done in the old days, *chica*. Most cattle are still branded that way, and a few big ranches still burn-brand their horses too. But a freeze-brand is much prettier. And it doesn't harm the animal's hide. In about six weeks the hair will turn white in the exact shape of the brand."

A double crown, Gabrielle noticed. How strange! The brand was almost identical to the birthmark on her hip. If she was a horse or cow, the cowboys wouldn't have to bother marking her. It was as if she already belonged to this ranch.

But how could that be? She didn't belong here on this fabulous ranch. She wasn't sure she belonged anywhere, or to anybody. The birthmark had to be an odd coincidence. She couldn't think of a more reasonable explanation.

The sound of a vehicle pulling to a stop behind them had her twisting her head. Through the smoked lenses of her sunglasses, she watched Wyatt step out of his pickup. He was dressed as a sheriff this evening in a khaki shirt and blue jeans, a revolver strapped to his hip. As he approached them with long purposeful strides, her heart kicked into a happy rhythm.

Silly. She was downright stupid for allowing her body to react to him the way it did. But as she turned to greet him, she wasn't at all sure it was just her body that was succumbing to the hard sheriff. She was desperately afraid her heart was becoming involved too. And that would never do.

"Hello, Wyatt," Ruben greeted him with a friendly grin. "What brings you down here to the ranch yard? Decided you want to do some real work?"

Laughing, Wyatt reached to shake the older man's hand. "If I only had the time, I'd love to work you down, old man."

Ruben chuckled. "You'd never get it done, son." He poked at Wyatt's flat belly. "You young bucks are just too soft. After an hour in the heat, you wilt like a morning glory."

Wyatt slapped Ruben's thick shoulder. "You might be

right at that, Ruben. It's hot enough out here now to singe a scorpion's tail.''

He glanced at Gabrielle, who'd been silently watching the friendly interaction between the two men. A sleeveless white blouse exposed her slender arms, and blue jeans hugged the curves of her hips and long legs. A wide-brimmed straw hat shaded her face while a pair of sunglasses hid her eyes. She looked wan and pale, but never more beautiful to him.

"You must be feeling better," he said.

"Today I do," she said. "And Ruben kindly offered to let me ride down here to the ranch yard with him for a few minutes."

"She's gonna turn into a mushroom if she keeps staying in that house," Ruben spoke up as he glanced affectionately at Gabrielle. "And she's too pretty to let that happen. If you don't find her folks soon, Wyatt, I think me and Rosita are gonna adopt her. We'll have an even half-dozen then."

Gabrielle smiled at him. "Once you got me, Ruben, you might want to get rid of me pretty quick. Everyone says girls are a lot of trouble. I'm sure Wyatt would agree to that."

Ruben laughed as he glanced back and forth between Wyatt and Gabrielle. "Wyatt doesn't know half of what he thinks he knows about girls. Now me, I've raised four beautiful daughters. And now that Maggie's married and moved out of the house, it would be a pleasure to have another one."

Wyatt watched Gabrielle reach for the older man's hand and give it an affectionate squeeze. It was a natural, father-daughter exchange, yet for some reason he was envious. Though he wasn't sure why. Unless it was because he knew Ruben honestly would like Gabrielle to be his daughter.

And maybe, deep down, he wished that his own father could have been the kind, hardworking man Ruben was. That Leonard could have loved Wyatt the way Ruben had loved and nurtured his own five children.

"Ruben, can you help me with this gelding's shoe?" A wrangler called to him from across the ranch yard. "I think he's about to lose it."

Shrugging, Ruben grinned at Wyatt and Gabrielle. "A cowboy's work is never done. Can you see that Gabrielle gets back to the house?" he asked Wyatt.

"Sure," he answered. "We'll see you later, Ruben."

Gabrielle watched the old ranch hand tug at the brim of his beat-up straw hat, then walk across the dusty work yard to where the young wrangler waited.

"You know," she said to Wyatt, her gaze still following Ruben, "Maggie is a very lucky woman."

"Why? Because she married a millionaire?"

She shot him a disgusted look. "No. Because she has Ruben for a father and Rosita for a mother."

He noticed she rarely mentioned the Fortunes' wealth, nor did she make reference to money in general. From the report his police friend in Los Angeles had given him, Gabrielle's address was in a clean, but very modest part of town. A small apartment with no yard, pool, or anything more than a parking lot. Just rooms connected to more rooms of neighboring apartments. He had not told Gabrielle that he knew what her home was like. He saw no point in it. Especially when Matthew had suggested it would be better for her to remember these things on her own.

"Who knows? You might have parents just as kind and loving as Ruben and Rosita," he said.

She shook her head and glanced away from him to a pen of yearlings. Two of the young horses were reared on their hind legs, pawing at each other. Gabrielle wondered if they ever hurt one another with their rough play. Like siblings in a backyard wrestling over a ball or a bike. Would it simply be wishful thinking to imagine she had a brother or sister? she wondered.

"No. I don't think I have parents like the Perezes."

He glanced at her sharply, but her pensive profile told him little. "Why? You say you have amnesia. You don't know if you have parents or not."

"You're right. I can't be certain," she agreed. "But more and more I'm getting these feelings."

He grimaced. "Feelings? What are you talking about?"

Her gaze settled back on his face. "I don't know. Maybe I've been around Rosita so much I'm getting psychic too. But I've come to the conclusion that I either didn't have parents to begin with, or don't get along with them for some reason."

Wyatt was surprised she would admit such a thing to him, and it made him wonder if he'd been judging her wrongly from the start. It could be that everything about her story was true.

But women are born liars, a voice inside him shouted back. *You'd be a fool for believing everything Gabrielle said.*

The dejected look on her face bothered him, though. In spite of all his doubts about her being here on the ranch, Wyatt wanted to see Gabrielle happy.

"You're only guessing, Gabrielle. And until you remember the past, that's all you'll be doing." He reached for her arm. "It's too hot out here for you. Are you ready to head back?"

She wasn't. But she wouldn't argue. He was a busy man and she didn't want to push her luck and risk another hammering headache by trying to walk the half-mile back to the ranch house.

"Yes. Were you stopping by the house anyway?" she asked.

His fingers remained on her elbow as he guided her across the hard dusty ground to his truck. "I need to discuss some things with Ryan," he told her. "Have you eaten yet?"

"No. Rosita normally doesn't have the evening meal ready until six-thirty or seven. It's only six now."

"While I talk to Ryan, change your clothes. When I'm finished we'll go eat."

She glanced at him with mocking surprise. "Are you asking me out on a date?"

His expression aloof, he helped her into the cab of the truck. "I'm telling you we'll have a meal together. If you don't like the idea, you can stay home."

She rolled her eyes. "Do you ever *ask* a woman rather than tell her?"

His hand on the door, he paused and looked at her with eyes full of hard resolution. "It's been a long time. These past few years I haven't been guilty of asking a woman for…anything."

Gabrielle didn't reply to that. She felt that he was most likely telling the truth. And though she wondered why he had such a barbaric attitude toward women, now was not the time to question him.

"I'll need at least ten minutes," she told him. "And then I'll be waiting in the great room."

Once they reached the ranch house, it took Gabrielle three minutes to shower, one to slip into a cool cotton shift, and five to dab on a meager amount of makeup and wind her hair into a French braid. By the time she fastened silver hoops in her ears and grabbed up her handbag, she was in danger of passing the ten-minute mark.

However, when she stepped into the great room, Wyatt

was nowhere around. Only Mary Ellen was there, sitting on the couch, staring vilely at the telephone on the coffee table.

The day after the ransom note had arrived, a complicated listening device and tracer had been placed on the instrument. But so far the kidnapper had not attempted to communicate over the telephone or any other way.

"I really hate this intrusion on our lives," Mary Ellen said, gesturing to the telephone. "Those FBI agents think it's nothing to have your telephone tapped and bodyguards crawling all over the house. They've even got the phone over at my house tapped, just in case."

"They're only trying to help," Gabrielle tried to reassure her. "And it would be awful if someone else were taken from the family."

Mary Ellen gave her an apologetic smile. "Of course you're right, honey. I'm sorry for sounding so haggish." She sighed wearily and ran her fingers through her red hair. "I just wish things around here could be normal again."

Gabrielle eased down on the couch a couple of cushions away from Ryan's sister-in-law. Though she lived in her own home on the ranch, about two miles away from Ryan's, Gabrielle had seen her often. During her stay here, Gabrielle had learned Mary Ellen had been married to Cameron Fortune, a man who was the total opposite of his younger brother, Ryan. The man had spent most of his time enjoying women and booze, and the wealth that their father, Kingston, had left them. From the story Gabrielle had been told, Cameron Fortune would have floundered long before he died in a car crash more than five years ago, if it hadn't been for Mary Ellen's hard work and sharp mind taking care of her husband's business holdings. As for Cameron's adulterous ways, Mary Ellen had apparently turned her back on his behavior and focused her love and attention on raising her children instead.

The pretty redhead wasn't the least bit pretentious, and she never looked down on Gabrielle as the pitiful waif with amnesia. She was a respected woman both in and out of the family, and Gabrielle had grown very fond of her.

"I have the impression there's always something going on in the Fortune family," Gabrielle told her.

Mary Ellen chuckled. "That's certainly the truth," she agreed, then frowned. "But I'm worried about this whole thing with the ransom and getting Bryan back. I have bad vibes about it all."

"You sound like Rosita now."

She tried to smile. "Well, God knows, I'm not going to let Ryan hear my concerns. He has enough to worry about."

"Has Lily decided to wear the engagement ring yet?"

Mary Ellen's lips pursed with disapproval. "I don't think so." She waved one hand in a complacent gesture. "And I can understand the woman's reasoning, up to a certain point. But it would make Ryan so very happy. After all he's been through, you'd think she'd want to give the man that much."

Gabrielle's brows lifted. "You don't like Lily?"

Mary Ellen looked properly stunned by the question. "Oh, of course I do. I guess it didn't sound that way, though, now did it?" Before Gabrielle could reply, Mary Ellen waved her hand again and went on, "I think Lily is perfect for Ryan. And she loves him. That's what really counts. I guess...well, I'm trying to say Ryan is more like a brother to me than a brother-in-law, and I don't like anyone putting extra worry on his shoulders."

Gabrielle nodded. "I understand. And sometimes I worry that my being in the house is only adding to the problems around here. I talked to Matthew last night about going home, but he advised me to forget it for now.''

''And so you should,'' Mary Ellen agreed. ''Two days ago you were bedridden with a headache and dizziness. You're not completely well yet, Gabrielle. And besides, you're not causing anyone around here problems.''

Only *him*, Wyatt thought, as he caught the last of the two women's conversation. Gabrielle was causing him all sorts of problems. But as of yet, none of them were criminal. They only felt that way.

His boot steps echoed on the tile, and both women turned their heads to see him entering the room. Mary Ellen instantly stood and, with a smile radiating on her face, crossed the floor to greet him.

''Wyatt!'' Taking both his hands in hers, she raised on tiptoe and kissed his cheek. ''You look exhausted. When are you going to get some rest?''

He smiled down at her. ''There is no rest for the wicked, Mary Ellen.''

Then you must never sleep, Gabrielle wanted to say. Instead she watched Wyatt touch fingertips to the spot Mary Ellen had kissed. From the sheepish grin on his face, he obviously didn't always get such an affectionate greeting from the woman.

''What was that for?'' he asked.

Mary Ellen laughed softly. ''For all the time and hard work you put in on this family. Maybe one of these days everything will get quiet and back to normal around here, and you can have a nice, long rest.''

''After two days I wouldn't know what to do with myself,'' he joked, then his expression grew serious. ''I really don't care how many long hours I have to put in, Mary Ellen. I'd do it all over again and more to get little Bryan back.''

Mary Ellen sighed and patted his hand. "Yes. We all would."

Wyatt glanced at Gabrielle, who'd left the couch to join them. "Are you ready?"

She nodded, and Mary Ellen's brows lifted as she glanced back and forth between Wyatt and Gabrielle. "You two going somewhere?"

"Wyatt is taking me out for supper. Or maybe it's to jail and I just don't know it yet," Gabrielle joked with the other woman.

Mary Ellen laughed. "If Wyatt puts you in jail, I'll be the first one there to get you out." She gave Wyatt a look of warning. "Take her somewhere special, Wyatt."

A sly grin on his face, Wyatt reached for Gabrielle's arm. "I intend to, Mary Ellen."

When they drove away from the ranch a few minutes later, the sun was still blazing on the western horizon. Gabrielle slid her sunglasses on her nose, then glanced at Wyatt as she explained, "I'm not really trying to hide behind these things. The bright light seems to aggravate my headaches, and Matthew said I should keep my eyes protected when I go out in daytime."

"He's a good doctor. You should do what he says."

He reached to turn the air conditioner to a colder setting, and Gabrielle welcomed the icy air on her face.

"Is it always this hot and humid here? When does it cool down?"

"We don't have much cool weather here. We're not all that far from the Gulf of Mexico, so it's almost always humid. In the dead of winter you might need a light coat."

"I'm sure it must have been hot in Los Angeles, too," she remarked. "I just don't remember it."

"I doubt Los Angeles heat feels like Texas heat." He glanced at her, amazed that she'd done so much to herself while he'd been talking to Ryan. The figure-hugging jeans had been replaced with a clingy little dress that stopped just short of her knees. The white background was splashed with blue flowers, and the color was a bold contrast against her tanned skin. Other than a few wisps of bangs swept to one side of her forehead, her hair was bound in an elaborate braid. Her skin glowed fresh and dewy, and her lips and cheeks blushed with just a hint of rosy brown. He couldn't imagine a plate of food that could look any tastier than she did at this moment.

"What do you think you did back in Los Angeles?" he asked.

She shrugged, wondering who was asking—the sheriff in him, or the man. "I've been asking myself the same thing. If I had a house or apartment, I must have had a job of some sort. And I don't appear to be ignorant. Since I've been on the Double Crown, I've done quite a bit of reading, and I seem to be knowledgeable in a wide variety of subjects. It makes me wonder if I have a college education, or maybe was in the process of getting one. But nothing has gone through my mind to tell me if my wonderings are actually right or wrong."

Sighing, she folded her hands in her lap, then glanced at him from the corner of her eye. "Wyatt, have you thought of having someone search my apartment? There might be something in there that could tell us things. Like my bills or bank statement."

His gaze remained on the highway as he contemplated her suggestion. "The idea has crossed my mind," he admitted. "But what good would a bunch of facts do you? Sure, it would tell you where you banked, if you went to school or where you worked. And you would probably learn who your friends and family are. But what would those names mean, if you didn't remember them?"

She pressed her lips together and tried not to feel so lost and forsaken. "I suppose you're right. None of that would tell me who I really am inside. But at least I wouldn't be totally in the dark about my life."

He turned his head and cast her a quizzical look. If she was willing to chance exposing herself, then she couldn't be hiding much. But then, maybe she already knew there was nothing in her apartment to give her plans away, and this was all just a ploy to gain his trust. Dear God, he wished he knew. "Do you really want to know that badly?"

"I'm not sure I can keep going on like this," she said quietly. "My whole life is in limbo."

"Have you been that miserable at the Double Crown?"

The thing that was causing her the real misery was him. But there was no way she could tell him such a thing. To do so would admit he was an important factor in her life. And she didn't have to be told to know that Wyatt Grayhawk didn't want to be an influence in *any* woman's life.

"No. But—"

"Then let it go for now, Gabrielle," he interrupted roughly. "I figure it will all come back soon enough."

And when it did, she would be out of his life. He was shocked at how barren the idea left him feeling.

Wyatt took her to an older part of town where a little café was tucked between a saddle shop and a tavern. Above the wooden screen door covering the entrance was a faded sign that read Jose's.

Inside, Gabrielle looked around her with charmed interest. The ceilings were low and the floor no more than bare board planks. Small round tables covered with white tablecloths were scattered throughout a main area and smaller connecting rooms. Succulents, many of which Gabrielle didn't recognize, grew in large pots alongside the windows and anywhere else there was available space. Brightly striped serapés, battered sombreros, old bits, spurs and bridles all adorned the stucco walls.

A hostess quickly greeted them at the door and, after a quick exchange in Spanish with Wyatt, led them to a secluded room with one private table. After lighting a fat candle in the middle, she passed them each a folded menu, then left with a promise to quickly send a waitress for their orders.

"I didn't have any idea you spoke Spanish," Gabrielle said as she opened the worn menu.

"When you live around a language all your life, you naturally pick it up. And in my line of work it's practically a necessity to be able to communicate."

"What about the Cherokee language? Do you know any of it?"

His eyes remained on the menu. "No," he said curtly. "My father could have cared less about his heritage."

"That's a shame," Gabrielle replied.

"Where Leonard Grayhawk was concerned, there was a lot to be shamed."

She forgot the menu as she studied his face. "Was? Is your father dead?"

One of his shoulders lifted, then fell. "Who knows? He left this area years ago to go back to Oklahoma. I haven't heard from him since. And I don't want to."

There was nothing but bitterness in his voice. Gabrielle decided it would be best to let the subject of his father alone for the time being. He'd been kind enough to ask her out for supper. She didn't want to ruin their evening by opening old wounds.

She turned her attention to the menu. It was written in Spanish, and she could only manage to translate a few words here and there. "I'm afraid you're going to have to order for me, Wyatt. I don't know what any of these things are."

Across the table, he gave her a wry smile. "Do you like your food hot?"

"How hot is 'hot'?"

He chuckled. "You know what it feels like outside. Well, double or triple that temperature."

"Oh, well, I definitely couldn't handle hot. Get me something mild."

His smile turned sly. "So you're not feeling adventurous tonight?"

As her gaze lingered on the sharp angles of his face, she was suddenly swamped with broken images of his lips pressed to hers, the look in his eyes when he'd tossed her dress aside, the feel of his hands on her breasts and belly. That brief time with him seemed like weeks ago rather than days. Yet she remembered every second of it as though it had happened yesterday.

"Not *that* adventurous."

He chuckled. "Then I'll try to find something that won't burn your tongue."

She drew in a deep breath, then released it as she tried to push away the lingering erotic images of the two of them. "Do you come here often?"

He shook his head. "I would if I had more time. It's my favorite place to eat. But this past year has been too busy. Usually I throw something into the microwave and call that supper."

"I think when I finally do leave the ranch, I'm going to be very spoiled from Rosita's cooking."

"Living on the Double Crown would spoil most anybody," he said.

She sighed. "Having someone waiting on me or doing

my housecleaning isn't important to me. I don't believe I came from that sort of life."

"Why do you think that?" he asked, his eyes narrowed keenly on her face.

"Because it doesn't feel natural for someone else to be making my bed or cooking my meals. I feel as though I should be doing it myself."

"Maybe that's subconscious guilt."

Her eyes filled with shadows as they lifted and met his. "Did you have to say that?"

For once Wyatt wished he hadn't. He didn't want to keep thinking of her as a potential criminal. Yet if he didn't, he might find himself in the bottom of a deep pit before he ever realized he'd fallen.

"It's second nature to me, Gabrielle. It's my job to be suspicious."

"Especially of women," she said with disgust.

He opened his mouth to warn her that she was treading on dangerous ground, but the sudden arrival of a waitress forced him to turn his attention to ordering.

Once the young woman disappeared from the cozy little room, Wyatt leveled his gaze back on Gabrielle. "Now, you were saying something about me and women…"

There was something in his voice that taunted her to speak her mind even though she knew it was bound to rile him. "What can I say—other than the fact that you don't trust females? You put them in the same category as a toothache or a honey locust thorn in your foot. Why?"

He tapped his fingertips atop the table in a slow, menacing rhythm. "You don't want to know why."

"That's where you're wrong, Wyatt. I've never known a man like you. I want to know why you are like you are."

His brows pulled together. His eyes narrowed even more.

"How do you know you've never known a man like me? You say you have amnesia."

"Damn it, Wyatt! You're changing the subject. I do have amnesia, but I think the memory of a man like you would be…impossible to forget. Anyway, we were talking about you."

He glanced around at the open doorway as though he expected to see the waitress returning at any second.

"What's the matter?" she asked. "Are the women you've been connected with a secret?

He glowered at her. "Do you think if you'd had your heart broken and stepped on by a man, you would want to talk about it?"

His words stunned her, and she stared at him for what felt like a long time. "Am I supposed to believe you've had your heart broken?"

"Why does that seem impossible? Because you think I don't have one?" Disgust twisted his face. "Maybe I don't have one. At least not a whole one."

"Why?"

He muttered a curse under his breath, then looked up just as the waitress appeared with their drinks of iced water and coffee.

Gabrielle waited until the woman had served them and left the room before she repeated, "Why is your heart not whole?"

His eyes bore into hers. "Because I believed a woman. First in high school. I fell in love with a girl my age. I wanted to marry her, have a family with her. And she swore she would always love me. But her affluent parents would have no part of their daughter marrying a half-breed."

"If she honestly loved you, she would have married you anyway," Gabrielle pointed out.

One corner of his lips lifted in mocking agreement.

"You think so? Well, Kelly's parents put it to her this way—marry him and you'll lose your allowance and inheritance. Was that a difficult choice?"

It wouldn't have been a hard choice for Gabrielle. Compared to having Wyatt, money would mean nothing. "What happened?"

He glanced away from her, and pain lanced Gabrielle's chest as she realized it was hurting him to admit he'd been deserted and looked down on.

"She chose the money and eventually married a lieutenant over at Lackland Air Force Base."

"So you never let yourself fall in love again?"

Glancing back at her, he snorted cynically. "Kelly shed me like a snakeskin, and that's just about how low I felt at the time. I swore I'd never get near another woman, and for several years I stuck by the promise. But then..." He shook his head as his features twisted with self-disgust. "I still had the foolish notion I wanted a woman in my life. And when I met Rita, I was completely smitten. She was fiery and beautiful and exciting. Idiot that I was, I thought I could tame her and make her into the perfect wife." He laughed bitterly. "When I caught her in bed with another man, she didn't even bother to apologize."

"Oh, Wyatt," she said in an anguished whisper. "I'm so sorry."

He reached for his coffee. "No need to be sorry, Gabrielle. They were great lessons. They'll not be forgotten. Ever."

Ten

The food Wyatt ordered for their supper was delicious. There were just enough spices to make the meat, cheeses and rice tasty, but not enough heat to make eating uncomfortable. Yet the enjoyment of the meal was somewhat dimmed for Gabrielle. As she ate, all she could think about was Wyatt as a young man—falling in love, planning a family and then having his dreams thrown back in his face by not one, but two different women.

It was no wonder he was embittered toward females. And to a certain point, she could understand why he was wary of them. But he was an intelligent man, she silently argued with herself, he had a job that required him to be able to judge people quickly, male or female. Surely he ought to see that all women were not like Kelly or Rita. *She* was not like them. It didn't matter that her past was a blank— Gabrielle's heart assured her she could never intentionally hurt the man she loved.

For the most part Wyatt was quiet during the meal, and she felt a twinge of regret for pushing him about his past. It wasn't her business why the man looked at life with a frown on his face. It shouldn't matter to her if he ever opened his heart again. Common sense told her she should let his past stay with him and simply worry about getting her own back. But common sense wasn't what she felt every time she looked at Wyatt's dark brooding face.

When the two of them left the café, the air was still and

heavy. To the south, jagged streaks of lightning had moved considerably closer. The sight was as ominous as the grim expression on Wyatt's face, and she shivered slightly as he helped her into the truck. But whether her reaction was to the oncoming storm or to Wyatt, she didn't know.

As he pulled the truck back into the flow of city traffic, Gabrielle didn't ask him where they were going. She figured he was all too ready to get her back to the Double Crown. However, several minutes later they entered a residential area that seemed vaguely familiar to Gabrielle. When he pulled to a stop in front of a large brick home, she knew why.

Surprise arching her brows, she glanced across the seat at him. "This is your house," she said. "I thought we were going back to the Double Crown."

"Not yet. I want to show you something."

Gabrielle wondered if it was the *something* he'd been about to show her several nights ago, but she didn't ask. Making love to her appeared to be the last thing on his mind.

This time when they entered the foyer he switched on the light, and she followed him into a large living area furnished with comfortable leather armchairs and a long matching couch. In one corner was an entertainment center with a wide-screen television and VCR, plus a stereo unit. Packed in the adjoining shelves were stacks of CDs, vinyl albums and videotapes.

Wyatt turned to her, his eyes darkening. "So you wanted to know about my past. I think it's time I showed you," he said.

"Wyatt, I—"

She broke off as he tugged her out of the room.

"Don't bothering arguing. Your curiosity about me

needs to be quenched. Then maybe you'll see you're wasting your time trying to—''

"To what?" she prompted as he propelled her down a wide, dimly lit hallway.

"To resurrect me."

What a strange choice of words, Gabrielle thought. Had Wyatt considered his life close to dead all these years? She couldn't imagine anything more terrible.

A few steps farther and he guided her into a bedroom. When he switched on a table lamp by the queen-size bed, she glanced around her, wondering if this was his bedroom. When he began to unbuckle his gun and holster and place them on top of a chest of drawers, she figured it had to be the room he slept in. Because she doubted, even in sleep, he was ever very far away from his weapon. He was too cautious a man not to be.

With the Colt safely out of the way, Wyatt opened the second drawer of the chest and searched among the things inside. From where Gabrielle stood several steps away, she couldn't see inside. Whatever he'd wanted to show her was obviously something he kept out of sight.

Eventually he lifted out a plain white envelope, then turned and crossed the small space to where Gabrielle stood quietly waiting.

"What is that?" she asked, nodding toward the envelope in his hand. "A marriage license or will?"

Grooves of bitter cynicism bracketed his mouth and lined his forehead. "If my parents had a marriage license, I don't know what happened to it. As for my will, it's secured in a safety-deposit box. Not that I have anyone to will anything to. But it's there just the same."

It suddenly struck Gabrielle that in a way Wyatt was somewhat like her. He didn't have a family. Or if he did, they weren't close enough to count.

"You don't have siblings? Or aunts and uncles any-where?"

"No brothers or sisters. If my father had family, I never knew them or heard him speak of them. My mother had a sister somewhere, but, like my mom, she's never tried to contact me."

"I wonder why?" Gabrielle's softly spoken question was directed at herself as much as to him.

"Don't bother yourself wondering, Gabrielle. I'm a half-breed. My mother didn't want me. She only married my father because she was pregnant and he forced her to. It's a cinch her sister didn't want any part of me either."

Gabrielle winced inwardly at the brutal bluntness of his words. "There are many people of mixed races, Wyatt. It's not something that should make you feel sorry for yourself."

His jaw hardened to granite as his gaze ripped across her face. "Don't tell me you know how I feel. You don't. You couldn't."

Determined not to cower beneath the anger simmering in his eyes, she straightened her shoulders. "I didn't say I knew how you felt. But, Wyatt, I have no idea who gave birth to me. Much less anything else. And I don't see that being part Native American and part white is anything to warrant carrying a chip on your shoulder."

A muscle ticked in his rigid jaw. "Who says I'm carrying a chip on my shoulder?" The question was spoken in a dangerously soft voice.

Gabrielle swallowed, but firmly held his gaze. "It sounds to me like you have a big chip. Just because some silly girl turned her back on you all those years ago. How could that possibly be important to you now?"

Silly girl. The two words jolted him, and slowly as he stood there staring at Gabrielle, he realized she was right.

What Kelly had done to him, thought of him, didn't really matter anymore. It was Gabrielle's opinion that meant the most to him. Dammit!

"It isn't," he snapped. Then with a weary sigh, he passed a hand over his face. "I'm trying to explain…you wanted to know about the women in my life. Well, here's the first. And believe me, her story is the best."

Frozen by his words, she watched in silence as he drew a ragged snapshot out of the envelope and handed it to Gabrielle. The corners were bent and there was a faded streak running through the right side of the small photo, but the image was still clear enough for Gabrielle to recognize Wyatt.

He was only a small boy of about three or four, she would guess. Even at that young age he'd been tall, coming well above the woman's knees. His hair was black and covered his forehead with a thick wave. There was a grin on his face that was both impish and contented. The sight of it tugged at Gabrielle's heart and made her wonder if the woman standing next to him, her hand resting lovingly on Wyatt's shoulder, had been the reason for his happiness.

"I take it this is your mother?" she asked softly.

"Yes. Marilyn Grayhawk."

"She's so beautiful. Was her hair strawberry-blond? That's the color it appears to be in this photo."

"It was red-gold, and long and wavy. I thought she was an angel because she looked like the pictures of the angels in my Bible. But I was seeing her through a child's eyes. I never realized she was planning to leave me."

Earlier at supper when Wyatt had talked about the two women who'd betrayed him, acid had filled his voice. But now it was husky with pain and loss. And Gabrielle suddenly knew if Wyatt had ever loved anything or anyone in his life, it had been Marilyn Grayhawk.

"How do you know she left you?" Gabrielle dared to ask.

He didn't answer immediately, and she glanced up from the photo to see his expression was both puzzled and disgusted.

"What the hell does that mean? She isn't here, is she?"

Gabrielle shrugged. "No. But...I mean what happened? When did she go? How?"

"I was five at the time, so I don't really know how she left. In the old wrecked car we had back then, I suppose. I woke up one morning with my father standing over my bed, telling me my mother had left. He said she was gone for good and not to be whining and bawling for her to come back. She didn't want no half-breed kid."

With grim disbelief, Gabrielle shook her head. "What sort of man could have done such a thing? Was he crazy?"

Wyatt's nostrils flared. "No. He was mean. A mean, drunk man."

He took the photo from Gabrielle's fingers and shoved it back inside the envelope.

"Do you have a picture of him?"

Surprise flickered in his hazel eyes. "Why would you want to see one?"

"Because he was your father."

Slowly he walked back over to the open drawer and pulled out a cigar box. Gabrielle followed him, and he handed her the tattered photo from among the box's collection of odds and ends.

The image was black-and-white and grainy, but Gabrielle could make out the man's impressive stature and thick dark hair. He was standing in front of a small run-down house. There was no son by his side, but a spotted dog with a chain around its neck, sitting on his haunches.

"Did he beat you?" Gabrielle asked as she tried to imagine what Wyatt's growing-up years had been like.

"Not really. He swatted me from time to time. But he didn't beat me. No, Leonard's abuse came in the form of words and neglect."

She sighed sorrowfully and handed the photo back to him. "What about your mother? Was he good to her?"

"I was just a little kid when she was home. But—I don't know. When I look back at that time now, I have to admit things couldn't have been good for her. We were poor, and I can't remember my father trying to make things any better. He rarely worked. My mother kept money in the house from her job as a waitress. At night when I lay in bed, I could hear my parents fighting. And sometimes I knew he hit her, even if I never actually witnessed it with my own eyes."

"Then how do you know she deliberately left you?" Gabrielle asked him softly.

Wyatt put the cigar box back and pushed the drawer shut. "She never came back," he said. Then, turning, he stared at her with naked pain on his face. "You couldn't know how I would stand at the window for hours on end, watching the road for that old car to drive up. For my mother to return."

Gabrielle could see how it was tearing at him to speak of his mother and her desertion, and her heart ached for him. But she also knew he would never rid himself of the festering pain if he kept hiding it all away inside him.

"No. I couldn't know that. And I don't think you could know what really happened with your mother either. Your father might have forced her to go."

"Why? It doesn't make sense."

Gabrielle walked over to the bed and sat down on the edge. "Who knows?" she said, clasping her hands around one bare knee. "Could've been he was jealous and thought she had a lover. After all, she was obviously a beautiful woman. Or it could have been he simply didn't want a wife around telling him what to do. Some men are like that, aren't they?"

He leveled a dark gaze on her. "You think I would be that way?"

She shook her head, surprised that he believed she was thinking of him as a husband. He'd made it clear he would never trust any woman enough to marry her.

"In your line of work, I'm sure you see all sorts of domestic violence cases. What causes them?"

He shrugged one shoulder. "Money. Work. Kids. Drugs and alcohol. Any number of things."

"That's what I mean. Something sent your mother away. Did she ever talk to you about leaving or wanting to live somewhere else?"

"Once she told me she was going to take me away with her...somewhere better." His lips twisted and his eyes grew distant. "That wasn't long before she left. Sometimes I wonder if she really was planning on taking me. But...hell, I've spent years wondering, asking myself what happened. I'm tired of trying to figure it out."

She shot him a disgusted look. "So it's easier to simply say she didn't want you because you were a half-breed."

Resentment flared his nostrils. "You really don't know when to stop pushing your luck, do you?"

Gabrielle refused to cower beneath his soft warning. "You're a stubborn man. I'm just trying to make you open your eyes. As it is, you don't even know if the woman's alive."

For a moment Gabrielle's suggestion took him aback. Then slowly his eyes widened as he considered the ramifications. The notion that his mother might not be living had struck Wyatt from time to time. But hearing Gabrielle say it out loud made the likelihood seem stronger.

"Marilyn would be somewhere in her mid-fifties now. Around Mary Ellen's age," he reasoned. "That's still young. But there's always the possibility she could have had a fatal accident or a terminal illness."

Gabrielle drew in a long breath and let it out as she tried to decide whether to speak her thoughts. "Or it could be, she didn't live a day past the one on which you last saw her."

Wyatt was a sheriff, yet he'd never suspected his mother being a victim of foul play. But then he had to stop and remember he'd always seen her through the eyes of a young boy, not those of a lawman. "Are you suggesting my father might have killed her?"

Gabrielle made a palms-up gesture. "All I'm saying is I think you owe it to yourself and her memory to try to find out. You have a job that accesses you to all sorts of investigative sources. Why don't you use them to try to find her?"

Was there any sense to what Gabrielle was suggesting? Wyatt asked himself. Could he have gone all these years hating his mother for leaving him, when she might not really have deserted him at all? Just thinking about it made him sick with regret. And yet if he did find the courage to hunt for her, to find her, how could he bear it if his mother rejected him? It was a risk that carried the promise of great pleasure...or deep pain. Just as did the risk of loving Gabrielle.

But Wyatt didn't have to *love* Gabrielle to enjoy her, he thought. He'd decided a long time ago that grabbing pleasure for the moment was just about all a person could expect out of life.

"Can you guarantee anything good would come of my search?"

"No. But I can guarantee you'll never be truly satisfied until you make an effort to find out what happened to Marilyn Grayhawk."

A long breath slipped out. "Maybe you're right, Gabrielle."

It was more than she'd expected him to say. She scooted closer and reached for his hand. "Does that mean you'll try?"

His gaze dropped from her face down to the small fingers wrapped tightly around his. No woman had ever dared to say the things Gabrielle had said to him tonight. But then, no woman he'd ever known had cared about his childhood or his mother. No woman had ever really cared for him. Not with love or deep devotion. Yet he would be crazy, he told himself, to think that Gabrielle felt more than physical attraction for him.

"Maybe," he repeated. "I'll think about it."

His gaze lifted back to her face, and she smiled gently. "I hope you do."

Slowly, he reached up and pulled the badge from his shirt pocket, then lifted his hat from his head and dropped the badge inside. Gabrielle's heart began to thump with wild anticipation as he leaned over and placed the items on the nightstand behind him.

Outside the row of windows to their left, lightning flashed closer, and the low rumble of thunder gently rattled the glass panes. Wyatt turned back to her and the raw, hungry expression on his dark face had her heart flying to her throat.

"I think a storm is coming," she said in little more than a whisper.

He leaned closer and his fingers gently brushed at the wisps of hair on her forehead. "I'm sure of it," he agreed.

Like the wings of a trapped bird, her heart continued to flutter in her throat. She breathed deeply and moistened her parched lips with the tip of her tongue.

"Do you think we should get back to the Double Crown?"

His palm cupped her jaw and chin. "Eventually."

Gabrielle didn't bother to ask him what that meant. His face and the warm touch of his hand told her. He wanted her.

"Or do you want me to take you back to the ranch now?" he asked softly.

Wyatt's question was more than tantalizing. The part of her that was still living in darkness prodded her to answer, yes. But the rest of her refused to get the simple word past her lips. She needed her memory to have a future. But for tonight she was content to simply make memories with Wyatt.

"No. I don't want to go back to the ranch right now."

A spark suddenly flickered in his eyes. "You know what I am. How I am. I can't make you promises."

From the very moment she'd met Wyatt Grayhawk, she'd thought he was a strong man both inside and out. And now that she was beginning to really know him, she could see she'd been right about his strength. The thing she'd been wrong about was his heart. It wasn't the unfeeling rock she'd first imagined. He'd once felt joy and love and pain. But so much of the latter that he'd closed himself off to anything more than a friendly acquaintance-ship.

"I already knew that," she whispered.

One corner of his lips curved upward as his fingers moved to the back of her head. As he fumbled with the pins holding her hair, he said, "You're a foolish young woman to get next to me like this. You know that too, don't you?"

The corners of her lips tilted into a beseeching smile. "Yes. But I can't help myself."

His groan said neither could he.

One by one, he continued to slip the pins from her hair. Once they joined his hat and badge on the nightstand, he pushed his fingers through the intricately wrapped strands until her hair lay like wind-rippled waves upon her shoulders.

Gabrielle forgot to breathe as his hands cupped her face and drew her lips to within a fraction of an inch of his.

"You're not a woman I should be wanting," he murmured huskily, "but, God help me, I do."

His name was all she could manage to get past her lips before he possessed them with a fierceness that made her head reel. She gripped his shoulders as his tongue delved past her teeth and twined with hers. As he tasted the intimate recesses of her mouth, the zipper at the back of her dress slowly parted, his fingers tugging downward until his hand was resting at the base of her backbone. The soft material fell from her shoulders and pooled around her waist.

Without breaking the contact of their mouths, his hands cupped around her lace-encased breasts, and Gabrielle groaned in the back of her throat.

"Stand up," he whispered against her throbbing lips.

Shaking, she rose from the bed, and the short dress slid down her hips and onto the floor. She stepped out of the material and her sandals, then stood before him as an offering.

The white scraps of lace covering her breasts and hips reminded Wyatt of her virginity, and for moments he questioned the rightness of taking that from her. But as he'd told her before, rightness or fairness never factored into what life dealt a person. He wanted her and she wanted him. Nothing else mattered.

With one hand, he snagged her waist and tugged her back down beside him. "You're so beautiful, Gabrielle. Beautiful," he repeated softly. "But you've already been told that, haven't you?"

If she had, she didn't remember it. She doubted any man had spoken the words to her and made them sound the way Wyatt just had, as though he worshipped the very sight of her. The idea sent the power of her femininity surging through her.

"You're making me crazy," she accused.

He chuckled under his breath as his hands slid around her back. His palms and the pads of his fingers were rough and callused. The friction they made against her smooth skin was terribly erotic and arousing. She closed her eyes as he unhooked the clasp of her bra; the satin straps slipped from her shoulders, allowing the fabric to slide away from her body.

Once he'd tossed it aside, his eyes devoured her nakedness. Her breasts were round and firm, the nipples rose-brown and puckered with excitement. And just seeing she already wanted him made Wyatt's heart thud like a drum in his chest. He rubbed his thumbs across the rigid rosebuds, then bent his head and circled each with his tongue.

Fire shot through Gabrielle's loins, and her fingers pushed into his black hair and tightened against his scalp. She had no memory. Yet she was sure no man had ever touched her this way. No man had ever made her ache with this hot need that was coiling more and more tightly inside her.

He suckled both nipples, then tasted the soft outer flesh

of her breasts, before returning his lips to hers. This time when he kissed her, the two of them leaned sideways until they fell on the mattress.

With his lips still feasting on hers, he crushed her tightly in the circle of his arms. His hands roamed the silky naked skin of her back, then cupped her bottom.

Gabrielle gasped as he quickly jerked the juncture of her thighs against the hard bulge of desire in his jeans, then, with a husky growl of his own, rocked her hips back and forth against him.

Her breathing labored, she spoke between gasps. "Wyatt—I can't—I need—"

"You don't have to tell me," he countered in a voice rough with desire. "I know what you need."

And he did.

Heat scorched her entire body as his hand slipped into her panties and his finger found the moist throbbing ache between her legs.

"Don't be afraid," he whispered against her lips. "Kiss me while I feel you."

The room spun around her as she obeyed him, and his finger began to work glorious magic. Her bones turned to liquid fire, and soon she was whimpering with a desire so great that it totally consumed her.

She clutched at the folds of his shirt, then fumbled with the snaps as the need to touch him grew ever more desperate. When the front of his shirt parted and her palms found the heated flesh of his chest, he eased away from her and quickly shed the rest of his clothing.

The fact that he didn't bother to turn off the lamp surprised Gabrielle. He was a man who kept so much of his inner self hidden, and she'd expected him to be the same with the outside.

She wondered if he realized how much he resembled a

tall, bronze warrior. His long legs and arms were hard corded muscles, his belly was washboard flat, his chest broad and smooth, the male nipples small and dark. As for his jutting arousal, she tried not to stare, but heat filled her cheeks just the same as he turned to face her.

He turned his back to her for a moment to open a foil packet, and Gabrielle realized he'd already anticipated her lack of birth control. Yet behind that thought also came the shocking awareness that even the risk of becoming pregnant was not enough to make her turn away from this man. He created a feverish need. And not just in her body. Each time he touched her, she could feel her heart melt just a bit more. And she couldn't let herself think of what kind of shape it would be in after tonight.

A gust of wind suddenly rattled the windows, and through the slatted blinds Gabrielle could see tree branches bending beneath the storm.

As Wyatt slid down beside her on the bed, drops of rain began to pelt the glass. "Are you frightened?" he asked, his eyes searching hers.

"Of you? Or the storm?"

The question made him smile, and as his fingers gently pushed through the hair at her temple, she knew she would never regret giving herself to this lonely lawman.

"Both," he said.

"No," she answered. "But I'm sure you're going to tell me I should be."

His white teeth continued to glint in the darkness. "I'm not going to bother. And anyway, I have you where I want you for tonight."

For tonight. The words made Gabrielle realize that this was where she wanted to be—always. With Wyatt touching her, loving her, smiling at her as he was now. But in the back of her mind she acknowledged she was living a fairy tale. Tonight's memory would more than likely be the only thing Wyatt ever gave her.

Reaching out with one arm, he snapped off the lamp, allowing nature's light to illuminate the room. Beyond the window the intermittent lightning exploded like bright fireworks. Yet the storm outside was mild compared to what was going on inside Gabrielle.

Wyatt pulled her close against him, and she eagerly slipped her arms around his neck. The sudden contact of his heated flesh, smooth and hard against hers, was a giddy shock to her senses. Like naked power wires, her breasts, belly and thighs sizzled as his lips once again sought the sweet curves of her lips.

Over and over he kissed her, until her breath was gone and she lay limp against the mattress. All the while his hands made a foray of her body, his fingers discovering sensitive little spots that left her groaning and throbbing with need.

Eventually his lips followed the slow meandering path of his hands until he reached the soft mound of curls that decorated her womanhood. Then his head lifted and he caught her eyes with his.

In the depths of his gaze Gabrielle could see both awe and pain, and the sight seized her heart like the grip of a fist. "Is something wrong?" she whispered hoarsely.

Terribly wrong, Wyatt could have told her. He'd never wanted anything, anyone, the way he wanted Gabrielle. He was visibly shaking with need. And the magnitude of his desire left him feeling exposed and vulnerable—two things he never wanted to be with a woman. But it was too late to hide or turn back. He had to bury himself inside her— or he'd die from the wanting.

"No," he said with a throaty growl.

With a sigh, she reached up and touched his cheek with

her fingertips. He caught her hand and kissed each finger, then with a groan of surrender, his knee nudged her thighs apart.

Gabrielle wasn't prepared for the sharp slice of pain or the explosion of pleasure behind it, and for a moment she was too stunned to do anything but grip the rigid muscles of his forearms and try to recapture her lost breath.

"Oh...oh, Wyatt," she whispered with shocked wonderment.

"I know, my little darling. I know," he said thickly, then, bending his head, he kissed her slowly, sweetly as he gave her body the time it needed to adjust to his invasion.

Like a white-hot sun, pleasure surged through every part of her and soon she was moving against him, with him. Wind slammed against the windows, while on the bed Gabrielle locked her legs around him and welcomed the storm.

Hours later Wyatt woke to the patter of gentle rain against the roof and the feel of Gabrielle's soft warm body curled next to him. Her head was pillowed on his arm, and for a long time he studied the precious lines and angles of her sleeping face.

No woman had ever slept in his bed—with or without him in it. He'd never been able to tolerate that much closeness. But then, he had never made love to a woman before.

The admission was worse than the knife wounds he'd suffered in his shoulder and thigh. The stab of the switch-blade had healed, but he wasn't sure he would ever recover from his coupling with Gabrielle. Everything inside him had poured into her, and he very much doubted he would ever get all of himself back.

Glancing at the faint light coming in the windows, his inner alarm clock told him morning wasn't far off. Carefully, he eased out from under the arm she'd thrown around his waist and reached for his clothes.

Several minutes later, he returned to the bedroom with a cup of steaming coffee. After placing the mug on the nightstand and switching on the lamp, he sat down on the edge of the bed and touched Gabrielle's shoulder. When she failed to stir, he pushed a wave of brown hair back from her cheek, then leaned down and pressed his lips to her slightly parted ones.

With a tiny moan, her eyes fluttered open and she looked at him with sleepy, confused eyes.

"Wyatt?"

One corner of his mouth lifted wryly at the idea of her sleeping so soundly and trustingly in his bed. "It's almost four in the morning," he told her. "I think I'd better get you back to the ranch before someone misses you and starts to worry. They probably already have."

She raised up on her elbow and glanced around the room. Suddenly everything came rushing back to her. Their supper and the talk about his mother. Then the long hours of making love. The merest thought of what had transpired between them was enough to curl her toes and scorch her senses.

"Is it still storming?"

"No. There's only a little rain falling." He offered her the mug of coffee. She scooted up in the bed and carefully tucked the sheet under her arms before she accepted the hot drink.

Wyatt watched her cradle the mug with both hands and sip gratefully. The sight of the white sheet tucked demurely around her naked body made him want to smile. There wasn't any part of her that he hadn't touched or tasted last night. And he wondered if she had the idea that covering herself would make him forget about wanting to make love to her all over again.

If so, he could have told her it wasn't working. Even though it was four in the morning, and he'd broken all the rules by allowing a woman to stay in his house—his bed— overnight, he couldn't stop a rage of desire from licking the edges of his brain and firing his loins. Before he even realized what he was doing, his fingers were sliding up her bare arm and onto her shoulders.

Gabrielle lowered the coffee cup and tilted her head to one side as she studied the sensual glint in his eyes.

"I thought you were ready to leave," she said huskily.

"I was."

His fingers caught in her hair and tugged ever so lightly.

"Was?" she breathed the question.

"I've changed my mind. I don't give a damn who's worried about you."

Before she could think of a reply, he took the mug from her hands and placed it out of the way on the nightstand, then switched off the lamp.

Gabrielle's heart began a rapid thump as he turned back and reached for her. "Don't you have to go to work soon?" she asked softly.

He tugged the sheet from beneath her arms, and it fell past her waist. His eyes smoldered as he cupped one breast in his callused palm. "I'm the boss. I make my own hours. And right now...this is the only work on my mind."

Gabrielle had thought they were both sated and drained. But now just seeing that he wanted her all over again made her breath catch in her throat and her body ache to give him what he needed.

Her eyelids fell shut as she thrust her fingers into his thick hair, then, with a groan of pleasure, tugged his head down toward her breast.

Daylight was breaking by the time Wyatt dropped Gabrielle off at the Double Crown. He didn't kiss her or even tell her goodbye. But after she'd opened the door, he looked at her for long moments as though she was a butterfly he'd captured and admired for a few hours and was now letting go forever.

It was a look that chilled her.

Gabrielle tried to push it out of her mind as he drove away, and she hurried through the gates in the sandstone wall. She wasn't going to think about returning to the ranch now. She wasn't going to think about anything. Except making love to Wyatt.

Eleven

Wyatt glanced at the digital clock on the dashboard of his pickup. Eleven-thirty. Six minutes later than the last time he'd looked. The woods were quiet, the air so still and heavy that it could have been cut and served on a platter. Across from him in the confines of the cab, Matthew strained his eyes for any sign of headlights in the far distance.

A hundred feet or more from their hidden position at the edge of the thick woods, a row of mailboxes lined one corner of the intersection. Beside the post of the last box, Wyatt had placed the brown bag holding several million dollars.

So far no one had driven past them, much less stopped to collect the cash. Wyatt was beginning to get an uneasy feeling about the whole setup. However, he kept the negative notion to himself. Matthew was already about to break apart from the strain.

"What if someone comes by, spots the bag and stops out of curiosity?" Matthew asked worriedly. "You can't allow just anyone to take it. If the kidnapper doesn't see the money, we might never get Bryan back."

"Damn it, Matthew, don't start losing your grip now," Wyatt ordered sternly. "I'm not about to let just anyone pick up the ransom bag. If a baby isn't first set out of the vehicle, the driver better be ready to answer to me."

Matthew wiped a nervous hand over his face and let out

a shaky breath. "And what if he or she *does* put Bryan out?"

Wyatt tried to hide his impatience, because he knew his friend was close to being out of his mind with worry for his child. "We've been all through this, Matthew. We're going to grab the baby and make sure he's Bryan, while my deputies and the FBI follow the kidnapper."

"Yes. Okay. But...oh, God, Wyatt, I just don't think I can take much more of this!"

"You can if you have to," he told him firmly. "It's a quarter to twelve now, and the note said twelve midnight would be the pickup time. Think of it this way, Matthew— in fifteen minutes you could possibly have your son back."

Several miles west, on the outskirts of the small town of Leather Bucket, Lily's daughter, Maria Cassidy, paced back and forth in the tiny living room of a shabby trailer house. The continual thrust of her fingers into her long dark hair had left it hanging in limp hanks around her thin face. Her brown eyes darted frantically to the corner of the room where a playpen was shoved against the wall. The sleeping toddler was worth millions. The money would be waiting there at the mailboxes by now. All she had to do was drive to the lonesome intersection of dirt roads and get it.

But who would be waiting there for her? she asked herself. More than likely that damn Sheriff Grayhawk. Knowing him, he wouldn't be content to sit back and let those bumbling FBI men handle the switch on their own. Maria feared the local sheriff far more than she did the government men. He was a shrewd, mean bastard. If anyone could put two and two together and figure out that she had Bryan Fortune, it would be Grayhawk.

But so far he hadn't managed it, and now the money was there for the taking. Just the idea brought a savage glow to her dark eyes. She could finally get out of this dump, buy all the clothes and jewelry she wanted, travel and live the life of a queen—instead of working her butt off in a slimy café, waiting on men who wanted to get their hands on her, get her into bed and give her nothing in return.

But even more than what the money could buy her, she would finally see the Fortunes pay for all they'd done to her mother. Lily might be all soft and forgiving, but her daughter sure as hell wasn't going to let them off so easily. Her mother was still stupid enough to believe Ryan Fortune was really going to marry her.

Snorting with contempt, Maria snatched up a pack of cigarettes and a lighter from a wobbly end table. Once she had the tip glowing, she sucked the nicotine deep into her lungs. "Marry her," she spat mockingly under her breath. Ryan Fortune wasn't going to do anything but use her mother as a bed partner. Just the way one of the Fortune men had used Lily all those years ago.

She paced over to the playpen and glanced down at the sleeping toddler. Claudia and Matthew had baby James now. The child they called Taylor. They were raising her kid! No one had the slightest suspicion that Maria had given birth to the little boy. The idea had her stifling down a high cackle.

From the bits of information she'd gleaned from her mother and sister, Sheriff Grayhawk had discovered Matthew was James's father, and Claudia was giving her husband hell over the fact. The stupid woman believed her husband had had an affair. Maria could have told her the fool doctor was too goody-goody to look at another woman sideways, much less make a baby with her.

But none of that mattered at the moment, Maria reminded herself. Right now, she had to decide whether or not to pick up the money.

Puffing heavily on the cigarette, she hurried across the room once again and into a cluttered kitchen where a clock on the wall showed 11:55.

Cursing, she flopped down in a plastic chair and drummed her fingers on top of the card table that served as a dinette. Five minutes! In five minutes she was supposed to be sitting Bryan out by the mailboxes and getting the money. *Her money!*

But what if Grayhawk or the FBI grabbed her when she stopped to put the baby out? There were woods nearby, her mind raced on, with plenty of trees and underbrush to hide a whole posse.

No, she had to think of some other way to handle this. She couldn't spend the money if she was rotting away in jail! And besides, she thought as her gaze drifted through the open doorway to the playpen, the longer she kept the kid, the more the Fortunes would suffer.

With that gleeful thought, she took one last drag on the cigarette, crushed it out in a jar lid, and decided to make herself a sandwich.

Three hours passed before Matthew would accept the fact that the kidnapper wasn't going to show. On the way back to the ranch, the young doctor was so devastated he could hardly choke out one word. As for Wyatt, he wanted to bust something, anything, to vent the anger he was feeling.

Ryan met them at the door, his face mottled with fear and frustration. "What the hell happened? Didn't anyone show up?"

Matthew's head swung from side to side, and Mary Ellen appeared at that moment and quietly took her nephew by the arm and led him into the great room.

Wyatt stayed where he was to answer Ryan's questions.

"No one showed. Just a rancher driving home with a trailer load of horses. Two of my deputies and the FBI are still out there keeping vigil. I told them to give it another hour, then pick up the money and bring it back here to you. I don't want to leave the bag out in the open after daylight."

"No," Ryan agreed. "It wouldn't do any good anyway," he added, then cursed at the helplessness of it all. "I have more money than I can spend, Wyatt, but that isn't enough to get my grandson back."

Wyatt had never had a child, but he knew what it meant to lose someone. It wasn't hard to imagine what this man was feeling, what the whole family was going through, at this moment.

"There's no way of telling what happened with the kidnapper, or why he or she didn't show," Wyatt told him. "But this whole incident makes me lean toward the culprit being a woman. For some reason the kidnapper doesn't want to give the baby up. A woman is more likely to make those sort of attachments than a man."

"You believe it's a woman. And you still think she's close by?" Ryan asked sharply.

"I also believe she isn't going to harm the baby. Not after this length of time."

"Hell, Wyatt, if you know all this, why can't you catch her?"

Wyatt released a weary breath. "I'm trying, Ryan. That's all I can tell you."

With a sigh of resignation Ryan clapped Wyatt on the shoulder, then nudged him toward the great room. "If I sound like I'm blaming you, Wyatt, I'm sorry. I realize you're a sheriff, not a miracle worker. I was just so hopeful...and I feel so damn helpless."

"Well, I can tell you, Ryan, I feel pretty damn inept right

now. And Matthew is crushed. I'm worried about him. Especially now that Claudia isn't standing behind him.''

As the two men stepped into the large room filled with other family members, Ryan said in a voice just for Wyatt's ears, ''Frankly, I'm worried about him too. He truly believed he was going to get his son back tonight. I don't know how much more he can take.''

Pausing beside Ryan, Wyatt took a quick survey of the large room. The atmosphere was grim. Everyone was talking in hushed tones, the way people do when they receive word of a death and are stunned by the news. He noticed Claudia had returned to the ranch for tonight, and was for the moment sitting beside her husband. She was dabbing a handkerchief at her eyes. Obviously she was devastated that the negotiations with the kidnapper had fallen through. As for the young doctor, he was clutching Taylor close to his chest as though he were afraid to let the boy get more than an inch away from him.

At least Matthew had *one* child, Wyatt thought. But one son had been traded for another. And Wyatt didn't see the interchange as coincidence. That's why he had to find Taylor's mother. And once he did, he believed Bryan wouldn't be far behind.

''If I could find out who gave birth to Taylor, it would certainly help matters.'' He spoke his thoughts to Ryan.

Ryan Fortune slanted him a keen glance. ''You don't believe my son had an affair, do you?''

''Not in a million years.''

Ryan rubbed a weary hand over his face. ''He has Fortune blood in him, Wyatt. You should remember that.''

''I realize some of the Fortune men are known for their philandering. But Matthew is like his father. He's not an adulterer.''

Ryan squeezed his shoulder. ''Thanks for that much,

Wyatt. Now I think I'll go have a word with the FBI agent who's been watching the house. The way Fortune luck is going tonight, he's probably asleep.''

Wyatt watched the older man walk away, wishing for the thousandth time that there was something he could do to end this family's misery.

"Wyatt, would you like coffee?''

Gabrielle's voice sounded behind him, and before he could even glance over his shoulder at her, his heart drummed with pleasure. Damn fool, he silently cursed himself.

Slowly he turned to see her carrying a tray loaded with an insulated pot, several mugs and coffee fixings. Grinning faintly, his eyes met hers.

"Are you taking Rosita's place tonight?''

"She's gone home. And I thought most everyone could use something to revive them.''

He took the heavy tray from her and carried it to a small wooden table situated in an out-of-the-way corner of the room. Gabrielle followed and quickly poured each of them a cupful.

Wyatt accepted the mug, then watched her stir cream into hers. He hadn't seen her since he'd brought her home the morning after the storm, more than two days ago.

During that time he'd thought of nothing but her. Even tonight as he'd sat with Matthew watching and waiting for the kidnapper to make an appearance, images of Gabrielle kept straying into his mind. For the past two days he'd fought with himself to keep from driving out here to the ranch. To see her. To take her to some secluded place where he could make love to her again.

The notion caused a strange mixture of emotions to ball in his throat, making his voice unusually husky when he spoke. "All you have to do is look around this room to see it was a no-show tonight."

"Yes," she said with a sad sigh. "I was sitting with the family when you called from your truck. I thought Claudia was going to faint, poor thing. All the while you and Matthew were gone tonight, she kept staring at the picture the kidnapper sent of Bryan and talking about all the things she was going to do with her son once you brought him home. Dallas finally took the thing away from her. Zane thought he was being cruel, but I think he was just trying to spare her any more pain."

Something in her voice said she truly cared about these people, thought Wyatt, that she hated seeing them or anyone in pain. Or was that just something he wanted to hear?

As his eyes explored the length of her, it suddenly dawned on him that she was a different woman from the one who'd collided her rental car with a tree. She seemed less West Coast than Texan now. Tonight she was dressed in indigo blue jeans and a yellow short-sleeved shirt. The color matched the buttery streaks in her hair, which was piled atop her head in a loose mass of curls. Her skin had paled to light golden from its original beach-burned brown.

Yet it wasn't exactly her appearance that made her seem different. Her voice had slowed and softened, along with her mannerisms. She'd come here to Texas with her inner motor racing at full throttle; now it was simply idling, waiting. For what, he didn't know. Over the past few days there had been brief moments when the very deepest part of Wyatt wanted Gabrielle's waiting to be for him.

But as soon as the thought flickered inside him, he squashed it. He wasn't going to let any woman get a hold on him. Not even one as beautiful and delicious as Gabrielle.

"Claudia no doubt loves her son and wants him back,"

Wyatt finally replied. "I'm just wondering if she feels the same about Matthew."

Gabrielle glanced across the room to where the couple still sat talking on the couch. Taylor was on the verge of falling asleep in his father's arms. For the moment, they appeared to be a regular family. "Claudia believes her husband has had an affair. That would be a hard pill to swallow."

One of Wyatt's brows cocked upward at the sharpness in her voice. "You sound like you might be a jealous woman."

She glanced at him, her expression full of conviction. "Not of you. I already know you wouldn't love a woman, much less be true to her."

Though it shouldn't have, her opinion riled him. "Believe me, Gabrielle, if I was ever crazy enough to love a woman, she would be all I'd want."

"Are you trying to tell me you have morals?"

He actually grinned. "I am the sheriff of this county."

She sipped her coffee as she felt her insides begin to quiver. Seeing Wyatt again, standing this close to him, smelling his skin as his shoulder brushed against hers, was like standing at the gates of heaven looking in on the pleasures inside.

"Does that mean you always do what's right?"

"I try. But I am human," he drawled.

Her eyes lifted and met his. The dark glow she saw there made her breath catch in her throat. The desperate urge to taste him and touch him had been building from the moment she'd seen him walk into the room, and she wondered if he could read on her face what she was feeling.

"Wyatt, I—"

Suddenly she didn't have to wonder anymore. His hand clamped around her upper arm. "Let's go outside."

She didn't say anything as she set her coffee down and allowed him to lead her across the large room to the curved glass doors leading out to the courtyard. Along the way, she felt certain all eyes were on the two of them, but a quick glance as they went out told her no one had even noticed their exit.

Wyatt didn't stop until they were deep into the shadowed recesses of the courtyard, where tall pampas grass hid them from view, and the night blossoms of moonflower vines filled the air with their scent.

"Wyatt—" she began again, but stopped when he jerked her into the hard circle of his arms.

"Dammit, do you know how much I've been wanting you?" He breathed the words against her neck.

She swallowed and closed her eyes as the sweet sensations of having him next to her swamped her. "You make it sound like a sin."

"It is!"

His teeth sank into her earlobe, and his hands delved beneath the hem of her T-shirt and didn't stop until they were on her breasts, kneading their fullness, teasing the nipples to hard buttons.

"You said you were a man of morals," she reminded him between gulps for air.

"Not where you're concerned. I've been fighting with myself for nearly three days to stay away from you and this. I can't!"

"Why would you want to?"

Her simple question made him groan and crush his mouth over hers.

"You taste so good. So good," he whispered, his teeth nipping at her lips, her tongue, her cheeks.

She clung to him, her legs shaking, her body on fire. "I've missed you, Wyatt. You can't know how much."

Yes, he knew. But he could hardly admit it to himself. Much less to her.

His hands splayed across her bottom and jerked her hips up against his arousal. "I want you, Gabrielle. God, how I want you!"

She groaned and searched for his mouth in the darkness—

A few feet away, the sound of a man clearing his throat drifted to their hidden alcove. Wyatt instantly put her from him and cursed under his breath. "I forgot about the men guarding the house. We'll have to leave."

"Wyatt! We can't leave the ranch tonight. Not after what's happened! The Fortunes might need you later on."

"I need you right now!" he growled.

To underscore his words, he kissed her fiercely, his tongue plunging into the warm wetness of her mouth. Gabrielle was lost long before he lifted his head.

Taking her by the hand, he led her out of their dark, fragrant lair and down the walkway, until they reached the door leading into her room. She quietly opened the glass enclosure, and Wyatt followed. There was a small lamp burning on a desk near the bed. But dark shadows filled the sitting area where they stood.

Wyatt carefully locked the door behind them, then nodded toward the door that opened onto the hallway leading back into the house. "Can that door be locked?"

For an answer, Gabrielle crossed the room and twisted shut the dead bolt. Then, with her heart throbbing in her chest, she returned to him.

"Wyatt, what if—" she began in a whisper.

"Don't worry. Don't talk," he interrupted thickly as his hands spanned her waist. "Just let me love you."

With his lips on hers, his hands still on her waist, he propelled her backwards until her back met the wall. Then his fingers were on the front of her jeans, releasing the button and tugging down the zipper. Once he got the denim down past her hips, the jeans fell to her ankles and were quickly followed by her panties.

Then he crushed her between him and the wall as his lips captured hers and his tongue began a mating dance that fired her senses to the boiling point.

Vaguely she heard the slice of his zipper as he released himself, and then he was plunging into her, deep and swift. Gasping with stunned pleasure, Gabrielle wrapped her arms around his neck.

With a guttural sound of pleasure, he clutched her bare bottom and lifted her against him, then began to move urgently, desperately toward the release they were both seeking.

The explosion between them was too frantic to last long. When it ended, Gabrielle was panting hungrily for snatches of air while her legs were trembling to the point of collapse. Wyatt fastened her jeans back in place, then lifted her in his arms and carried her to the bed.

The dim light cast upon the bed allowed him to see that her hair had fallen to her shoulders; her lips were puffy and had darkened to the color of a ripe strawberry. Yet it was her eyes that grabbed his heart. They were wet, flooded with the overwhelming emotion that had just passed between them. Wyatt had tried not to feel it, had tried to simply concentrate on the pleasures of her body. But his mind, his heart had also poured into her. And God, how that scared him.

"Are you all right?" he asked softly.

She swallowed, then nodded. He pushed the tumbled hair from her face, then bent and gently kissed her lips.

Her hand went weakly to the back of his head and she sighed against his neck as her heart cried, *I love you. I love you, Wyatt.* Aloud she asked, "Why did you wait so long to come to the ranch—to me?"

He eased her head back against the mattress, then cupped her flushed cheek with his palm. "Because I knew what would happen."

Her shadowed eyes fell to the badge pinned to his shirt pocket. "It makes you unhappy to want me, doesn't it?"

That odd pressure was back in his chest, making him long to cradle her in his arms. "I don't want to need anyone or anything. Even you," he added bluntly.

She tried not to blanch at his words. After all, she'd understood how he felt long before he'd ever touched her. "I guess not needing would make things easier for people. The Fortunes wouldn't be miserable right now if they didn't need to get their loved one back."

"You make me sound like a rock. I do feel, Gabrielle."

His remark had her hazel eyes slowly searching his dark, handsome face. Oh, yes, he felt, she thought sadly. A few moments ago, he'd shown her just how passionate he could be. But it wasn't about love. And she was beginning to see that was the thing she needed most from this man.

Not wanting him to read the thoughts behind her eyes, she turned her face away and fought to gather her spent body and scattered senses back together.

"Are you angry with me?" he asked after a moment.

Angry? Dear Lord, she would make love to him all over again this very minute if only he asked with a word or a touch. Turning back to him, she lifted her fingers to the front of his shirt. "No."

The corners of his mouth turned downward as he studied her sad face. "But what we shared a few moments ago isn't enough for you. Is that what you're trying to tell me?"

"I understand it's all you have to give."

He groaned with frustration. She was being agreeable.

She seemed to know and understand him better than he did himself. Yet her easy acceptance of his attitude didn't make him feel happy or contented. Some perverted part of him wanted her to slap his face, to tell him what a sorry bastard he was—taking her body and giving her nothing in return.

Another thought suddenly struck him, and he turned his back to her and wiped a shaky hand over his face. "I may have given you something neither of us bargained for," he muttered lowly. He glanced over his shoulder at her. No woman had ever made him lose track of himself. She made him forget everything. Everything but *her.* "I didn't use any protection."

Gabrielle had realized their recklessness long before he'd shuddered to a climax inside her. But by then she'd known it was too late for either one of them to do anything about it.

"Don't worry. I'm pretty sure it's the wrong time of the month for anything to happen. And anyway, I wouldn't... hold you responsible."

Maybe she wouldn't, Wyatt thought. But he sure as hell would. The whole idea made him realize he was getting in deep. Far too deep.

Gabrielle could sense him drawing away from her even before he rose from the bed and tucked his shirttail back inside his jeans. But she recognized that to try to cling to him now would only send him running faster.

Sitting up on the side of the bed, she said, "I don't know who I am. Or what I am. I don't even know where I'll be next week or the week after that. Maybe—" she drew in a deep breath and let it out slowly as she shoved back her tousled hair "—maybe it isn't a good idea for us to have a physical relationship."

"It *never* was a good idea," he snapped. "But it's kinda late in the day to be worrying about that now."

Gabrielle had to agree. Because this time she had made love to him with her heart, too. She couldn't continue to lay it out in the open, only to have him unconsciously crush it.

"It's not too late to stop it." The words felt like roofing tacks in her mouth, but she had to say them. Her past was blank; her future was no better. She couldn't face it with a broken heart. Not if she intended to survive.

He turned and his gaze held hers. "Is that what you want?"

She lifted her chin and prayed the tears at the back of her eyes would remain there. "It's what we both want. I just said it for you."

"You're right. I don't want or need this," he said, but he was lying. His mind could see his deceit. Every inch of him felt it. But did she?

He headed toward the door, then paused with his hand on the knob. "Don't leave town without letting me know," he said gruffly. "As a sheriff I'm not finished with you."

But as a man he was.

And it was all Gabrielle could do to hold back her sobs as he walked out the door.

Twelve

Twenty-six years had passed since Marilyn Grayhawk had disappeared. From past police records, Wyatt couldn't find a missing persons report that had been filed during that time. Nor had any unidentified female bodies been discovered in the area. If Leonard had killed his mother, he'd hidden the body well.

But Wyatt refused to believe his father had been that sadistic. The man had been a mean son of a bitch, all right. But not a murderer.

The day his father had told him his mother was gone, Wyatt could remember going into his parents' bedroom. Clothes had been strewn on the floor, the bed, the dresser. Drawers in the chest had been partially open, with things spilling over their edges. At the time he hadn't been old enough to understand what the messy scene had meant. But now the dim image in his mind told him someone had packed and left in a hurry. But had she left of her own accord, or had someone forced her to go?

With a heavy sigh, Wyatt propped his elbows on the cluttered desk in front of him and glanced out the dusty windowpanes looking over Red Rock's main street. Twenty-six years ago there had been no relatives of his mother or father living in this area. At least, not any that a five-year-old boy could recall seeing or visiting. Who would still be around here that might remember his mother?

Dammit, why had Gabrielle ever put this fool notion into

his head! It wasn't like the whole thing had happened two weeks ago, or even two years ago. The way he figured it, Marilyn had gotten damn tired of living with a lazy drunk and a half-breed kid. She'd wanted out of the whole mess. And one night she'd finally taken flight without so much as telling her son goodbye.

Was that the easy way to look at it? he wondered. Gabrielle had said so. But then, Gabrielle hadn't known his parents or the way his life had been back then. Hell, she didn't even know her *own* parents.

Or did she? He wasn't sure what to believe anymore.

Groaning, he swiped a hand across his face. He hadn't seen her in almost a week. In spite of his busy job, the time had crawled at a tormenting pace. He didn't want to eat. He couldn't sleep. All he could think about was Gabrielle. Her face, her voice, her body as he'd buried himself inside her. And then her parting words before he'd left.

At thirty-one, Wyatt had been in lust more than once. And he'd certainly had a case of it for Rita. But this was not like those times. Gabrielle was not those women. Just looking at her, hearing her voice, pleased him in ways he didn't understand. When he was with her he felt things, thought things he never had before.

He refused to believe he could be falling in love with her. Hell, he didn't know how to fall in love, or even what that expression was all about. But he had to admit that he wanted her with a fierceness that refused to die.

But now she didn't want him. Or so she said. Wyatt hadn't been expecting anything like that from her. At least not this soon. She'd given herself to him so wildly. So willingly. If her words hadn't told him how much she'd wanted him, her body had certainly conveyed the message. Over and over. So what had prompted her to put a stop to their relationship? Had she started to remember her past and hadn't wanted him to find out about it? Or perhaps she had never forgotten and was planning to hightail it once her mission here was accomplished? If only he knew what that mission might be. And why the hell did any of it matter to him?

Rising from the comfortable leather chair, he walked across the small room and poured himself a cup of coffee. Doughnuts and sweet rolls were stacked on a paper plate by the coffeemaker. An enticement put there by his secretary, Alta, who thought he was wasting away of late from the heavy workload.

Thank God, the older woman didn't know about Gabrielle. She was a matchmaker of the worst kind. She'd already married off three of his best deputies.

Ignoring the sweets, he carried his coffee over to the window and gazed out at the shops and passing traffic. He needed to forget about Gabrielle, and turn his thoughts back to the hunt for his mother. Not that it was ever a hunt. A hunt had to begin somewhere—and he had nothing to begin with.

He needed a link. Something or someone that might have a clue as to where she'd gone when she left here. But he'd only been a small boy then. He hadn't known any of her friends. No one had ever come to their house. Maybe Marilyn had been embarrassed of the place or her husband. Or maybe even of her son, he thought with a cringe.

He did remember she'd been a waitress at a café. He'd even gone there once or twice with his father. What had been the name of the place? He strained to conjure up the image of the plate glass on the front—the name printed there. And what had his mother called it? Merle's? Berle's? Yes, *Berle's.* Maybe he'd write the café owner and see if he or she knew anything—

The phone rang, interrupting his thoughts. The glowing

button at the bottom told him that it was his secretary calling from her office in the adjoining room. He lifted the receiver to his ear and punched the connection. "Yes, Alta. What is it? Isn't it time for you to go home?"

"Five minutes. But who's counting? There's a young woman here asking to see you. Says her name is Gabrielle Carter. You got time for her?"

Wyatt's hand gripped the receiver as his heart plunged off a cliff. "Plenty. Send her in."

"Sure thing, boss."

He hung up the telephone and tossed away the cup holding the last swallow of coffee. She knocked on the door before he could take a seat behind his desk.

Standing at one corner of the messy desktop, he called, "Come in."

Gabrielle opened the door and quietly stepped inside. Her gaze darted around the small confines of the room, then settled on him. Wyatt felt as if he'd been whacked in the chest with a two-by-four. His breath refused to go in or out, and for a moment he wondered if his lungs had been paralyzed by the sight of her.

She was a sight in white linen slacks and a white silk blouse that fluttered against the tips of her breasts like teasing fingers. Pearls, or the equivalent thereof, glistened against her throat and hung from her earlobes. More gifts from the Fortunes, he supposed. And then it struck him that he hadn't given her anything. Except that part of himself he'd wanted to keep.

"Hello, Wyatt." She moistened her lips with her tongue, then took a step closer. "I hope I'm not interrupting anything."

Only his misery. "How did you get here?"

"Rosita let me borrow her car. I drove here by myself."

He was finally able to breathe, and the air escaped him

so fast that it nearly whistled past his teeth. "You haven't driven since your wreck. You must have wanted to get away from the ranch pretty badly to venture out on your own."

"I wanted to see you."

His lips flattened to a thin line as he turned away from her and returned to his vigil at the window. Only this time when he stood in front of the dusty panes, he wasn't seeing a thing except the dirty glass.

"Really?" he asked with sarcasm. "That's not what you said before I left the ranch the other night."

Behind him, he could hear her sighing, and then her soft footsteps approaching his back. It was all he could do to keep from turning and grabbing her.

"I didn't say anything about not wanting to see you. I said—"

He whirled around, his features tight and edged with anger. "I know what you said! Do you honestly think you can separate the two? Do you think we can be in each other's company without making love?"

This was the second time he'd called it love, Gabrielle thought. Once the other night in her room, and just now. But she knew better than to put much stock in his words. To him it was a figure of speech, not a reality.

"We are civilized human beings," she pointed out.

He damn well didn't feel civilized whenever she was near him. He felt downright savage. And maybe he was, he thought grimly. That's what Leonard used to call him: a little half-breed savage. His father had thought the title amusing, but Wyatt was beginning to believe it was fitting. Strange that Gabrielle had made him see the truth about himself.

"What do you want, Gabrielle? I don't have time for chitchat."

His hard bluntness made her wince inwardly. She stepped around to his side and looked up at his brooding face. He wasn't wearing his hat, and the hank of hair falling onto his forehead glistened blue-black beneath the fluorescent lighting. There were sunken shadows beneath his eyes and gaunt hollows in his cheeks. He didn't appear to be a happy man. But then, she doubted Wyatt had ever been truly happy. And that was the thing that hurt her most.

"I wanted to—to put your mind at ease."

His eyes remained on the window. "You think I've been worried about something?"

"Yes. What happened the other night at the ranch. Our—uh…well, you don't have to be concerned about an unwanted pregnancy. My monthly cycle has come and gone."

Unwanted. Unwanted! If only someone had wanted *him* as a child. And if Gabrielle had become pregnant, would he have wanted her baby? Their baby? In any case, the chance was gone now. The same way she soon would be. The same way everything had come and gone in his life.

"You could have told me that over the phone," he said flatly.

Her eyes widened at his suggestion. "That isn't something I wanted to discuss over the phone! I wanted to tell you to your face. But you don't even care enough to look me in the eye! I was right the other night," she went on, her voice growing low and wobbly, "when I said we should end things. You can't—"

Like a flash of lightning, he turned and gripped her upper arm. "You know I can't look at you without wanting you! And yet you come here like Eve, tempting, wanting me to take a bite anyway. What is it with you, Gabrielle? Do you want to torture me? Is that your intention?"

Her lips parted as her wounded gaze searched his twisted features.

Torture was being without him, she thought. Didn't he understand that? "The last thing I want to do is torment you, Wyatt," she said hoarsely. "You probably don't believe me, but I can't help that. I'm trying to do what's best for both of us. And I can see our relationship can go nowhere. Not with you feeling the way you do."

He sneered. "Just what do you want, Gabrielle? A marriage license stating everything is legal and binding? What would that really give you?"

She swallowed as she fought the urge to fling herself against his chest and kiss him until neither of them could breathe or think beyond the next second. "Nothing, if it wasn't bound in love. I want a man who will believe in me, stand behind me, love me and give me one child or ten. You can't do that. So I'm not going to waste my time asking."

His fingers bit deeper into her flesh as his face dipped down to hers. "You knew how I was before any of this ever started! Before I took you to my bed, I reminded you I wouldn't make you promises. You said it didn't matter!"

Her head swung from side to side as she stared up at his embittered face. "I didn't think it would. But then I...I started to care about you."

His laughter mocked her words and the ache in her heart. "Care! Oh, God, tell me another one! The only thing you care about is what you can get out of the Fortunes. And me."

Her hand reared back to slap him, but he instantly caught her wrist and twisted her arm behind her back. The movement caused her upper body to thrust forward and crush her breasts against his chest.

"You're despicable!" she lashed at him between gritted teeth. "Hateful! And I—"

"And you want me anyway," he growled, his eyes glinting with raw hunger. "We both know just how much."

His accusation should have infuriated her. But she couldn't be angry because he'd simply spoken the truth.

"Wyatt. Oh, Wyatt," she whispered achingly. Then, before he had the chance to do anything, she raised up on tiptoe and covered his mouth with hers.

For a moment he was stunned motionless, and then nothing else mattered except that she was in his arms again, kissing him, murmuring his name as though he were the most precious thing she'd ever known.

Outside his office and down the hallway he could hear an arrestee cursing one of the deputies. And in the next room, the *tap, tap* of Alta's keyboard. Beyond, in another room, a phone was ringing. Yet the outside world made no difference to Wyatt. He tasted her with his lips, his teeth, his tongue. And all the while she clung to him and whispered his name.

It wasn't until the phone on his own desk began to ring that he was finally forced to put her away from him.

Through watery eyes Gabrielle watched him go to the desk and pick up the receiver. When he started to speak, she walked to the door on shaky legs and let herself out. To stay would be like begging him to break her heart. But the ache in her chest said she was too late.

When Gabrielle returned to the Double Crown, she peeked into the large study, hoping to talk to Matthew. He was sitting at a long oak desk, and didn't appear to be doing any work. Rather, he was staring off into space, his features pinched and weary.

For a moment Gabrielle considered backing out of the open doorway. The young doctor had a lot to worry about, and she didn't want to burden him any more than necessary.

But before she had a chance to leave, he spotted her and motioned for her to come in.

She approached the desk where he remained seated. "I don't want to disturb you, Matthew. And you looked like you were deep in thought."

"You're not disturbing me. Besides, thinking about my problems won't make them go away."

There was a leather armchair positioned at a comfortable angle in front of the desk. Gabrielle sank into it and folded her hands on her lap. "I wanted to talk to you about my health."

He nodded. "I hope you've been feeling well. Any headaches lately? Or blurry vision?"

"Not for a couple of days. And then it was only a light headache."

"Good," he said with a smile. "Sounds like you're making progress."

"That's what I wanted to discuss with you. Do you think I'm well enough to go home now?"

His smile faded to a frown as he tapped his pen against the ink blotter. "I suppose it would be possible. But why? Are you starting to remember?"

Gabrielle glumly shook her head. "Not anything. I sometimes have vague impressions fly through my head. But nothing I can hold on to."

He propped his elbows on the desktop and looked at her frankly. "Then why would you want to go back to California? You call it home, yet you don't know anyone there. Even if you found friends or relatives, they would be virtual strangers to you. Until your memory returns."

It was obvious he didn't agree with the idea of her going back anytime soon. Desperation surged through her. "Do you think seeing someone from my past might jar my memory?"

He considered her question for a moment. "Not necessarily. In fact, something or someone from your past might be the reason you haven't regained your memory."

She leaned forward in the chair, a puzzled frown on her face. "What do you mean?"

"I'm not a neurologist or a psychotherapist, Gabrielle, but I have studied a little about these problems. There might be something or someone in your past you don't want to deal with. Subconsciously blocking it out of your mind could be your way of dealing with the unpleasantness."

She let out a long breath. "So in other words, you're telling me you don't think going back to California is a good idea. Until I remember who and what I'm going back to?"

"That's just my opinion, Gabrielle. But I can understand your urgency. And if your amnesia continues on, I can see where you'll eventually have to go back to gather your identification and tend to business such as bills and so forth." He studied her more closely. "Is that what's worrying you? Your financial situation? If it is, you shouldn't be concerned. My father will see that everything is taken care of for you."

Gabrielle gasped at the generosity. "Oh, no! That's not my worry. And I'd never allow Ryan to pay any debts I might have incurred before I came here. No, I guess I'm just getting a little desperate to learn who I am."

She had to leave here, she thought frantically. She couldn't go on being so close to Wyatt. He was in her blood like a disease; she wouldn't be able to resist him for long. And if she didn't resist him…well, she hated to think how much deeper she could fall in love with the man.

The doctor smiled gently at her. "I suspect with each day that passes you're learning more about yourself. You just don't realize it."

Oh, yes. She was learning what she wanted out of life. Who she wanted. And she had to put a stop to it. Wyatt would only use her until the passion between them faded. Then it would all be over. She'd have no past or future. She couldn't let that happen.

Rising to her feet, Gabrielle clutched the edge of the desk with both hands. "Isn't there some sort of treatment they can give me at the hospital to make me remember? Shock treatment? Or what if you injected me with Pentothal? Isn't that supposed to make people spill their guts about themselves?"

The faint smile on his face disappeared and his expression turned to one of real concern. "Gabrielle, these are very extreme measures you're talking about. Shock treatments are rarely used nowadays. Anyway, they would further erase your memory. Sodium thiopental might have you reciting your past while you were under the influence of the drug, but, like hypnosis, you might not remember anything once it wore off. Why have you suddenly become so desperate? I thought you were happy here on the Double Crown?"

Heat crept into her cheeks. "I'm not ungrateful, Matthew. Believe me, I love your family. And Rosita and Ruben. Everyone is so good to me. Just like I belong here. But it bothers me that I don't belong. If I stay much longer I'll be sponging. That's something I don't want to do."

He made a dismissive wave with one hand. "Claudia spends more on her weekly visits to the hairdresser than you could possibly eat in three months. Believe me, Gabrielle, you're not costing the Fortunes anything. And even if you were, we have plenty."

She closed her eyes for a moment and pressed her fingertips against her forehead. "Matthew, I feel like I'm stuck. I can't have any future until I know what was going on in my past. Can I?''

Studying her troubled face, the young doctor leaned back in his chair and folded his arms across his chest. ''I suppose that depends on what sort of future you're talking about. You do need to know what sort of education you've had for job purposes. And of course you need to know if you have family out there who might be worried and trying to locate you.''

Her eyes hardened. ''They're not!''

Matthew's brows lifted. ''How could you know that if you don't remember?''

She realized she was almost angry. Why? It didn't make sense. ''You sound like Wyatt now,'' she muttered. Shoving back her tousled hair, she went on, ''It's pretty obvious no one is looking for me. I've been gone from California for several weeks now and no one has filed a missing persons report with the police. Wyatt has kept a careful watch for a bulletin on me. None has shown up. That's how much I'm wanted.''

The doctor didn't say anything to that. Instead he leaned forward in his chair, studied her for a few more moments, then said, ''I was under the impression you and Wyatt had become interested in each other. I had the idea you would stay here. Because of him.''

It was all Gabrielle could do to keep from groaning aloud. If only Matthew knew just how interested she was in Wyatt. Turning her back to the doctor, she said, ''I understand you and your brothers have been friends with Wyatt since childhood. You ought to know as well as I do that Wyatt isn't interested in settling down with any woman.''

There was a long pause before Matthew finally replied. ''Sometimes a man's mind can be changed, Gabrielle. Especially by the right woman.''

She swallowed at the painful lump in her throat. "Well, I'm by no means special." She drew in a shaky breath. "So I guess what I need to know the most from you is if I'm well enough to travel. The rest I'll…have to deal with when I get to California."

He sighed. "If you're that determined to leave, then I suppose I have to agree you're well enough to fly back to California. No driving, though."

She turned back around to look at him. "You said it was okay to drive today to Wyatt's office. Why can't I rent a car and drive back to California? That's obviously how I came."

He shook his head. "You only drove to his office and back. If you'd gotten blurry vision or a headache, all you had to do was pull over and use the cellular to call the ranch. Heading across country for more than fifteen-hundred miles would be quite different. It would be too physically taxing. If you want to go anytime soon, you'll have to fly."

Gabrielle did some swift calculating in her head. "I suppose flying one way wouldn't cost much more than renting a car for three days. And since I don't have a penny to my name, it doesn't make a whole lot of difference. One way or the other I'm at the mercy of your father. I'll ask him about loaning me the money for a plane ticket. And I promise I'll pay him back just as quickly as I can."

Matthew left his chair and came around the desk to stand in front of Gabrielle. "Any one of us would be glad to give you the money, Gabrielle. As I said before, money is not a concern with the Fortunes. But we do want to see you well and happy."

Her gaze dropped to her feet. If Matthew realized she was running from Wyatt, she couldn't help it. "Thank you, Matthew. And I will be…happy. I promise."

"I truly hope so, Gabrielle."

She glanced up at him at the same time her eyes filled with tears—but before they could fall onto her cheeks, she hurried away from him and out of the study.

Thirteen

Wyatt was sitting at his desk, contemplating the letters he'd sent off in an attempt to locate his mother, when the telephone rang. When he answered it, Matthew was on the other end.

"Hello, Matthew. What's up? Do you have that list for me?"

"Yes. I know you asked for it more than a week ago, Wyatt, but trying to remember that far back was harder than I thought. I've gone through my old address book and also my senior college yearbook. I couldn't find any woman with the name of Megan Brown."

"I really didn't expect you to, Matthew. The woman obviously used a phony name. I'll start with the ones you've listed. Did you have any addresses to go with any of them?"

"Three or four. But I doubt they'll be up to date after all these years. Dammit, Wyatt, this is like trying to find a needle in a haystack. It's hopeless. Do you honestly think the Megan Brown who registered at the sperm bank could be some woman from my past?"

"Maybe it does sound hopeless. But I have to cover every angle."

Wyatt closed his eyes and rubbed the burning lids. The past week had been even worse than the one before. If his job didn't wind up killing him, his desperate need to see Gabrielle would. "What do you want to do, Matthew, just roll over and give up? Just forget about finding Bryan or Taylor's mother?''

The other man sighed wearily, then said in a choked voice, ''No. I can't give up. Claudia is still living in the penthouse in San Antonio. She's little more than civil to me these days.''

''Claudia is a woman,'' Wyatt said, his voice full of acid. ''She's thinking about herself. When you get right down to it, that's what all of them do.''

''Claudia is hurting,'' Matthew tried to reason with his friend.

''And what the hell are you doing? Laughing about it all? Dancing a Bob Will's two-step every night?'' Wyatt sighed and pressed his fingers harder against his aching eyes. ''I'm sorry, Matthew. Your wife's behavior is none of my business. If you have the list ready, drop it by my office tomorrow. Gonzolez and I will get to work on it and see what we can come up with.''

''I thought you might come out to the ranch and pick it up tonight,'' Matthew said.

Wyatt dropped his hand from his face. ''Why? Is something else the matter?''

''No,'' he answered in a careful tone. ''I just wanted you to come to the ranch this evening—if you could.''

Wyatt drew in a deep breath and let it out. ''Well, I can't. I'm busy.'' He glanced down at the letter lying next to the phone. He wasn't going to write his mother tonight. He had to give himself time to think about it, prepare himself for another rejection. But he couldn't go to the Double Crown. Gabrielle didn't want them to be together. And Wyatt sure as hell wasn't going to beg her to change her mind.

''Oh. Well in that case, I'll drop by your office in the morning.''

"I'd appreciate it, Matthew. I know you're a busy man too."

"It's not that I'm busy. I really wanted you to come out to the ranch this evening because…well, I thought you might want to see Gabrielle before she leaves tomorrow."

Wyatt shot straight to his feet. "Before she leaves tomorrow! What are you saying? Leaves for where?"

The line went silent for a moment, then Matthew said in a troubled voice, "I figured you probably didn't know. She talked to me a few minutes ago to see if I would agree to allow her to travel. She's already made plans to fly to California tomorrow."

"Why? Has her memory returned? What's happened to her?"

"You. I think."

"Me!"

"I don't think that should shock you, Wyatt. I've been going through some hell of my own here lately, but I'm not blind. And neither are you, old friend."

Wyatt didn't say anything. He felt frozen.

Matthew went on. "Gabrielle is running away from you because she thinks you don't care about her. I had the foolish notion you did. But then, I've been wrong before. I can't even make my own wife happy," he added bitterly.

Wyatt's lips felt stiff when he finally forced himself to speak. "Did you decide she was healthy enough to travel, or is she going against your wishes?"

"No. I gave her the okay. I could see how desperate she was."

Anger and pain boiled up in him. "I told her not to leave without contacting me. She knows she's still under suspicion!"

"Hell, Wyatt! Suspicion of what? She's hardly an ax murderer!"

"No. But she could be something—" He didn't go on. He couldn't. All he could think about was the future without Gabrielle in it, and the blackness wasn't a pretty sight.

"Forget it, Matthew. I'll be out there in a bit. And whatever the hell you do, don't tell her I'm coming!"

Matthew usually hated it when people hung up on him, but this time when the phone slammed dead in his ear, he smiled.

Miles away from the Double Crown in a cheap motel room, Clint Lockhart paced across the worn carpet. His long stride ate up the small space between the two walls as his blue eyes shot daggers at the voluptuous woman sitting on the edge of the sagging mattress.

In the past, Clint would already have had her in the sack. She liked rough sex, and he used to take pleasure in giving her what she wanted. Each time she'd begged him for more, it was like stabbing a knife in Ryan Fortune's chest.

For years now Clint had been waiting to get his revenge on the Fortunes. To him, the old man, Kingston, had been nothing but greedy, stealing the Lockhart family ranch while pretending to be a friend and neighbor. A ranch that Clint would have inherited one day.

It did not matter to him that his older sisters had married into the Fortune family. Janine and Mary Ellen had been fools, but not him. He was determined to make the Fortunes pay for all the wealth they had stolen from him.

But Ryan didn't give a damn about his cheating wife anymore, and that had taken most of the fun out of the sexual games he'd played with Sophia. That—and her greedy, lying ways. In the past few months he'd learned she was a bit too much like himself to suit his taste.

"What do you take me for, Sophia? I'm not one of those

wimpy fools you lead around by the nose. I'm getting damn tired of your stalling! I want the money we agreed on.''

"Clint," she cooed in a patronizing tone, "I've told you these things take time."

He stopped in his tracks and glared at her. "Time! Don't talk to me about time. I've waited years to get my revenge on the Fortunes. A hell of a lot longer than you have! And I'm fed up with waiting. If you don't come up with something soon—"

Rising to her feet, Sophia planted her hands on her hips and faced him. "You'll what?" she taunted brazenly. "Botch another kidnapping?" She laughed, sneering at him. "That's just what we both need!"

When Clint had first come up with the plan to kidnap Ryan's grandson, Bryan, he'd thought it a surefire way to get millions from the Fortunes. But everything about the plan had gone haywire. First they'd stolen the wrong baby. Then the thugs Sophia had hired to help them carry out the kidnapping had bungled the switch for the money and had nearly gotten caught by the FBI. If the idiots hadn't escaped, he and Sophia would, more than likely, be in prison now.

Two strides had him towering over her. At his sides, anger clenched his hands into tight, angry fists. "If you hadn't messed that whole thing up, we could have already been spending millions of the Fortunes' money! Instead, we're getting old waiting around for those half-assed lawyers of yours to get a divorce settlement."

Looking up at him, her pink pouty lips formed a catty smile. "It'll be good when we get it. I promise." Her hand slid up his arm and her fingers toyed temptingly with the dark auburn hair brushing his collar. "Now, why don't we forget about money for a while. It's been too long since we've, uh…connected." She purred the invitation.

His blue eyes hardened even more as he slung her hand away from him. "Yeah, and it's gonna be a helluva lot longer if you don't pay up, Sophia."

Furious that she could no longer entice him with her sexual charms, she crossed the room and plucked up a pack of cigarettes from a scarred dresser. Of all the men she'd bedded, none of them had come close to satisfying her the way Clint did. The macho cowboy was good-looking and arrogant. She'd reveled in his lovemaking. But now it appeared their bedroom games were over, and he was getting too greedy and demanding for his own good. She had to find a way to get him off her back. Get rid of him once and for all.

"All right, Clint, if you must know, I've agreed to settle with Ryan for twenty-five million. The lawyers will be drawing up the papers soon."

His eyes narrowed suspiciously as he watched her jam a cigarette between her lips. "Twenty-five million! What happened to fifty-million? That's what we both agreed on. What the hell has come over you, Sophia?"

Shrugging, she took a deep drag on the cigarette and blew the smoke straight at him. "I'm almost busted and I don't like it. Twenty-five million is better than nothing. Besides, you just said you didn't want to wait any longer."

Crossing the space between them, he snatched a handful of her strawberry-blond hair and tugged her face up close to his. "You'd better not be lying to me, Sophia. If you are, I'll find out. And when I do, I'll—"

"You'll what?" she taunted, a smug smile tilting her lips. "You're not going to do anything to me. I'm your link to the money. And we both know it."

His hard blue eyes raked over her face for a few more moments, then he dropped his hold on her hair and stalked to the door. "One of these days you're going to push me too far, Sophia," he warned. "Just remember that."

Her answering laugh followed him out the door.

Gabrielle had packed a small carryon bag for the trip to California. She'd boxed up all the clothes Maggie had given her, saying they should be donated to charity. When packing a few essentials, she had come across the Bible Wyatt had found in her car. It seemed to be the only link to her past. The Bible looked old. But not so ancient that the pages were tattered and yellowed. Gabrielle really couldn't be certain about the book's age. The fire that had turned her rental car into a pile of crisp aluminum had scorched the edges of the pages and parts of the leather covering. There was no way of telling what condition the book had been in before the flames had threatened to destroy it.

Wearily, she glanced up from where she sat in the courtyard. Evening shadows were beginning to lengthen on the ground in front of her feet. Soon it would be too dark to read. For the past thirty minutes she'd been leafing through the testament, reading a verse here and there, hoping by some miracle that something in the words would snap the chains binding her memory. She'd even gripped the book and prayed for God to help her.

If only her memory would return, she thought miserably. She wouldn't have to face an unknown life in California. She wouldn't even necessarily have to go back there. If she knew about herself she might have the courage—the right—to stay and try to win Wyatt's love. As it was, she couldn't convince him of her goodness. Not without a past to back it up.

Footsteps alerted her that someone was approaching the end of the courtyard, where she sat out of sight of the main part of the house. Expecting it to be one of the bodyguards Ryan still had posted on the ranch, she glanced around briefly. Then her heart suddenly clutched.

Wyatt was walking slowly toward her. His face was grim. Black brows were drawn together above his hazel-green eyes, forming one long slash across his forehead. His lips were flat and hard, his jaw unmoving.

Deciding it would be a waste of time to bother with the niceties of a greeting, she asked, "What are you doing here?"

"Matthew told me you were leaving tomorrow," he said cuttingly. "I wondered when I was going to hear about it. After you got to California?"

She blanched at his words. "I was going to call you in the morning before I caught my flight."

"Really."

She huffed out a breath. "Yes. Really."

He sank down beside her on the swinging love seat. "What if I said you couldn't go?"

She glanced at him sharply and tried not to let the beautiful, rugged lines of his face sway her determination. "I haven't done anything wrong. You can't stop me."

No. He couldn't legally stop her. He wasn't sure he could stop her any other way, or even if he should try. Everything inside him was sick and torn apart.

"Matthew says you're running away from me."

Coming from Wyatt, the statement jolted her. It was one thing for Matthew and Maggie to see how she felt, but it was altogether different to expose her feelings to this hard man beside her.

"I can't continue to live here on the Double Crown forever. It wouldn't be good for the Fortunes, or me."

Her fingers were nervously sliding up and down her thighs. He itched to place his hand over them and still their movement. But he didn't. He knew once he touched her he wouldn't be able to stop.

"So, Matthew was wrong. Your going has nothing to do with me?"

How was she ever going to bear leaving this place and Wyatt behind? she wondered. The idea of never seeing his face, hearing his voice or touching him was crushing everything inside her.

"Matthew was a lot right," she confessed in a small voice. Then, fixing her gaze on the bible in her lap, she went on, "I'm frightened of what you do to me, Wyatt. Of how you make me feel. I guess...I want you too much. And you...well, what you feel for me is skin-deep."

There was pain in her voice. Wyatt hated to think he'd caused it. He didn't want Gabrielle ever to hurt. Over anything. Did that mean he loved her? Dear Lord, the answer was beyond him. He was a different man from the one he'd been before Gabrielle crashed into his life. Whether the difference in him was good or bad, he didn't know.

"Maybe you're right to go, Gabrielle. I can't offer you anything," he said flatly.

The breath she drew in stabbed her chest like a thousand needles. "You mean, you don't *want* to offer me anything."

He kept his groan of frustration inside where she couldn't hear it. "You're young. Much younger than I am. You don't know who might have been in your past. There might be some guy in California waiting for you to return to him."

Gabrielle found the courage to look at him. "If there was such a guy, it's pretty obvious I didn't get as close to him as I have to you," she said wryly.

Wyatt closed his eyes and swallowed. The idea of another man touching her as he had made him feel absolutely murderous. She belonged to him! All this past week he'd imagined those hundred acres as his. He'd pictured a ranch house with himself and Gabrielle in it—making love and babies.

Yet he wasn't a fool. His house in the suburbs had never been a home because it wasn't filled with love. His parents' house had rotted and crumbled because there'd been no love to keep it strong. And if Wyatt ever did have the courage to build a ranch house in its place, the structure would have to have love to be anything more than a house. Was he crazy to dare think Gabrielle could give him that love?

When minutes began to pass and he didn't reply, Gabrielle decided he'd said all he had to say on the matter.

Sighing, she rose to her feet. "I think I'll go to the kitchen for some iced tea. Would you like to go in? Or I'll bring the drinks back here."

Her voice finally penetrated his deep thoughts. He glanced up at her as though he was surprised to see her standing. "Were you saying something about drinks?"

It wasn't like Wyatt to be distracted. But he was a man who always had a lot on his plate, she reasoned. She was just a morsel among his other problems.

"Iced tea. I'm going to the kitchen after some." She handed him the Bible. "Would you keep that beside you until I get back?"

He accepted the partially damaged book. "What were you doing with this thing?"

She shrugged. "Praying for a miracle. Why don't you read a few verses while I go fetch the tea? There's plenty of things in there about faith and trust. And love."

She looked so beautiful. Even in a pair of plain khaki shorts and a navy blouse, with her hair in tangled waves upon her shoulders, she was enough to turn any man's head. And she would, he thought sickly, once she got to California.

"Yeah," he muttered. "But would a man like me understand any of it?"

She shrugged again, then as she turned toward the house, tossed over her shoulder, "Why don't you try?"

Wyatt watched her until she disappeared into the house, then he placed the partially scorched Bible on the seat beside him. Gabrielle must believe the sacred book could tell her something. When he'd walked up on her, she'd been leafing through the pages, a frown of desperation on her face. Had she been searching for a certain passage? He realized many people had a favorite quote from the scriptures to help guide them in life.

Curious now, he picked up the Bible and quickly flipped through the brown-edged pages. As far as he could tell, no lines had been marked or highlighted. And though Wyatt wasn't an overly religious man, by any means, he attended church from time to time and knew it was a natural thing to mark verses that the preacher's sermon touched upon. The appearance of this Bible gave him the impression that it had been used for something other than church-going.

He closed it, studied the front and back, then opened the front cover. No names or dates written. No clues as to why Gabrielle had carried it all the way from California—

His gaze suddenly zeroed in on a piece of cellophane tape pressed near the edge of the inside seam. Quickly he stripped away the tape and discovered a slit had been cut through part of the covering to make a secret envelope. Certain he was on to something now, he fished inside with one finger and was rewarded when it came into contact with something. Heedless of damaging the cover any more, he ripped the slit wider and dumped the contents onto his lap.

"What in the hell?" he muttered, his hand slowly reach-

ing for one of the two photos. It was a snapshot of Ryan
and Cameron and their sister Miranda before she'd run
away from the family. Quickly, he studied the faces, then
flipped the photos over and read the names listed on the
back. The second picture was of Kingston and Selena Fortune, parents of the three siblings.

His mind buzzed. Where had the photos come from? He
picked up the other item that had tumbled out with the
snapshots. Unfolding it, he quickly scanned the document,
which appeared to be part of an insurance policy.

What did any of this mean? Had his worst nightmare just
become true? Had Gabrielle been playing him for a sucker
all this time?

Fourteen

When Gabrielle returned to the courtyard, Wyatt was still seated on the swing, waiting for her.

"Here's the tea," she announced. Then with little more than mild curiosity, she nodded at the items on his lap. "What's that?"

Wyatt took the glass from her offered hand, and she sat back down beside him as though nothing had changed since she'd left a few moments ago. He looked at her with shock and disbelief.

"You tell *me*," he said. "I found it in your Bible."

Her brows slowly lifted as her gaze fell from his accusing face down to the photos and the folded piece of heavy paper.

"In my Bible? But…there wasn't anything in my Bible," she argued. "I leafed through it over and over. I even held it upside down and shook it, hoping a card or something might be stuck between the pages. I couldn't find anything."

"Well, I did. They were hidden between the cover and inside paper liner. Take a look."

Uneasy now, Gabrielle set her glass of tea aside and reached for one of the photos. After studying it, she said in a confused voice, "I don't think I know these people."

"Hmm. Well, those two people are Ryan's mother and father," he said dryly. "What about this one?"

She took the other photo and carefully scanned the features of the three people standing together. "I'm not sure. But I believe the man in the middle resembles Ryan. If it is, he must have been little more than a teenager here."

"It is Ryan. You don't know the other two?"

She shook her head, then suddenly her eyes popped wide open. "Wyatt! What were photos of the Fortunes doing in my Bible?"

"You tell me," he repeated.

Once again she shook her head in bewilderment. "But I have no idea! Do you think I knew the Fortunes before I lost my memory?"

His lips spread to a thin line. "None of them recognized you when you arrived here," he pointed out.

Her mind began to whirl with all sorts of questions and implications. Yet she could remember nothing. "Is that something else you found with the pictures?" she asked, gesturing toward the paper on his lap.

Without saying a word, he handed her the document. Gabrielle opened it and quickly scanned the information. It didn't make sense to her. These things must somehow be connected to her. But how?

"I...I don't understand any of this. Who is Miranda Fortune? Why would I have a part of the woman's insurance policy?"

Wyatt felt cold as his gaze met hers. "You really are good, Gabrielle. You must have come from an acting family to have this much talent."

Her jaw dropped as she realized where his suggestion was leading. "You think I'm acting?" she practically shrieked. "You believe I really know about all of this?"

"It came from your Bible, didn't it?"

She looked down at the damaged book. It had traveled with her all the way from California for some reason. The photos and insurance document had to be the purpose.

"Let's go in the house," he said roughly. "I want the Fortunes to see all of this. They think you've been innocent all this time. Now they can see for themselves that you were up to something. Why don't you tell me what it was, and save yourself the embarrassment of confessing in front of them."

She jumped to her feet and glared at him. "I have nothing to confess! I have no memory! I can't tell you why I had any of these things, but I know it wasn't for sinister reasons! But you obviously believe otherwise," she added sickly.

With the photos and document in one hand, he rose from the love seat and gripped her arm. They entered the house through the glass doors off the great room. Ryan, Lily and Mary Ellen were sitting on the couch having a glass of wine. The three of them looked up with mild surprise as Wyatt led Gabrielle over to them.

Ryan quickly spotted the dark look on Wyatt's face and rose to his feet. "What's wrong?"

"I'm not sure, Ryan. I thought maybe you or some of your family might be able to put this little puzzle together." He handed Ryan the photos and paper. "I found these in a secret compartment in Gabrielle's Bible. She says she didn't know they were there, or anything else about them."

Ryan took one look at the pictures and gasped. The two women behind them quickly rose to their feet. "What is it, darling?" Lily asked.

"I'm not sure," he answered in a voice that was suddenly quivering with excitement. "This is…Miranda. Little Miranda. My sister." He handed the photos to the two women, then unfolded the insurance policy. "Oh, God, this is her. The date she was born. Her name. Everything. The policy was dated a few years ago—but this is proof! Proof Miranda is still alive!"

This wasn't the response Wyatt had been expecting from the older man. "What do you think Gabrielle was doing with these things? Why was she coming here to the ranch with them?"

Ryan glanced up from the paper. His hands were trembling, and there was an incredulous smile on his face as he looked at Gabrielle. "You must be her daughter, honey! You must be my niece!" He tossed the paper down on the coffee table, then came around to Gabrielle and took her face in both his hands. "Let me look at you—*really* look at you. Why didn't I see it before?"

A few steps away, Mary Ellen carefully studied the photos. "This is the three of you," she agreed. "Cameron, Ryan and Miranda. My goodness, this was taken years ago!"

Ryan said, "I'm trying to remember how Miranda looked before she went away, and now I'm sure." His smile broadened as he looked from Wyatt's shocked face back to Miranda's bemused one. "Yes. You have her features. You can't remember her? Or tell us where she is?"

Gabrielle's expression was pitifully blank and regretful. Ryan dropped his hands from her face and sighed with disappointment.

"I'm so sorry, Ryan. I can't. Are you certain about all of this?" she asked hoarsely. "I mean…I can't believe I'm a Fortune."

"I don't believe it!" Wyatt practically growled.

Gabrielle couldn't look at him. His doubts and accusations were simply too much for her heart to handle.

"Wyatt, I know it's your job to be suspicious, but this is one time you're wrong." Ryan said, walking over to the telephone. "I'm going to call the rest of the family here to the house. I can't wait to tell them we've got a new blood relative!"

Wyatt threw up his hands in a gesture of helpless disgust.

Certain her legs had turned to rubber, Gabrielle said weakly, "I think I'd better sit down."

She sank into the nearest armchair. Lily filled another goblet of wine and carried it over to Gabrielle. "Here, honey, drink this. You must be feeling pretty shocked right now. It isn't every day a girl learns she's an heiress."

Gabrielle darted a doubtful glance at Wyatt, who was now pacing around the large room like an angry mountain lion. Obviously he believed she was some sort of con artist. That she'd deliberately hidden the information about the Fortunes in the Bible to somehow use against them. The idea crushed her. Yet she could see how the whole thing would look suspicious. And Wyatt was every inch a lawman.

"Ryan can't be sure about me. I might have had those documents for some other reason," Gabrielle said.

Mary Ellen shook her head as she came to stand just behind Lily. "Now that Ryan has put the notion in my head, you do favor Miranda. Especially if I think of her without all that lipstick and makeup she wore."

"You knew Miranda Fortune?" Gabrielle asked her.

"Yes. We were neighbors back then."

"I've never heard any of you speak of the woman. I didn't realize there was a missing sister in the family."

Mary Ellen waved her hand dismissively. "We don't speak of Miranda much. She left so long ago. And there have been so many other pressing problems for the family here of late. When Cameron died in the car crash, we were all hoping Miranda would hear about it and come to the funeral. Both Ryan and Cameron had feared their sister had met with foul play. But from the looks of that insurance policy, she was alive a few years ago."

Across the room, Ryan hung up the telephone, then

turned to the others. ''They'll all be here in a few minutes,'' he said happily. ''In the meantime, I think we should have Rosita put some champagne on ice and bring out the best dishes for supper. This calls for a celebration!''

Glad to see her fiancé finally smiling with good news for a change, Lily went over and linked her arm through his. ''That's a wonderful idea, Ryan. Would you like me to go to the kitchen and tell her?''

He bent his head and kissed her cheek. ''If you don't mind.''

''I'll be right back,'' she promised him.

Lily left for the kitchen. Wyatt stopped his pacing and walked over to the older man. ''Ryan, this family has been in a hell of a mess here lately. Don't you think you're jumping the gun with an impromptu celebration? For all we know, Gabrielle could have come here trying to extort money from you.''

''Hell, Wyatt! Does that beautiful woman look like she could harm a fly? She wouldn't do that to any of us!''

Wyatt turned hard, unyielding eyes on Gabrielle's pale face. ''Sofia's good looks haven't kept her from dealing you plenty of misery.''

Ryan glared at him. ''You would have to bring that up. Let's not talk about that…woman. I don't want to spoil the evening.''

''I don't want to spoil your evening or anything else,'' Wyatt assured him. ''I just want you to be prepared when all of this turns out to be fraud.''

Ryan shot him a glance. ''I believe you're the one who needs to get prepared to accept the fact that Gabrielle is really one of us.''

By the time Dallas, Maggie, Matthew and Zane had arrived, the great room resembled a rowdy family reunion. The pictures and the document were passed from one relative to the next. While they were inspected and discussed, Ryan explained to Gabrielle how Miranda had left home at the age of seventeen.

With her attention still captured by Ryan Fortune, who was sitting in an armchair directly across from her, Gabrielle said, "But she wasn't of age, Ryan. I'm surprised your father allowed it. From all you've told me about Kingston Fortune, he sounded like a hard and strict man."

Ryan nodded, his expression full of wry fondness. "He was very strict with his two sons—he demanded and expected a lot out of Cameron and me. But Miranda was the apple of Kingston's eye. He gave her anything she wanted. And the more he gave, the more she took. She went wild. I can't think of any better way to describe my sister's behavior back then. Anyway, after she left the ranch, Dad couldn't stand it. He went all the way to California after her. But he was never able to track her down. Losing her broke his heart."

Gabrielle found it difficult to imagine a girl so young wanting to leave her home and family. Even then the Fortunes must have been rich. Miranda had siblings, a mother and father, and anything else she might have wanted. Yet she left it all. For what and why?

"A movie star," Gabrielle repeated, weighing the words, wondering about the woman whom Ryan believed was her mother. "Do you think that dream is really what pushed her to leave Texas? Did she ever write or contact any of you?"

"Shortly after she left, we received one postcard. It was postmarked Nevada, and there was nothing written on it to explain what she was really doing or where she was staying."

Gabrielle pressed her hand against her forehead. A dull throb was beginning to build behind her eyes. She hoped it didn't grow into a full-fledged headache before the night was over.

Matthew came to stand near his father's chair. The young doctor looked at Gabrielle. "You're not going to catch the flight you had booked for tomorrow, are you?"

Gabrielle glanced from the two Fortune men to Wyatt, who was seated in an armchair directly to her right. "I…I haven't thought that far ahead," she told Matthew. "This is all such a shock."

"Of course she isn't going to leave," Ryan spoke up. "Gabrielle has found her home."

Her home! She'd made this her temporary home, but never had she imagined she might truly belong here as a member of the Fortune family. The whole thing was beyond her wildest dreams. But then, she'd had those photos and the paper with Miranda's name.

"I can tell you right now, Gabrielle isn't going on a plane to anywhere until we get to the bottom of this," Wyatt spoke up, making all heads swivel toward him. "If Gabrielle can't remember why she had your personal family items in her possession, then you don't know what the hell she was up to!"

"Wyatt! What is the matter with you?" Matthew exclaimed. "Gabrielle hasn't attempted to hurt anyone while she's been here. Or take anything from us. Can't you give her the benefit of the doubt?"

Gabrielle might not have tried to hurt anyone, Wyatt thought, but she had. Right now, he felt as if his world had been torn apart. In spite of her suspicious arrival on the Double Crown, he was gradually finding himself trusting her more and more. She was the first woman in years who'd made him think of trying to have a family of his own. And she was the only woman who'd made him stop and wonder if Marilyn's leaving might have been a forced disappearance rather than a desertion. But now he had to wonder if he'd been made a fool of all over again by a smooth little gold digger.

"Wyatt is looking at this whole situation from a sheriff's point of view," Ryan told his son. "If you were in his shoes you'd have to do the same thing." Pausing, he directed his gaze at Wyatt. "But that doesn't mean I agree with you."

Wyatt threw up his hands. "Look, you're all simply assuming Gabrielle is your relative. The daughter of a sister who's been gone from the family for thirty years. You need some sort of concrete proof. Something more than a couple of old photos."

"There's also the document with Miranda's name on it," Zane spoke up.

Wyatt frowned. "So she has an insurance policy with Miranda's name on it. There's nothing on the document linking her to the woman."

"Wyatt is right," Gabrielle had to agree. "There might have been some other motive for me having those things hidden in the Bible."

A few steps away, Rosita paused as she carried a tray full of iced drinks to the coffee table. "There is proof Gabrielle is a Fortune," she said to no one in particular. Then, directing her attention solely on Ryan, she said, "I'm surprised you haven't thought of the Fortune birthmark before now."

Sudden dawning streaked across his face, and snapping his fingers, he jumped to his feet. "You're right, Rosita!"

Matthew turned stunned looks on his brothers. "Why didn't we think of our birthmark? If Gabrielle is a Fortune, she'll surely have one."

"That's right," Zane echoed. "We all do. Even Taylor. And we don't even know where he came from."

"Gabrielle has the crown-shaped birthmark on her hip. I saw it on her some time ago," Rosita said before Ryan could ask.

Gabrielle had never seen Ryan angry with the housekeeper before. He always treated the woman with fondness and respect, but now he was practically shouting at her. "Rosita! You saw the birthmark and didn't come straight to me?"

Rosita shrugged, clearly unalarmed by her boss's frustration. "I told Ruben about it, and we decided you had enough troubles to deal with besides wondering about a birthmark. And we figured if Gabrielle really was a family member, you'd find it out anyway."

Dallas looked at his wife and groaned. Shaking her head, Maggie went to her mother and gently draped her arm around her shoulders. "Mother, don't you think Gabrielle might have wanted to know? She's been trying to get her memory back."

"I warned Wyatt that I felt Gabrielle was connected to the family. I could feel a strong urge had drawn her here. Just like I told you about the striking serpent that caused her wreck. But you paid me no heed," she told her daughter. "No one around here wants to hear what I know or see."

"Mother—"

"Don't badger her, Maggie," Dallas spoke up. "Your parents were only trying to mind their own business."

Gabrielle glanced from one face to another. It seemed they'd all forgotten she was in the room. Except for Wyatt. His eyes were boring a hole straight through her.

Trying not to let his anger pulverize her any more than it already had, she spoke up in a voice loud enough to be heard by all. "If anyone is interested, I do have a birthmark on my hip. It looks almost identical to the brand you put on your horses. When I saw it down at the corrals, I kept thinking how strange it was that I was marked with the Double Crown brand.''

Everyone stared at her with wide eyes and slack jaws. Everyone but Wyatt. A quick glance from the corner of Gabrielle's eye assured her he didn't believe any more of the story than he had ten minutes ago.

"Maggie, you and Gabrielle go to the bedroom where you can take a look for yourself," Ryan said to his daughter-in-law. To Gabrielle he asked, "Would you mind?"

Quickly Gabrielle rose from the chair. "Of course not. I want to know about this as much as you Fortunes.''

As the two women left the great room, Wyatt got to his feet and walked over to the glass doors leading out to the courtyard. Not long ago, it seemed, he and Gabrielle had escaped to the hidden shadows among the gardens. At that time he'd been certain her need for him had been as feverish as his own for her. Now he could only wonder if everything about her had been a lie. Even the way she'd given her body to him.

Hell, what did it matter? She'd been planning to leave tomorrow anyway. And he'd been going to let her go. But when tomorrow came would he really have been able to see her walk away?

He didn't have time to consider the agony of that question. Behind him the two women had returned to the room, and things were in an uproar. Wyatt's long strides carried him to the midst of the commotion.

"The birthmark is there," Ryan told him, his face wreathed in smiles. "Gabrielle is really a Fortune."

Wyatt felt as if someone had knocked him sideways. "I don't believe it. Everybody has *some* sort of birthmark."

"Not like ours," Dallas insisted. "We're branded on the hip in a certain spot with a crown-shaped mark.''

Wyatt glanced at the other man without really seeing him. "I understand all you Fortunes have the same birthmark. But did you ever consider it could be copied? Think about it. People will do a damn sight more than put a mark on their bodies to get into the money you Fortunes have!"

"What do you mean, copied?" Gabrielle spoke directly to Wyatt for the first time since they'd left the courtyard.

"I mean that mark is probably a fake. A tattoo."

"It didn't look like ink to me," Maggie remarked.

"Matthew is a doctor. He can verify whether the birthmark is real or fake," Ryan said.

Wyatt looked around at the faces in the group, wondering how they could all be so trusting and accepting after the heartache they'd been through this past year. Were they crazy, or was it him?

"Forget it! You all want to believe Gabrielle is a Fortune, so go ahead—take her into your family. Just don't forget I warned you."

The room went terribly quiet. Gabrielle was certain she could hear her heart breaking, shattering into a million pieces on the tiled floor at her feet. Without even glancing her way, Wyatt stalked away from the group and toward the door.

"Wyatt, are you leaving?" Ryan called.

Wyatt glanced over his shoulder. "I've got work to do and it's obvious I'm wasting my time here."

As he disappeared into the entryway, Maggie put her hands on Gabrielle's shoulders and gave her a little nudge. "Go after him, Gabrielle."

Her eyes full of pain, Gabrielle shook her head. "He doesn't believe me," she said hoarsely.

"He's in shock," Mary Ellen suggested gently.

Maggie nudged her again, and this time Gabrielle's heart

refused to listen to the logic in her head. She raced across the room and out to the front steps.

"Wyatt!"

Without turning to look, he paused on the walkway. She hurried down the steps to join him.

"If you came out here to plead your case with me, forget it," he said tightly.

Moving in front of him, she looked up at his dark face. His features were so rock hard, he didn't appear human.

"I didn't come out here to plead my case, Wyatt. I don't know what my case is," she said softly. "For all I know, you're right about me. I could be a con artist, a gold digger who came here to get money from the Fortunes any way I could. If I had my memory, I might be able to defend myself. As it is I can only hope you're wrong."

A sneer twisted his features. "You're going to milk your amnesia story for all it's worth, aren't you? Do you honestly still expect me to believe your memory was lost when you crashed into that tree?"

Shadows of pain filled her eyes as she continued to search his forbidding face. "It was."

"Hah!" he scoffed bitterly. "I think you've lied to all of us from the very start. Unfortunately, the Fortunes are still believing you. But I'm not."

Moving closer, she gripped his forearm as her eyes pleaded with him to understand. "Do you think I was lying when I made love to you? I was a virgin, Wyatt! You know that!"

For a split second she thought she saw regret flicker in his eyes. But then he deliberately picked her hand from his arm, and dropped it back at her side as though her touch was abhorrent to her.

"Like I said before. People will do anything for money."

She wanted to slap him. But why bother? He'd made up

his mind about her, and she couldn't think of one thing that might change it. Besides, she could feel the throb in her head growing to the size of a bass drum beat. Sweat was beading on her forehead and upper lip, and trickling in rivulets beneath her shirt. The hysterical thought struck her that her head was going to burst right along with her heart.

"I'm sorry for you, Wyatt. Truly sorry," she whispered brokenly, then pressing her hand against her forehead, she turned away from him and hurried back into the house.

By the time she staggered into the great room, she was on the verge of collapsing. Her legs were shaking and intermittent explosions of pain were going off behind her eyes.

Mary Ellen was the first one to notice her return. The woman rushed over to her and took hold of her arm. "Gabrielle, what's wrong?"

"I…I'm getting sick. My head is pounding."

"Oh, this has all been too much for you, honey. To learn who you are would have been traumatic enough, but to learn you're a Fortune, well, I can't imagine what you must be feeling." She brought her arm around Gabrielle's back and urged her forward. "Come along, and I'll help you down to your room."

When the others spotted Gabrielle and Mary Ellen slowly making their way toward the kitchen, the whole family rushed over to them.

"Gabrielle, what happened?" Maggie cried in dismay.

Matthew stepped forward and quickly scanned her pale, sweat-dampened face. "Is your head hurting?"

She nodded. "Terribly. Worse than it ever has."

Matthew glanced at Mary Ellen. "Help her to bed, and I'll go get my bag."

"Do you need help?" Lily asked Mary Ellen.

"I'll go with them," Maggie said as she hurried around to support Gabrielle's other side.

"Don't worry about anything, Gabrielle," Ryan said. "You might have lived in California before, but you're home now. We'll take care of you."

Gabrielle thanked him, then the two women helped her back to her room and into bed.

"I'm so sorry you're ill," Mary Ellen said as she smoothed the sheet across Gabrielle. "We were getting ready to celebrate."

"I'm sorry I spoiled the evening," Gabrielle said in a voice tight with pain.

Mary Ellen smiled gently. "Oh, my dear, you haven't spoiled anything."

"You're the first happy news we've had in a while," Maggie added. "We'll celebrate when you're feeling better."

Gabrielle squeezed her eyes shut and pressed her fingers against her forehead. If it turned out she was truly a Fortune, she would be glad. Yet the pleasure would be shadowed by the heartbreak of knowing Wyatt didn't believe in her. And most of all, that he didn't love her.

"Wyatt doesn't believe I'm cause for celebration. He'd jail me if he could find a legal reason."

Maggie came to stand by the end of the bed. "Wyatt isn't behaving like himself," she said. "He's always been a tough nut to crack, but he's usually not so hard-nosed or unreasonable."

Mary Ellen reached down and patted her shoulder. "He's just afraid he loves you. That's the only thing wrong with Wyatt."

Her eyes filled with pain, Gabrielle glanced up at Mary Ellen. "He thinks I lied to him."

"He'll see the truth of things eventually," Mary Ellen

tried to reassure her. "Now, forget about Wyatt and try to get some rest."

A light knock sounded on the door and the three women looked around to see Matthew entering the room. He quickly took Gabrielle's blood pressure and pulse, then examined her eyes with a penlight.

"I don't think the concussion you suffered last month is connected to this headache. I'm inclined to believe it's an old-fashioned migraine brought on by nerves." He reached into his bag and brought out two pain capsules. "Take these," he said, handing them to Gabrielle. "If it doesn't let up in about an hour, we'll do something else. The best thing you can do now is turn off the light and try to sleep."

"Matthew," Maggie began as he put his things back into his medical bag, "since you're here, why don't you take a look at Gabrielle's birthmark. It might ease her mind to have a doctor confirm whether it's real or not."

He glanced questioningly at Gabrielle. "I'm perfectly satisfied with Maggie's opinion, but if you want me to look, I will."

Wyatt's mistrust had affected her so deeply that she was still doubting herself. If Matthew could give her the truth, she needed to hear it. As for exposing her hip to the man, he was a doctor, and the area he had to see was small and not anywhere embarrassing.

"I would appreciate your opinion, Matthew," she told him. "I believe Maggie is right. I'll feel better knowing one way or the other."

He motioned for Maggie to flip on the overhead light, and Gabrielle slipped her pajama bottom down just far enough for him to see the mark.

Leaning closer, Matthew peered at the distinctive crown on her hip. "Hmm. This is really something," he murmured.

Fear clutched Gabrielle's heart. Maybe Wyatt was right. Maybe she was really a gold-digging con artist. "What is it?" she asked frantically.

He glanced at her and smiled. "We're bona fide cousins, Gabrielle."

After the doctor and the two women left her room, a long time passed before Gabrielle truly digested the news Matthew had given her. The birthmark wasn't ink or dye. It hadn't been put there artificially to gain access to the Fortunes' millions. She *was* a Fortune! As much as were Dallas and Matthew and Zane and all the children belonging to Cameron and Ryan. It was amazing.

Eventually the drug Matthew had given her began to dull the pain. As sleep crept closer, she wondered what Wyatt was going to think when he heard the news. He might admit he was wrong about her. But it was hardly enough to make him love her. Somehow she was going to have to make herself accept the fact that everything between them was over.

Fifteen

Wyatt was sitting on the couch in his living room, staring into the darkness, when the telephone rang. He cursed as the sound intruded on his anguished thoughts. He didn't want to talk to anyone. He didn't want to see anyone.

But he was the county's sheriff. He couldn't neglect his duties. And the call could very well be an emergency from his office. He leaned over and picked up the receiver, then grunted a greeting.

"Hello," a woman replied. "Is this Wyatt? Wyatt Grayhawk?"

The female voice was unfamiliar and hesitant. Wyatt answered a bit warily. "Yes, this is Wyatt Grayhawk. And if you're selling something, lady. I don't want it."

"Wyatt."

She said his name again in a choked voice, and Wyatt was suddenly gripping the receiver with full attention. "Are you in trouble, lady? Don't dally around. Tell me, dammit!"

"No. I'm sorry. I just don't know what to say."

Without warning his heart started to pound. He stood, then swallowed. "Who...who is this?" he asked, his voice suddenly going very quiet.

"This is...Marilyn. Your mother."

Wyatt was certain the room was tilting around him. His throat was too tight to speak, then when he finally thought he could get a word out, he didn't know what to say.

"Wyatt? Are you still there?"

"Yes. Yes, I'm here." His heart was still pumping like a locomotive and his hands had started to shake. "I…how did you know—how did you get my number?"

"Information. I received a letter from Ruby Mendoza. She told me you wrote to Berle Atkins hoping he'd know how to contact me. Ruby used to work at Berle's and she still kept in touch with me and Berle. I—I didn't know what to think. I couldn't believe it."

He swallowed again. Just hearing the woman's voice was so strange and yet somehow achingly familiar. "I wasn't even sure you were still alive," he admitted in an awed whisper.

"Oh, Wyatt. Oh, Wyatt. I'm so…you can't imagine how much I've thought of you. How much I've missed you. Are you—I guess you're all grown up now," she said with a tearful laugh. "And I know you must be handsome. You were a gorgeous little boy."

Like clawing hands, regret tore at him. "I'm the sheriff of Red Rock now. That's what I do for a living."

"Oooh! Oh, that's…that's wonderful," she said, her voice full of surprise and pride. "I knew you'd be a success. I prayed you would be. And prayed that…"

She didn't go on and Wyatt quickly prodded, "What?"

"That you wouldn't turn out to be like Leonard," she confessed, then followed the words with a deep sigh.

He didn't have to ask her what she meant. He'd lived with Leonard for eighteen years, far longer than Marilyn had. As for being like his father, Wyatt could have assured her he didn't drink heavily nor was he lazy. But was he mean and embittered? Had he allowed himself to become that much like Leonard? He couldn't bear to admit it, even to himself.

"What are you doing? Where are you living?" he asked her.

"I'm in Kingman, Arizona. I own a little café here. It's doing pretty well."

He squeezed his eyes shut as he tried to picture her there in the desert town. "I don't understand…I guess the reason I wanted to contact you—" He stopped, drew in a deep breath and started again. "Why did you leave all those years ago? Why did you leave me?"

Once that last question died away, the line went quiet, and then he realized he could hear the muffled sound of sobbing. Finally she spoke, although her voice quivered badly, "I had to go, Wyatt. Your father beat me, then put a gun to my head and ordered me to pack and leave."

He suddenly thought of Gabrielle and how close she'd come to guessing the truth. "But why? I know the bastard was mean, but—"

"Because he threatened to harm you if I didn't leave," she interrupted. "He knew you were the one thing I truly loved, and he used you to hurt me."

"You never came back," he accused.

She gasped and lowered her voice as though she were still afraid Leonard might hear her. "I didn't dare. He promised if I ever returned to Red Rock, he would be waiting to kill me and you both. I couldn't take that chance, Wyatt. I knew as long as I stayed away, he wouldn't harm you. He didn't, did he? Please tell me he didn't beat you."

"No. He wasn't much of a father, but he didn't beat me. He…he always said you didn't want me because I was a half-breed. He said you were pregnant and had to marry him. And that you blamed him for ruining your life."

"Oh, God, how terrible," she said with a groan. "That couldn't be further from the truth. I was planning to take you with me. But he found out about it," Marilyn said.

"The crazy thing was, though, he thought I was going to run off with one of the men who came into the café every morning. He was convinced I was having an affair and that was his way of hurting me—banishing me from my own son."

Wyatt pinched the bridge of his nose as he tried to tell himself it was useless to hate and blame his father now. The past had already happened. It couldn't be changed. And he supposed in the end, Leonard had suffered more than anyone else.

"Were you having an affair?" Wyatt asked.

She gasped. "No! Though God knows I wished I had. Maybe some man could have helped me smuggle you out of there. As it was, I couldn't defend myself against a drunk maniac."

Wyatt could understand her fears back then. But twenty-six years had passed. She might never have contacted him if he hadn't started to search for her. "I realize you were frightened of Leonard all those years ago. But you...never tried to get in touch with me after I was grown."

"I couldn't!" she cried, and then in a voice full of dismay went on, "I mean—isn't Leonard still there in Red Rock?"

To think she was still so terrified of the man was pitiful, and proved how powerful abuse was over a woman or child. Wyatt supposed that in her mind, she pictured Leonard as he was back then, still capable of being a tyrant to mother and son. "No. He's been gone for about twelve years now."

"Where?"

"Somewhere in Oklahoma. I'm not sure. I really don't give a damn. Do you?"

"Lord, no. But I figured he was still there. I don't want

him to know I've talked to you, Wyatt. He might still try to hurt you.''

It was then that he realized the true depth of her fear, and realized, too, that it was all for him. ''Oh, Mother, the man can't hurt me now. He's gone from our lives.''

The fact that he'd called her ''Mother'' must have affected her, because she began to cry again. ''I wish I'd known, Wyatt. I wish I'd been brave enough to come back. I loved you so. I still do,'' she said brokenly.

His own voice was husky when he spoke. ''I thought you'd deserted me.''

''I guess I did, Wyatt,'' she said regretfully. ''But not in my heart. Never in my heart.'' She sniffed and drew in a calming breath. ''Every day after I left I wanted to come back for you, but I couldn't find a way. And no one really wanted to help me. All my friends were even more frightened of Leonard than I was. None of them wanted to get involved. Finally I decided there wasn't anything I could do. And as more time began to slip away...I figured you probably already hated me. That you wouldn't want to be with me anyway.''

''I've tried to hate you,'' Wyatt admitted. ''But I can't. I think we both need to forget the past and try to start over again. Is there any way you might come to Red Rock for a visit? I want to see you.''

Marilyn sniffed again, but this time Wyatt could hear happiness through her tears. As for himself, a warm sort of peace he'd never felt before poured through him.

''Are you certain Leonard won't hear about it and cause trouble?''

''I'm certain he'll never show his face around here again. I'm the sheriff now, Mom.''

She suddenly laughed with relief and a great amount of pride. ''Yes. I must remember my son is the sheriff. And

I'll find a way to get there,'' she promised. "I have a friend who can run the café a few days without me. Is next week too soon?"

"I'll send you a plane ticket by courier, and when your flight arrives at the airport in San Antonio, I'll be waiting to pick you up. In the meantime, you have my number now. Call me if you need anything,'' he told her.

The line went quiet again, and he realized she was too choked up to speak. It amazed him how much his heart went out to her, how easy it was to allow his mother back into his life.

"Mom? Are you okay?"

"Yes. I just wanted to say, I don't know who or what prompted you to hunt for me, but I thank God you did."

He suddenly smiled. "I'll tell you all about it when you get here."

"Yes. Goodbye, son. And…I love you."

Wyatt swallowed and closed his eyes. "I love you too."

When Gabrielle woke a few hours later, the pain in her head was mercifully gone. But where was she? Totally disoriented, she leaned up on her elbow and looked around the dim shadows of the long room. This wasn't her apartment.…

Oh, dear! Oh, God! It was the Double Crown! Her memory had returned!

Ripping back the bedcover, she raced over to the dresser and switched on a lamp. For some reason she expected to look different. And she did look somewhat changed from the young woman who'd been working her way through college as a waitress.

Shoving back her tousled hair, Gabrielle peered more closely at the image in the mirror. A few hours earlier she'd gone to sleep with a fierce headache. Now she was wide awake. And she remembered! Everything! Her mother, Miranda. Her older brother, Kane. Her father—the faceless rodeo rider, Lloyd Carter, who'd abandoned the three of them even before Gabrielle had been born.

She'd come here to Texas hunting the family she'd never had, and the family her mother would never speak about. And if it had been left up to Miranda, Gabrielle would never have found them. If she hadn't picked up the newspaper in the diner and noticed the article about Bryan Fortune being kidnapped, she would still have been in the dark about her heritage.

Gabrielle sank onto the dressing bench as she remembered back to the day she'd confronted her mother with the newspaper article. The name was Fortune—the same name she'd found on one of her mother's old insurance policies. The family lived on a ranch in Texas, and the kidnapped child had a birthmark described as exactly the same as Gabrielle's and her brother Kane's.

At first Miranda had laughingly called it an odd coincidence and nothing more. But Gabrielle had felt certain there was some sort of connection to the family back in Texas. She'd pushed her mother for more direct answers, and when Miranda had refused to give any, Gabrielle had informed her mother she was going to Texas to find out the truth for herself.

Miranda's reaction had been close to hysteria. She'd demanded Gabrielle to stay in California and forget her wild ideas. She'd warned her daughter that she would only find trouble in Texas. And when she did not to call her mother for help.

Why? Gabrielle wondered. For years, she had asked her mother about her family. But all Miranda would tell her was that she'd been raised on a ranch in Texas and hadn't gotten along with her parents, so she'd run away to California.

Well, that part pretty much matched what Ryan had told her earlier tonight. Still, it was hard to understand why Miranda had stayed away from these people for so long. Especially when they had millions, and she'd struggled to raise two children alone, waitressing and working odd acting jobs. Sometimes she'd landed a part in a local play, or once in awhile she'd lucked out and gotten a part in a low-budget film.

Even so, money had always been a scarce commodity for the Carters. Gabrielle had never minded living modestly, but she knew her mother had always wanted to live the high social life more fitting of a movie star. Gabrielle groaned at the idea. Her mother never had been, nor would be, a movie star.

Oh, Lord, what was Wyatt going to think of all this? He'd never in a thousand years believe her! And she seriously doubted the Fortunes would. All of them would think she'd used the wreck to fake her amnesia and to gain sympathy and a foothold with the family. They might even have the idea that Miranda sent her here as a way to gain part of the Fortune millions she'd deserted so long ago! As for Wyatt, he'd probably take great pleasure in denouncing her as a gold digger.

Groaning with misery, Gabrielle dropped her head in her hands. What was she going to do? What *could* she do?

As far as she could see, she had two choices. One, she could go wake the family, tell them everything she'd remembered, and hope they would all believe she'd come here with sincere intentions. Or two, she could pack a few things and leave without letting anyone know.

She tried to swallow down the pain that had started in her chest and was rising up in her throat. There really was no choice, she told herself. The Fortunes were too kind to cause them any more problems. If she slipped away and never came back, they would all see she didn't want money from them.

As for Wyatt, he didn't want her around anyway. He'd labeled her as trouble from the start. It didn't matter that she loved him. He would never return her feelings. The best thing she could do now was go back to the world she'd come from—and try to forget him.

A tear brimmed over her eye and slid down her cheek. She couldn't forget Wyatt. He was in her heart to stay. She'd simply have to go through the rest of her life wondering how things might have been if she'd come here under different circumstances, and if he'd been a man who could trust her.

In less than ten minutes, she'd changed into the clothes she'd worn from California and thrown a few essentials into a denim carryall. All the nice things Maggie and the rest of the Fortunes had given her were packed away in boxes to be sent to the Red Cross. As for the money Ryan had loaned her, she put all of it—except enough for bus fare and food—into an envelope, then added a short note.

Dear Ryan and family,
Thank you for the love and kindness you showed me while I was here in your home. Perhaps someday I can explain why I had to leave this way, and hopefully you'll understand. I promise to repay the rest of the money as soon as I can.

My love to you all,
Gabrielle

She sealed the envelope, then propped it on the base of the lamp on the nightstand. After she switched off the light, she carefully made her way to the door leading out to the courtyard.

Getting off the property without being seen by the guard was going to be tricky. But if she hung in the shadows, she thought she had a chance. Far more of a chance than Wyatt would ever give her, she thought sadly.

Wyatt was lying in bed, his mind churning, his heart aching. He didn't know why he'd bothered to lie down. He knew sleep would not come to him tonight. There was no way he could shut down his mind after all that had happened. First with Gabrielle, and then his mother.

How ironic that he had found one woman after losing the other.

Hell, he thought with a snort. Where was he getting the idea Gabrielle had been his to lose? She'd been playing him along just as she'd been duping the Fortunes. Hadn't she?

Groaning out loud, he slung his forearm over his aching eyes. Had she really been lying to him? he asked himself for the thousandth time. She'd seemed so genuinely confused about the pictures he'd found in the Bible, and she'd been so adamant about not wanting anything from the Fortunes. Why couldn't he simply take her word as the truth?

Because he loved her. God help him. He didn't know when his heart had refused to listen to his warnings or why. He only knew the feelings inside him were too strong to ignore. And that put him in an all-too-vulnerable position. If he allowed himself to believe in her, he was only bound to get hurt worse.

Dammit, he couldn't possibly hurt any more than he was hurting now! But he didn't know what to do about it. Or even if he *could* do anything to put things right between them. He'd ripped her feelings to shreds tonight. Maybe she could forgive him for that. But how was she going to view things, especially him, since she'd become a Fortune?

Money and the social status that went with the name would be rightfully hers. Once she had time to absorb what it meant to belong to one of Texas's richest families, she probably wouldn't be interested in a regular Joe like himself. But he'd been wrong about his mother all these years. Maybe he was wrong about Gabrielle, too. He desperately wanted to think so.

The telephone beside the bed shrilled loudly in the quiet bedroom. Frowning, he squinted at the digital clock, then lifted the receiver. "Hello."

"Wyatt, it's Matthew."

Expecting to hear one of the deputies on the other end of the line, the sound of Matthew's voice brought him straight up off the bed.

"Where are you?" he asked at the same time as he was reaching for his jeans.

"At home. On the ranch. I went to check on Gabrielle a few minutes ago and found her gone."

Wyatt's heart suddenly lodged in his throat. "Gone? What the hell do you mean 'gone'?"

Matthew breathed heavily. "After you left, she went to bed, and I medicated her for a severe headache. I told her to let me know if it didn't get better. A few minutes ago, I got a phone call from Rosita—something about a dream she'd had of Gabrielle running down a dark road. She wouldn't hang up until I promised to go check on her. That's when I found Gabrielle gone from her room."

"Have you searched the whole house? If she was ill, she might have collapsed."

"She didn't collapse, Wyatt. She left a note and the money Dad had given her. All the clothes and things Maggie bought for her—they're still here."

"She might have left hours ago!" Wyatt said hoarsely. "What did the note say?"

Matthew read the few short words. As Wyatt listened, fear and regret twisted through him like a dark tornado. "How did she leave?"

"On foot. There are no vehicles missing."

"On foot! My God! Doesn't Ryan still have a guard posted to the house?"

"She must have given him the slip."

Wyatt cursed again in Matthew's ear. "If she's on foot, she can't have gotten too far."

"Unless she caught a ride once she reached the highway."

Wyatt didn't even want to consider that possibility. "I'm leaving the house now to search for her. If she does show up back at the ranch, call my personal cellular number. You have it."

"Yes. Yes, we will. Find her, Wyatt."

"I won't stop until I do," he promised, then hung up the phone and reached for the rest of his clothing.

Sixteen

Where the hell was she? Wyatt desperately asked himself. She couldn't have gone far. Not on foot. Dear God, he hoped she hadn't been foolish enough to accept a ride.

As his eyes searched the shadows along the highway, he cursed himself for leaving the Double Crown earlier tonight. He should have stayed and reasoned the whole thing out with her. He should have tried to listen to her side, rather than accusing and berating her. But he'd never dreamed she would leave without letting anyone know. He'd left the ranch believing he still had tomorrow with her.

That's the trouble with you, Wyatt. You've always wanted to avoid matters of the heart. You've always wanted to wait about loving and needing. Now you might have waited too long.

The ominous voice was swirling through his head like a dark cloud, when he suddenly spotted the silhouette of a person several yards ahead on the side of the highway.

He sped up, then braked the pickup to a screeching halt as he came alongside the weaving figure.

Before Gabrielle could summon the energy to run or hide in the woods that bordered the highway, Wyatt jumped out of the truck and grabbed her.

"Gabrielle! What in God's name are you doing out here?"

She opened her mouth to speak, but nothing would come

out. With shaky hands she tried to pull her torn blouse back onto her shoulder.

"What's happened? Are you hurt?" he demanded urgently.

Before she could answer, he took her by the shoulders and led her into the glare of the headlights on his truck. The sight of her wild, tangled hair and torn clothing warned Wyatt something terrible had occurred. Then he saw the glazed terror in her eyes.

"My Lord, Gabrielle," he whispered roughly, "what caused this? Are you all right?"

She finally managed to nod, then speak. "I caught a ride with a trucker. He...told me he'd let me off at the bus station. But he..."

"He what?" Fear rushed through him with such force that he was certain every bit of air had been knocked from his lungs. Giving her shoulders a little shake, he urged her to tell him. "Did the bastard rape you?"

"No," she said on a broken sob. "I managed to fight him off, and somehow I got out of the cab of the truck. I thought he would chase me down. But I guess I must have kicked him pretty hard. He drove off, and I haven't seen him since."

Relief flooded through Wyatt. He grabbed her to him and cradled her head against his shoulder. "Thank God, you're not hurt."

This wasn't the same Wyatt who'd stalked out of the ranch house a few hours ago, Gabrielle realized. She didn't know what had caused the change, and right now it didn't matter as long as he kept holding her like this.

Fear for her safety still lingered in his voice as he gently scolded, "Don't you understand you could have been killed? I've been out of my mind searching up and down the highway!"

She tried to swallow her emotions. "I didn't...think the man would be crazy! I thought he was just a friendly trucker who was happy to give me a ride."

"I'll bet he was happy," Wyatt muttered. "Do you have his tag number? Or a description of the truck? The Texas Highway Patrol will be only too happy to stop him."

Gabrielle shook her head. "I couldn't get the number. I was too busy running. And I don't remember exactly what the truck looked like."

He let out a long breath. "Well, don't worry about it. The main thing is, you're okay," he said. Taking her by the arm, he led her around to the door of the truck. Once the two of them were inside, he found an old denim jacket behind the seat and draped it over her shoulders. "Here. This will help warm you up while I call the ranch and let them know you're safe."

Wyatt started the truck and drove to a wide pull-off where he could safely park. While he was on the telephone with the ranch, Gabrielle tried to pull herself together. He was going to want answers and explanations, and she very much doubted he would accept the truth of the matter.

The conversation with Ryan lasted less than two minutes. When it ended, Wyatt placed the cellular phone on the dash, then turned to Gabrielle. After pushing the tousled hair away from her face, he studied her stricken features beneath the dim cargo light. A red welt ran diagonally across one cheek and greasy dirt was smeared on her chin, but he spotted no other external injuries.

"You know, since you first came to the Double Crown, I've thought many things about you, Gabrielle. But I never once imagined you as a fool. This stunt you pulled tonight was worse than foolish. Why? Why did you leave like that?"

He was far more bewildered than angry, and that took

Gabrielle by complete surprise. From the moment he'd found her, she'd expected him to unleash a whip of fury. So far it was yet to come.

"I—because I had to," she answered. "There was no other way."

"No other way? That doesn't make sense. You had a plane ticket for tomorrow. Even if the Fortunes didn't want you to leave, you could have used it in spite of their wishes. Why were you trying to go to the bus station?"

His face was so dear, so beloved, that she had to drop her eyes from him and wait for the pain to ease in her chest. Drawing in a bracing breath, she lifted her gaze back to his. "I wanted to be gone before anyone noticed I wasn't on the ranch. Especially you," she added in a choked voice.

He stared at her as though she were speaking in a foreign language. "Gabrielle, you don't understand. Yes, I was angry—about the pictures, the birthmark. Everything! I didn't want to believe you were a Fortune. But I've been thinking—"

"Wyatt," she was compelled to interrupt, "I have to tell you something. I've remembered. When I woke up, my memory was there. Just as though it had never been gone."

He went stock-still and then his brows inched upward ever so slowly. "You know who you are? At least, who you were back in California?"

She nodded, her heart pounding with anticipation. Did she dare try to explain? If he didn't believe her now, her hopes and dreams—her very life—would be over.

"I know it sounds phony and crazy. And if I were in your place, I probably wouldn't believe it. But that's the way it happened. I woke up and for a moment I wondered why I wasn't in my apartment. And then, as everything started coming back to me, I realized you and the Fortunes would never believe I came here to Texas simply to find out if I was related to them. So I decided to leave without telling anyone. And then you would all know I—I wasn't a gold digger.''

He winced and told himself he'd paid for his mistake a thousand times over while he'd been searching the highway for her, gripped with fear.

''What did you remember?'' he asked. ''What made you suspect you might be related to the Fortunes in the first place?''

A wondrous expression slowly transformed her beleaguered face. ''You mean—you actually want to know? You…believe me?''

With a tortured groan, he tugged her into the tight circle of his arms. ''I *have* to believe you, Gabrielle. Because tonight I've learned I sure as hell can't live without you.''

Joy exploded within her, and she leaned back and gathered his face with her hands. ''Oh, Wyatt! Are you sure? When you hear about my past—well, you might not feel that way.''

''Tell me everything,'' he urged softly.

He couldn't know how sweet those three words sounded to her. ''Well, there's so much, I don't exactly know where to start. My father was a rodeo cowboy—Lloyd Carter. My mother was very young when she fell in love and married him. He left when my brother Kane was about a year old and Mother was pregnant with me.''

''He never came back or tried to contact your mother?'' Wyatt asked.

Gabrielle shook her head. ''Never. My mother raised us alone. We always just managed to scrape by on what she made at odd jobs. What Ryan said about Miranda wanting to be a movie star was right. She's never given up on that dream. But the closest she's ever come is a couple of minor parts in some terrible, low-budget films.''

"The address we found for you in California—it isn't with your mother?" he asked.

Gabrielle sighed. "No. As soon as I graduated high school, I moved out and got a place of my own. You see, Mother is—well, she likes men. She's had a string of affairs. Most of the time she thought of me as her nursemaid, and someone she could pour out all her troubles to. And the troubles were always men and money. I couldn't stand living with her. But I do live close enough to keep an eye on her. God only knows what she's gotten into while I've been gone."

"Did she know you were coming to Texas?"

Gabrielle nodded. "She was livid about it and forbade me to come."

A puzzled frown pulled his dark brows together. "I don't understand."

She rested her palms against his warm chest, loving the feel of him, the beat of his heart against her fingers. "I've never understood her. But I'm beginning to now. You see, all these years I wanted to know my family. I wanted to know my grandparents and cousins and uncles and aunts. I didn't have anybody but my brother and a mother—a mother who's never really been a mother in the proper sense. But she always refused to tell me or my brother about the family. Except that she'd come from a ranch in Texas and that her parents were really mean to her so she'd run away to save herself."

"Dear God. From what I've heard, Miranda was so spoiled by her father it was sickening. Kingston gave her anything she wanted."

"I know it doesn't make sense. But for as long as I've been old enough to realize the truth, mother has never been the sensible sort."

"And she never mentioned being a Fortune to you or your brother?"

Gabrielle's lips twisted as she recalled the many times she'd begged her mother to tell her about her family. Miranda had always refused. "No. If I had waited on her to tell me, I would never have known. Instead, I just happened to pick up a newspaper in the diner where I worked as a waitress, and I noticed an article about Bryan's kidnapping. The family lived on a ranch in Texas. The name was Fortune and the child had a birthmark just like the one my mother and brother and I have. I thought it was more than coincidence, so I had to come and find out for myself."

"The pictures and the document with Miranda Fortune's name on it—how did you happen to have those?"

"I've had those for a long time. When I was a teenager, I snooped through some of my mother's things, trying to come up with clues to my family's whereabouts. I thought they might eventually lead me somewhere." Her hands slid upward and curved around his shoulders as she studied his face for any sort of reaction. "I realize this whole thing sounds incredible, and that it looks like I really did come here wanting money. But that was never my intention. From the time I was old enough to work, I've supported myself. I'm proud of that. I don't need anything else."

Suddenly a wry smile lifted the corner of his lips. "I hope that's not true, Gabrielle. I hope now that you're a Fortune, you'll still need me."

His words stunned her, and for a moment all she could manage to do was stare at him. "Do you really mean that?" she finally whispered. "Are you—trying to tell me you love me?"

With a needy groan, he buried his face in the side of her neck. "I don't know much about loving or needing, Gabrielle. If I'm not saying it right, it's because I've never felt like this before. But I have an ache in the middle of my chest that won't go away unless I have you in my arms. If that means I love you, then I do."

Tears were suddenly sliding down her cheeks. "Oh, Wyatt, I didn't think you'd ever give me a chance to explain. And I never expected you to believe me."

His arms tightened around her as he leaned his head back far enough to look into her eyes. "I made you feel cheap. I made you doubt yourself as a person," he said in a voice tight with regret. "That's the way I am, Gabrielle. I'm no good. Especially no good for you. You're a Fortune now. We both know you can do much better than me."

Sniffing, she pressed her cheek against his. "Darling, in my eyes there is no one better than you. I'm going to love you for the rest of my life, whether you want me to or not."

"Oh, God, Gabrielle, I want you—your love—for always. I never dreamed I would say that to any woman. I never imagined I would want to." He cradled her face between his palms. "Will you marry me? Give me the family I've never had?"

"You—you want children?" she asked, her voice filled with wonder. "I thought you were dead set against having a family."

"I was scared to admit my wants to myself, much less to you. I've lost too many times in the past to think I could win with you now."

"Oh, Wyatt, Wyatt." She breathed his name, anguish and joy threaded through her voice. "You have won. We've both won. Before I came here I was working on a college degree to teach special education. Do you think I could raise our children and be a teacher, too?"

"I'm more than sure you're woman enough to handle both jobs," he murmured.

His lips came down on hers, and as he tenderly kissed her, Gabrielle couldn't help thinking that although in the Fortunes she'd found her lost family, in Wyatt she'd found her love, her true home.

On the way back to the ranch, Wyatt stopped by the old Grayhawk homestead and showed her the place where he'd lived. He admitted to Gabrielle how much he wanted to build them a home there and raise cattle and horses.

"And children," she added with a happy sigh as he stood with his arm curled around her shoulders. "I think we'll have a good crop."

A sly smile on his lips, he glanced down at her. "Of children or livestock?"

She laughed and so did he, and as their eyes met they both realized how close they'd come to losing something precious, something that would last their whole lifetime together.

"Both," she said.

He slipped his hand around hers. "Are you ready to go back to the ranch and give the Fortunes the good news?"

Smiling she nodded. Then, just as quickly, the smile was gone and a frown puckered her forehead. Seeing it, Wyatt asked, "What is it, Gabrielle? Lord, your amnesia isn't coming back, is it?"

"No. Actually, I was wondering...what will I do if the Fortunes don't believe me? You do, but that's because you love me. They might think—"

He broke in before she could go any further. "And you think the Fortunes *don't* love you?" He chuckled with disbelief.

Her head swung back and forth. "I'm not sure how they feel. They're basically kind, generous people. But when they hear about Miranda, they might believe she sent me here to try to extract money from them. If they think that…''

Seeing the turmoil on her face, he gathered her against his chest and stroked the back of her head. ''Darling, whatever they think, just remember I'm standing firmly behind you. But I promise, they aren't going to judge you by your mother's behavior. And speaking of mothers…I talked to mine earlier tonight,'' he said happily. ''She's coming to town next week.''

Gabrielle's head reared back from his chest and she stared at him with shock. ''You talked to your mother? How?''

He smiled. ''I'll tell you all about it on the way to the ranch,'' he said. ''But right now we need to get going. We have a lot of news to give the Fortunes.''

As Wyatt had predicted, the Fortunes greeted Gabrielle with open arms and generally made a happy fuss over her. None of them doubted her amnesia or the sudden return of her memory. Instead, they were all eager to hear about her life in California. Especially Ryan, who was overwhelmed with emotion to learn that his sister was alive and well.

''You must call her,'' Ryan insisted as everyone sat around the great room drinking coffee Rosita had made and served.

The housekeeper had gotten out of bed in the wee hours of the morning to come to the ranch house to see for herself that Gabrielle was all right. Gabrielle would always be eternally grateful to the woman for the dream she'd had, and for calling and alerting Matthew. Otherwise, she would have caught the bus, gone back to California and deliberately severed her ties here in Texas.

Gabrielle glanced at her uncle. ''Are you serious? Ryan, I've been trying to tell you how Miranda is. Apparently she hasn't changed since she lived at home with you and your brother and parents. She's unpredictable and self-absorbed and she loves men. I can't count how many times she's been engaged.''

Chuckling, Ryan glanced over at his sister-in-law. ''She sounds like a true Fortune, doesn't she?''

Mary Ellen laughed with him. ''Totally,'' she agreed, then smiled reassuringly at Gabrielle. ''Ryan is right, Gabrielle. You must call her and persuade her to come here to the ranch.''

''Come here!'' Gabrielle gasped. She turned to Wyatt, who was sitting close by her side on the couch. ''What do you think?'' she asked him.

''My mother is coming. You want yours to be at our wedding too, don't you?''

His question brought a roar of happy surprise from the whole group. After everyone gathered around the two of them and offered congratulations, Mary Ellen pulled Gabrielle to her feet and guided her across the room to the telephone. ''No more wasting time,'' she said firmly. ''Call her. It sounds to me like we've got a wedding to plan—and not a minute to waste.''

The hour was late, even for the Pacific coast, but Miranda finally answered the phone on the eighth ring. Her voice was full of sleep, but when she realized it was Gabrielle on the other end of the line, she came wide awake.

Quickly Gabrielle related the events of the past few weeks. Miranda was shocked, but relieved that her daughter was all right. Yet she refused to agree to come to the ranch. She was certain the whole family had disowned her by now and she felt she didn't have a right to be a Fortune after all these years of neglecting her relatives.

''Let me speak with her,'' Ryan said, already reaching to take the phone from Gabrielle's hand.

Gabrielle was more than glad to hand it over to her uncle. Miranda had needed her family for a long time, even though she didn't know it yet. But Gabrielle felt certain Ryan would eventually be able to show his sister they all needed each other.

During the phone call, Wyatt had left his spot on the couch to stand quietly by Gabrielle's side. Now that Ryan had taken over the task of persuading Miranda to come to Texas, Wyatt took Gabrielle by the elbow and led her out the glass doors and into the dark, quiet courtyard.

"This has been quite a night," he said as he pulled her into his arms.

"I'll never forget it," she agreed as she slipped her arms around his neck.

Wyatt's arms came around her waist and he pressed her body tightly against his. "Guess what I've been thinking for the last thirty minutes?"

Her lips tilted into a sexy smile. "I don't have to guess. You've been thinking you want to get me alone."

"Hmm. We're not even married yet, and you already know me."

Unwittingly her hips pressed even more tightly against his, and moved in a provocative motion that caused him to groan with pleasure.

"That's because I was thinking the same thing," she admitted with a low, lusty chuckle. "Do you know how long it's been since we made love?"

The memory of that short passionate explosion in her bedroom coiled his insides and burned through his mind. "Too long, Gabrielle," he whispered. "Much too long."

Bending his head, he covered her lips with his, then quickly speared his tongue between her teeth. She reciprocated by rising on her tiptoes and pressing her breasts against his chest.

They were both becoming lost in the embrace when one of the glass doors opened.

"Wyatt? Gabrielle? Where are you?"

Hearing Ryan's call, they reluctantly broke apart and stepped out into the light so he could see them.

"Oh, there you are," he said with a happier smile than Gabrielle had ever seen on his face. "I just wanted to let you two know, Miranda is coming back to Texas. My sister is finally coming home, and she's bringing your brother Kane with her. My grandson is gone, but getting you all back is—well, it's the best thing to happen to this family in a long time."

"Don't give up on Bryan," Wyatt urged him. "We'll get your grandson back, and then the family will be complete."

Ryan shook his head. "Not entirely. Teddy has been missing for years. And we were hoping Miranda might know something about him, but she says she hasn't heard from him and has no clue where he might be."

Wyatt and Gabrielle exchanged puzzled glances. "Who is Teddy?" Gabrielle asked Ryan. "I didn't realize there were more Fortunes missing!"

"Our father was married once before being wed to our mother. He had a son—Teddy. When he was a baby and our father was away at war, his maternal grandfather stole him. Dad was never able to find our half brother and get him back."

Gabrielle gave him an encouraging smile. "Well, he was never able to locate Miranda either, but now she'll be back in the family. Maybe the same thing will happen with Teddy."

"I hope you're right," Ryan said, then bent and kissed her cheek. "They're breaking out the champagne inside.

We've got a reunion and an engagement to celebrate. Are you two going to join us?''

Before Wyatt or Gabrielle could answer, Ryan grinned and waved away the question. "Forget I asked. Just go back to doing whatever you were doing before I came out here."

Once Ryan had left them and reentered the house, Wyatt stepped up behind Gabrielle and slipped his arms again around her waist.

"Now there's a smart man," he said against her ear. Before she could guess his intentions, he bent and picked her up in his arms.

"Wyatt! What are you doing? What about the celebration?"

With her safely cradled in his arms, he began walking across the courtyard, away from the main part of the house and down to the door that opened into her bedroom. "We have our own celebrating to do right now," he answered in a voice husky with love. "We'll join the others later."

Gabrielle couldn't have agreed more, and once they reached the dark seclusion of her room, she whispered against his lips, "Is it always going to be like this with us, Wyatt?"

His teeth gleamed white and taunting as he grinned and covered her breast with his hand. "What do you think?"

A sigh of pleasure whispered past her lips as her body began to melt against him. "I think we're going to be celebrating every day for the rest of our lives."

* * * * * *

Here's a preview of next month's

*When a sexy-as-sin wedding planner finds
herself undeniably attracted to a gorgeous,
marriage-wary lawyer, will she soon be
sending out invites to her own
happily ever after?*

LONE STAR WEDDING
by
Sandra Steffen

"It's a small world."

Hannah Cassidy recognized the deep voice coming from a few feet behind her. She took a calming breath, then turned to face Parker Malone. "Sometimes it seems that way."

There was something deliberate in the step he took in her direction, something just as deliberate in his smile. He'd removed his navy jacket, loosened his tie and rolled up the sleeves of his white dress shirt. By all rights, he should have looked less intimidating. Her heart pounded an erratic rhythm because he didn't look any less anything. She cleared her throat, pretending not to be affected.

"I'm Parker Malone."

Since it would have been impolite to refuse it, she took his outstretched hand, but only briefly. "I know."

Parker waited to see if she would add anything—for instance, her name. She didn't say a word. Evidently, she knew her etiquette, but she only took civility so far. He'd always been under the assumption that women were uncomfortable with long stretches of silence. Hell, now that he thought about it, most of the women he knew never shut up long enough to find out.

There was something different about this woman. He'd tried to dismiss memories of their brief meeting, but he'd had very little success putting her out of his mind. That wasn't so surprising. He'd always believed that first impressions were the most potent, and his first impression of Hannah Cassidy had been a fantasy in the making.

"Are you enjoying the party, Hannah?"

She acknowledged his use of her name with the barest lift of her eyebrows. "Yes, I am."

It might have been her intention to instill her voice with an overlying coldness, but Parker earned a very good living by paying attention to the most subtle nuances and inflections in his clients' voices. She wasn't as cold as she wanted him to believe. A smug feeling of satisfaction settled over him. No matter what she pretended, she was aware of him. He'd venture a little further and say she was attracted to him too.

"Nice night."

She glanced at the guests, the orchestra, and the lawns far beyond the patio, and nodded.

"Hannah?"

She turned her head very slowly, and looked up at him. There was a softness in her eyes, and a directness he liked very much. "Ryan was right about that orchestra. They're very good. Would you care to dance?"

She hesitated as if surprised by his question. "As a matter of fact," she said, the sound of her voice as dusky as secrets whispered in the dark, "I would love to."

Parker felt the way he did when he was nearing the end of an intense game of chess. Victory was close. Check.

She smiled sweetly at him. And he reacted in the most basic and masculine way.

He reached for her hand, but she'd backed up. Increasing the distance between them, she lowered her voice and said, "Perhaps if you combed the numbers on a public rest-room wall, you could find someone to accommodate you."

"If you'd care to explain, I'm all ears."

"In a sense, you're the enemy."

He wasn't really, she thought. He was all shoulders and planes and angles and...

He slid a hand into the pocket of his dress slacks, the action drawing attention to a place she really shouldn't be looking. She glanced up at his face, only to find herself staring at the cleft in his chin. For heaven's sake, did everything about him have to be riveting?

Taking control of her senses, she said, "I've overheard bits and pieces of several conversations tonight, and the general consensus around here seems to be that you don't want Ryan Fortune to see my mother, Lily. Something tells me it isn't a moral issue with you."

"At least you're not blinded by my brains and good looks."

He was very good at deprecating humor. And if this had been a laughing matter, she would have smiled. "At least it hasn't gone to your head."

"That isn't what's gone to my head, Hannah."

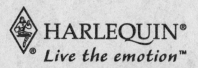

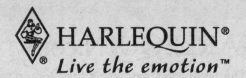

HARLEQUIN®
Live the emotion™

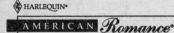